CROSSING ZERO

DALE BRANDON

Also by Dale Brandon

Fear Runner
Death Mountain
Dead Fall

CROSSING ZERO

TO: MARIAH

WITH WARM WISHES

Dale Brandon

6.6.19

DALE BRANDON

DISCLAIMER
This book is a work of fiction. Any real names appearing in the novel have been used to produce a sense of realism in the story. All of the character names are fictitious and are derived from the author's imagination. The author in no way suggests that the companies, persons, or organizations have, or will, act in the manner described in the novel. The events described herein are a product of the author's imagination and are used fictitiously. The sole purpose of the book is to entertain the reader.

For my siblings:

Bob, Carolyn, Sandy, and Shirley

ACKNOWLEDGEMENTS

My profound thanks to Joan Steiger for her editing and proof reading skills, and for her enthusiasm for the project. A special thanks to my wife, Kittie, for her continued support, and for a superb job of proof reading. The input from both of these exceptional women is greatly appreciated.

CROSSING ZERO

CHAPTER 1

Danny Fagan never killed anyone on an empty stomach. His motivation was feral and bone-raw; hunger diminished the exhilaration he felt while stalking his prey. After he committed four unsolved murders, Fagan's ritual meal had become an obsession. Dressed in khaki work clothes and a baseball cap, Fagan sauntered out of the Black Kettle coffee shop and lit a cigarette. He inhaled deeply, savoring the blend of nicotine and gravy residue. The sun would be up in half an hour. It was time.

He pulled out a disposal phone and punched in a number. He scanned the parking lot as he spoke. "I'll be at the site in about two hours. Three at the most."

"I'm on my way."

"I want the hole deeper this time," Fagan said coldly.

"I'll take care of it."

He walked down the street to a cargo van he had stolen six days earlier. He stopped and appraised his handiwork, which included a quick paint job and the placement of fictitious signs on the side doors. Plates from an abandoned Ford van completed the makeover. He exhaled on the glass on the driver's door and drew a cross on the fading moisture. It would be the only monument for his next victim.

He climbed into the back of the van and smiled at a lone homing pigeon cooing from a small cage in the rear corner. His thoughts softened as he opened a tiny wire door. He gently stroked the bird and whispered, "It won't be long now, Oscar." Fagan closed the cage, exchanged his shirt for a camouflage top with a matching hat, then he pulled onto the highway and headed south. Each twist in the road brought him closer to his next victim, increasing his excitement. This would be his first woman.

He thought back to the waitress at the coffee shop. The outline of her bra had been visible through the thin uniform, allowing him to see the faint silhouette of her dark areola beneath the fabric. She had strutted across the floor, hips swaying, breasts jiggling, playing to the men. The woman was a tease. They all were. Yet, her body had aroused him, stoking a discordant mixture of lust and hate. Women did that to him. For as long as he could remember, they had rejected his advances. He tightened his grip on the steering wheel and pressed down on the accelerator.

He passed the Sea Haven Lodge near Santa Cruz, turned onto a dirt road, and wound through several small redwood groves. He reached his destination and pulled into a stand of thick brush. Two cottontail rabbits scampered out of the bushes and bounded away.

Fagan checked his 9mm Sig Sauer, shoved a nylon cord into his pocket, winked at Oscar, and climbed out the rear door. He crept through the trees, his senses vigilant. He came to a trail, grabbed the end of a heavy limb he had cut the previous day, and dragged it across the path. He scanned the area, moved into the shrubs, and sat with his back against a stump.

Satisfied with his covert, Fagan chewed on a toothpick and thought about his target. Heather Coyne was attending a seminar at the lodge, and, each morning, she had used the trail for jogging. He had followed her routine for the last three days, but today he would do more than observe his prey. He had just switched ends of his toothpick when hikers topped a rise on the trail to his left. Two women strode along the path carrying small weights in each hand. Fagan shook his head. "Shit."

The women turned onto another trail and disappeared into the trees. If he saw them again, he would abandon his mission. He searched the path that led to the lodge and felt his pulse quicken at the sight of Heather Coyne in blue sweatpants and a yellow top.

He rose to a crouch, his muscles taut with anticipation.

A lone crow squawked nearby.

His target drew within thirty yards.

Fagan slipped the cord from his pocket and readied himself. At fifteen yards, he focused on his target's chest. Her large breasts heaved with each stride, the movement accentuating their size. Adrenaline pulsed through him when she passed the shrubs and stopped in front of the limb.

He glanced around—all clear. Swiftly, stealthily, he moved onto the trail and approached the woman just as she bent to grasp the limb.

She let go of the branch, cocked her head, and started to turn.

Fagan slipped the cord around her neck and yanked hard. She opened her mouth to scream, but only a muffled, gurgling sound escaped. She kicked wildly and fell to the ground. He pounced on her and tightened the cord.

Terror flashed across Heather Coyne's face as she thrashed about in a cloud of dust. Her eyes widened into beacons of horror protruding from a reddened, disbelieving face. Spittle bubbled from her mouth and dribbled down her chin.

Fagan straddled her and pulled the cord until she went limp. He hooked his arms under hers and dragged her off the trail, cursing the heel marks left by her sneakers. He lifted her into the van, loosened the cord, and laid her on her back.

Oscar cooed from his cage, an innocent witness.

Fagan exited through a side door and hurried to the trail to cover the heel marks. Satisfied, he went back to the van, got in, and headed toward the highway. Driving through the trees, he visualized salacious pictures of Heather Coyne's heaving breasts. His job was to kill the woman, but he became increasingly aroused as he considered future possibilities. Next time it would be different.

Women had always rejected him. The cruelty had started in high school when young girls, in groups of three or four, laughed about the acne speckled across his face. Over time, the girls blossomed into women, and the laughter turned to whispers. Why wouldn't they accept him the way he was?

Fagan turned onto Highway 9 and drove north. He wound through the mountains for nearly an hour; then, he turned onto an unpaved forestry access road that skirted the border of Big Basin State Park. He followed the rutted track for nearly two miles and then pulled into a grove of trees and stopped next to a blue pickup. Several layers of dry mud covered the bottom half of the vehicle. A man with an unkempt beard sat on the tailgate drinking a beer.

Fagan got out and walked to the rear of the truck. He grabbed the man by his shirt and shoved him backwards. "What the hell's wrong with you? You know we don't drink when we're on a job."

"Christ, man. Do you know how hard that ground is?"

Fagan glared at him. "Don't ever do that again." He grabbed the bottle and started to throw it into the trees, but he turned and tossed it into the pickup bed instead. He knew better than to leave evidence that he, or anyone, had been here. He stepped back. "That pit had better be finished."

Rick wiped sweat from his brow. "I'm done, but it was a tough job."

Fagan checked the surrounding area. "Have you seen anyone?"

"Not a soul."

"Let's get at it."

The two men rolled the woman's body inside a cotton blanket; then, they carried the sagging bundle through the trees to a freshly dug grave. After dropping Heather Coyne's remains into the hole, they grabbed shovels and worked swiftly. When they finished, Fagan removed a redwood sapling from the van and placed it on the center of the grave. They planted the tree and scattered leaves and debris over the area.

After Rick had left, Fagan went to the back of the van and opened Oscar's cage. Speaking softly, he removed the bird and ran his fingers gently over its gray feathers; then, he lifted his arms and set the pigeon free. "Home, Oscar. Go home." The bird soared into the air. After circling several times, Oscar's mysterious homing instinct locked on, and he disappeared over the treetops into a pathless, blue sky.

Fagan drove back to the highway and turned north. Thirty minutes later, he pulled out a disposable phone; then, he retrieved a business card from his pocket. It read:

SCANLAN EQUITY MANAGEMENT
Martin Scanlan

Fagan's original instructions had been to memorize Scanlan's private number, and then destroy the card, but he saw no reason to comply. Why should he? He was too good at what he did. The police would never catch him.

He dialed the number and said, "Finished."

Scanlan asked, "Any problems?"

"None."

Martin Scanlan's instructions had been to kill the woman, and to do it quickly. Fagan did not care why the woman had to be eliminated, that was none of his business. He had simply complied in a cold, heartless manner. End of story.

He headed for home, which consisted of a double-wide mobile home located on sixty heavily forested acres in the mountains southeast of Pescadero, California. Unknown to anyone but himself, there was a cave on the property he was converting for use as a prepper bunker. He was a loner, he knew it, and that was fine with him. The isolated property fit his life style perfectly. Screw those assholes on the other side of the mountain in Silicon Valley.

As he drove, his thoughts changed and he focused on Heather Coyne. Everything had happened too quickly. Things would be different next time—he would not have to rush.

CHAPTER 2

Kelly Sanborn learned a lot over the last eleven years, but one thing stood out—being a single mother is a tough job. Over time, she had conquered most of the challenges except one: she constantly worried about being able to provide for her small family. After years of struggle, she had finally secured a position capable of producing substantial income. Experienced stockbrokers often had comfortable incomes, but it usually took several years to build a strong customer base. Kelly worked hard to increase her client list, but she was in the early stages of a slow process.

After a prospect hung up on her, she listened to the hollow sound of a dead line for a few seconds; then, she leaned back and ran a hand through auburn hair. Rejection came with the territory, but that did not lessen her distaste for that part of her job. She opened her desk drawer and retrieved a chocolate truffle, her designated "crisis crutch." If Kelly had a worldly power that would allow her to categorize the nutritional value of food, chocolate would immediately vault to the top of the health food list; after all, that is where it belonged.

She picked up a folder as if it were a precious object and focused on the name on the cover: SCANLAN EQUITY MANAGEMENT. Signing an account this large would triple her commissions in a few months. If she did manage to obtain part of Scanlan's business, she planned to buy her son some badly needed clothes, and maybe even get a car that started every day. She reached across her desk for a photo of her eleven-year-old son and smiled at the freckles scattered across Cody's face.

She sighed as she considered her chances of landing the Scanlan account. Over the last six months, she had sent five letters and three profitable trade recommendations to Nathan Rosenberg, Scanlan's top analyst. He had not acknowledged her correspondence or returned any of her phone calls. She slipped off her shoes and rubbed one foot over the other, mulling her strategy. Rosenberg was an important contact, but her biggest hurdle had always been Martin Scanlan. Nothing would happen until she met with the top executive, but his secretary had refused every request for an appointment.

She needed a creative tactic that would demand Scanlan's attention. For the last eighteen months, she had been working on an innovative computerized trading system. She thought the new system would be the key to landing the Scanlan account, but it was also a source of concern. Lacking a final, elusive component, the current version of her software required more work.

Kelly's pessimism eased as bits of random ideas meshed to form a new strategy. She would work overtime to perfect her trading system; then, she would approach Martin Scanlan in a unique manner. It might work.

A burst of laughter startled her. She looked up and saw Zack Nichols, T. J. Halverson, and Eric Bradford throwing a Nerf football back and forth. Kelly had long been annoyed by the trio's puerile antics, and she wondered at what level testosterone poisoning became terminal.

In the past two decades, women had made significant inroads on Wall Street, and in the financial community in general, but not at Boucher & Crittenden, the small regional broker where Kelly worked. Much of the office's traditional, macho atmosphere remained intact.

Halverson walked by her desk. "What's wrong, Sticks. Having a bad day?"

He had begun calling her by that nickname after she politely declined his request for a date. She ignored the suspender-clad broker and turned her attention to a young black woman walking toward her.

Vanessa Pruitt plopped into a chair. "I just might have some good news." Vanessa hesitated, her smile broadening.

"You're a tease. Do you treat your men this way?"

"Of course. They love it." Vanessa pulled a sheet of paper from a folder. "You, Miss Sanborn, have just been declared the trading performance winner for the last quarter."

Kelly felt a stir of excitement. Over the last six weeks, she had tried a new computerized timing indicator on selected accounts. Even in its fledgling stage, her system had made a difference.

Vanessa patted Kelly's hand. "Mr. Crittenden wants to see you. I'll bet he's going to congratulate you on your performance."

When Kelly entered the president's outer office, Emmett Crittenden's secretary, the office snoop, looked over her reading glasses. "He's expecting you. Go right in."

9

Crittenden greeted her with his trademark false smile. His mouth curled up at the edges, but his eyes belied the gesture. He returned his attention to papers on his desk. "Shut the door, please."

Kelly had expected to sit in one of two chairs in front of his desk, but they had been moved against a wall.

He seemed to sense her hesitation. Without looking up, he gestured toward a sofa.

Feeling unusually self-conscious, she crossed the room and wondered why she always felt uncomfortable in his office. She took a seat, crossed her legs, and smoothed her skirt.

While waiting, she thought about the man behind the desk, the only son of the founder. Emmett Crittenden appeared to be in his early fifties, and he might have been handsome not too many years ago, but his notorious overindulgence in single malt scotch and rich food had obviously taken a toll. His body had reshaped itself into a portly silhouette and his complexion had turned ruddy.

As the seconds ticked by, Kelly became increasingly nervous and attempted to ease her anxiety by studying various objects around the room. Sensing her maneuver appeared obvious, she shifted her attention to the window. Distant spires of the Golden Gate Bridge loomed beyond the city, piercing a layer of fog like newborn herbage pushing toward the sun. The view had a calming effect.

She turned at a squeak from Crittenden's chair. He leaned forward and steepled his fingers. His eyes sent disturbing signals as his gaze moved down her body. She felt as if her dress were transparent, that his eyes were heat-seeking missiles streaking up her legs, spying on her flesh. She had always considered her legs one of her best physical assets, but she suddenly wished they were not.

Breaking the silence, Crittenden said, "You've been here a year and a half and, frankly, I'm disappointed with your performance."

"But I just won the quarterly portfolio con—"

He waved her off. "It's easy to show a large percentage increase with a small base. It's meaningless. I grade account managers on the commissions they generate." He raised a sheet of paper and used his pen as a pointer. "You're eighteenth out of twenty-one." He tossed the paper on the desk. "Unacceptable."

His declaration jolted her. "It's . . . it's only been ten months since I finished training."

Crittenden leaned forward and glared at her through passionless eyes. "That's enough time for a decent start in this market. We've been in a major bull phase for over six years, and the public always jumps in at times like this." He glanced at his report. "Dan Hawkins and Michael Musgrove finished training when you did. Do you want to hear their numbers?" He continued as if he had not expected an answer. "They have signed nearly twice as many new accounts as you have." He broke eye contact and gazed out the window. "I don't think you're going to fit in here."

His direction had taken on a sudden, startling clarity. She clasped her hands and stared at whitened knuckles.

Crittenden continued, "I'm putting you on probation."

My God, she couldn't lose her job. She thought of Cody. How would she provide for her son? Over the years, the fear had burrowed deep inside, awaiting a fragile moment—a moment like this.

Crittenden waited until she looked up. "You have sixty days to bring in fresh capital and generate a substantial growth in commissions. If you don't, I'll have no alternative but to release you."

A tense silence hung over the room.

A frisson of panic gripped her. It seemed as if her entire future depended on her next utterance. She had one chance. "I'm developing a new trading system that is showing dramatic potential. It may even be revolutionary."

Crittenden shook his head. "My God, Sanborn. Every major firm has rocket scientists working on computerized trading programs. The financial magazines are full of ads for that sort of thing. You can't compete with them. You need to concentrate on getting new clients."

"Can I at least tell you about it?"

Crittenden raised his hands, palms facing her. "It's too late."

Desperate now, Kelly sought a new tact. "I've also been working on Scanlan Equity Management. If I can land that account, I—"

"Nobody in this office has ever been able to get any of their business."

"I think I can crack the account."

Crittenden drummed his fingers and eyed her disapprovingly. "How many meetings have you had with Martin Scanlan?"

"I haven't met with him yet but, I expect to soon."

Crittenden shook his head. "That's blue-sky talk and you know it. Besides, there are rumors that Scanlan is having a tough time since the old man died. One of their best analysts quit last week after a big row."

"They still manage a lot of money, and they have a large house account."

"Yes, but you're overlooking the obvious. You're not going to get their business in sixty days. You don't have a chance."

It seemed hopeless when Crittenden crossed his arms and leaned back in his chair. She thought about his reputation for intransigence and sensed the futility of further arguments. He had obviously made up his mind before their appointment.

Kelly stared at the carpet and thought of Cody, the focal point of her life. A lump crept into her throat. After a moment, she looked up and caught him smiling oddly, staring at her legs. She uncrossed her legs, put her knees together, and tugged on the hem of her skirt.

He came from behind his desk. "I've already lost one female broker this year, and there are only two of you left." His voice took on a more conciliatory tone. "It would be a shame to lose another."

Twisting a ring on her finger, Kelly recalled rumors she had heard about a female broker's reluctant involvement with the president and her subsequent departure from the firm. She did not want this man near her.

Crittenden crossed the room, his potbelly bulging, his belt acting as a crude safety net for the protruding flesh. He sank onto the couch next to her.

Kelly leaned away and stared straight ahead.

"I can see I've been too harsh," he said, his words softer now. "Perhaps there's a way we can work this out."

Warning signs flashed as Crittenden inched toward her.

"W—what do you mean?" She wanted to snatch the words back as soon as they rolled from her lips.

He gestured with his arm as he spoke. "I have a solution for this problem." His hand came down to rest next to her leg in a clumsy, transparent maneuver. "I have discretion over the disposition of several house accounts. Institutional accounts—one quite large." The words came out slow and smooth, honey coated.

Her pulse quickened as her thoughts ran ahead, fearing his direction.

Crittenden said, "Do you realize how much commission a large institutional account can generate in a year?"

The bait.

Of course, she knew. Two or three of those accounts could catapult a broker into a higher tax bracket practically overnight.

His hand moved to her knee.

She flinched at the moist heat flowing through her hosiery, invading her skin.

"If we can work out a certain arrangement, I'll transfer some very important accounts to your desk."

Kelly's stomach churned, the muscles in her neck tightened, and she felt a sheen of sweat erupt on her face. Fighting to maintain control, she focused on Cody and his reliance on her, the sole provider for their small family. She felt herself at the edge of panic—she could not afford to lose her job.

Crittenden's fingertips inched under her skirt.

CHAPTER 3

Kelly was not about to let the manipulating sonofabitch have his way. She jumped to her feet. "Don't you ever touch me again. Do you understand? Never!" She backed across the office, frantically waving a hand behind her, searching for the door that seemed so far away.

Crittenden rose and extended both hands. "Easy, easy. You're overreacting." His voice carried a tone of self-assurance—as if he had been through this before. "If you think about this calmly, you'd realize it could develop into a pleasant and profitable experience."

Anger pushed its way through what little reserve Kelly had left. She spoke loudly, sharply. "You're using your position to gain sexual favors. There's no way in hell that will work with me."

Crittenden's face turned an ugly shade of red as he uttered a string of unintelligible sounds.

Kelly spun around and charged toward the door. Her chest rose and fell in great heaves as she grasped the brass knob.

He shouted, "You can't do it in sixty days, Sanborn. There's no way you—"

"The hell I can't."

She shut the door and hurried across the main floor, oblivious of her surroundings. The confrontation was over, but she knew her nightmare had only begun.

The phone rang when she reached her desk. Vanessa asked, "Well, did he congratulate you?"

"Not exactly."

"You sound upset. What happened?"

Kelly felt too fragile to attempt an explanation now. "I really have to go. I'll tell you about it Monday." She swept two binders into a drawer, grabbed her purse, and headed for the door. She took the elevator to the basement garage, then she trudged across an open area toward her car. Lowering her head, she disregarded her usual caution and purposely concentrated on the amplified reports of her heels clicking against the concrete. Her attempt to push the repulsive meeting from her mind failed immediately, and she knew she had experienced a watershed event capable of changing her life.

She searched a row of cars. It was always easy to find Huey; the name Cody had given to her sixteen-year-old car. Not many vehicles featured a shattered passenger window crisscrossed with professional-strength duct tape.

She got in, rested her head against the steering wheel, and replayed Crittenden's final words. She never imagined this kind of thing would happen to her. Eager to be home with her son, she inserted and turned the key.

Nothing.

She tried again. Silence.

How could Huey fail her now? She got out, looked under the hood, and, eventually, spotted a corroded cable that had broken loose from a battery post. She slammed the hood and kicked Huey on the front quarter panel. The heel from her right shoe snapped off and skidded across the concrete.

"Damn!" It seemed as if the entire world had turned against her. She leaned her forehead on Huey's cold roof and fought back tears. Crittenden's words echoed in her mind: "If we can work out a special arrangement." She saw a vision of his naked body bearing down on hers, his sweat flowing over her skin. She shuddered.

Kelly had lost track of the number of times she had seen Huey's front end hoisted by a tow truck. Enduring a familiar routine, she sat in the truck's cab while Huey rumbled along behind, attached by a steel bar and an electrified umbilical cord. Her auto club membership had turned out to be one of life's great bargains.

The truck delivered Huey to a nearby service station, and he was soon fitted with a new cable capable of breathing life back into his aging electrical system. She handed over her slightly past due credit card and worried that it might not be accepted.

She phoned home and told Miyako, her roommate, that she would be late. She walked to her car and ran her fingers over the duct tape on the passenger window. If she signed the Scanlan account, Huey would receive a proper retirement. The thought carried extra baggage—her confrontation with Crittenden.

With the events of the day churning in her mind, she pulled out of the station, anxious to reach her home in Half Moon Bay. She had forgotten it was Friday, getaway day for the city, and vehicles of all kinds clogged the streets. She drove to the Skyway and merged into heavy stop-and-go traffic; then, she maneuvered

Huey into the middle lane and competed for asphalt until she connected with Highway 280.

After a difficult commute, she pulled into her driveway and saw her roommate on the lawn. "Hi. Where's Cody?"

Miyako motioned toward the street. "He and Sparky are—"

"I know. They're playing ball." She shook her head at a familiar problem. Every time a ball floated through the air, Cody's concept of time attached itself with grappling hooks and went along for the ride. She encouraged her son's love of sports although it demanded considerable tolerance. Glancing toward the street she asked, "Did he pack?"

"I don't think so."

Kelly frowned. Cody was scheduled to stay at a friend's house overnight, and, then, leave early the next morning on a two-day scouting trip. The friend and his father would arrive in forty minutes. "I'm going to fetch him."

She stepped off the curb and saw two figures walking up the middle of the street. Both wore shorts, but the similarities ended there. Sparky Valentine stood a quarter of an inch over four feet. The dwarf plodded along with a choppy, bowlegged gait that never seemed to go in a straight line. His hair had an ever-increasing number of gray streaks.

Kelly was grateful for the way Sparky balanced the duties of landlord, neighbor, and friend. Moreover, he was a fine mentor for Cody. She had long ago accepted his eccentric, opinionated outbursts and had grown to love him as a member of the family.

Cody's lean frame towered half a foot above his companion. His cap had been shoved back, exposing a shock of blond hair above an affable face. A baseball glove hung from a bat balanced on his shoulder.

She observed Cody's expression as he approached. She had intended to reprimand him for being late, but his face softened her. Though she hated to admit it, he had his father's blue eyes, which were a shade of blue that reminded her of the New Mexico sky. The heavy sprinkling of childhood freckles had begun to lighten and flow into one another. He would be a handsome young man in a few years and he would probably, inadvertently, break the hearts of a few adoring girls along the way.

Cody handed his bat to Sparky and hugged her. "Hi, Mom."

"Don't try to butter me up. You're late."

"Aw, Mom. We were just playing ball."

She glanced at Sparky.

He shrugged and held up his hands as if to surrender. "My fault."

Sparky's way of admitting to minor lapses always disarmed her. Cognizant of shared guilt, she put her arm around Cody's shoulders and started up the street. She turned at the sound of grumbling from behind.

Sparky moaned and repeatedly flexed his right leg. "Good grief. My whole body aches." He straightened and rubbed his lower back. "Time steals strength from a man's body, but I won't give up without a fight." He twisted from side to side and grimaced. "You know you're getting old when your joints ache, and you can't find your reading glasses because there're on top of your head."

"But, Sparky, you're approaching your golden years."

"Whoever coined that phrase was obviously quite senile. You know what a guy once told me about those years? He said they should be called the metal years. You have silver in your hair, gold in your teeth, and lead in your ass."

Kelly could not help but laugh.

"And another thing. When you reach the pinnacle of wisdom, your body starts falling apart." He retrieved a protein bar from his fanny pack and headed next door, mumbling to himself as he went.

Kelly followed Cody into the house and steered him toward the bathroom. "Dan will be here in half an hour. I'll pack some of your things while you jump into the shower."

After a hectic thirty minutes, Kelly walked Cody to Dan's car and hugged him.

He looked up at her as she rubbed the last wet spots from his hair. "I love you, Mom."

Her heart melted. "I love you too." She watched him load his pack into the trunk and felt a pang of loneliness she always experienced when he stayed overnight with a friend. When the car eased from the curb, she waved and yelled, "Have a good time. And be careful." She wondered how many times mothers had said those exact words to departing children.

After Miyako had left to visit a friend, Kelly leaned against the kitchen counter examining her mail. Two bills and some junk mail. She opened the letter from the utility company, noting that it was not the envelope used for monthly statements. They would cut off her service if she failed to remit within seven business days. With payday more than a week away, she would have to call and request an extension.

She tossed the mail aside, poured a glass of red wine, and carried the beverage to her makeshift office in the dining room. A narrow aisle offered the only free space in the cluttered room. A table and three chairs occupied one wall. Two desks, one equipped with a laptop and one with a desktop computer, took up the entire opposite wall. The laptop was connected to a large monitor, which allowed her to share work with Miyako without changing chairs.

A small sign on her desk read: Hand Over The Chocolate And Nobody Gets Hurt.

Four small black and white fine art photographs covered part of one wall, which were the extent of a hobby she meant to pursue when finances permitted. One day, she hoped to obtain an original Ansel Adams, but that day was nowhere in sight.

Good luck had eluded Kelly over the last few years, but finding Miyako Soral had been providential. They had met while taking night classes. Kelly had studied economics and computer science, and she possessed a stunning memory, especially with numbers. However, she lacked the high-level training required for elaborate program design. Miyako, a freelance programmer, had agreed to help develop the trading system for a percentage of future profits. The arrangement had meshed compatible personalities, and Miyako became a close friend. Kelly felt blessed to have such a loving person look after Cody while she worked in the city. In return, Miyako paid only for her share of food and utilities.

Kelly stood at her desk sipping wine. Her thoughts cycled back to Crittenden, and she could almost feel the heat transferring from his sweaty palm to her skin. She shuddered and drained her glass. After a calming period, she realized she could not continually replay the episode. In that direction lay only fear and discomfort. She needed to attack the problem in her usual manner—analytically. She decided to work on a solution after dinner.

She warmed leftover ravioli, made a small salad, poured another glass of wine, and padded down the hall to her bedroom. She propped herself against the headboard and nibbled at her food. She finally pushed the plate aside and listed options on a yellow pad. She could file sexual harassment charges against Crittenden, but it would be his word against hers. He had not actually said he wanted her to have sex, though the implication had been clear. If she did file, they would brand her as a troublemaker and help with new leads would vanish.

Resign? Kelly listed the option although she would not quit, could not quit. Her commission checks were not large, but they should grow over time, especially if her trading system worked as she hoped. Her third option seemed the most prudent. She could blitz the next sixty days to obtain as many new clients as possible. However, the more she thought about this approach, the more she realized it would fail. Except for Scanlan Equity Management, most of her prospects were too small to bring in sufficient trading capital in such a short timeframe.

That left one alternative—sign the Scanlan account. A long shot, but her chances would improve if she could get Martin Scanlan to review a summary of historical trading results made by her software. If her system predicted enough market turns, he might agree to see her. She experienced a positive attitude for the first time since the confrontation and wondered if alcohol had dulled her logic. No one at Boucher & Crittenden had ever landed any of Scanlan's business. How could she possibly succeed where they had failed?

Of course, she could sleep with Crittenden. She dropped her pencil on the bed, refusing to dignify that possibility by listing it as an option. Although it would save her job and solve pressing financial problems, she would never succumb to his advances. Her anger swelled at his corrupt use of power. She put her glass aside and made a decision. She would expend every resource to finish her software, and, then, compile a list of historical trades the system would have made if active. If the results were good enough, she would devise a plan to gain an appointment with

Martin Scanlan. It seemed her best strategy, and it had to work. If not, she and Cody would be on the street.

She tossed her notes on the bed and rubbed her eyes. The day's events had worn on her, draining her energy. She put on a sleeping gown, went into Cody's room, and selected an extra-large piece of poster board they had purchased for a science project. She retrieved a black marker and then printed in large, block letters: PERSEVERE. The precept had been passed on to her by her father.

She tacked the sign on the wall above her computer, then she poured the rest of her wine into the kitchen sink. She would need a clear head in the morning.

CHAPTER 4

Kelly endured a fitful night, waking often. Her dreams were complex webs interlaced with visions of Emmett Crittenden and a faceless Martin Scanlan. Shortly after five, she swung her legs over the edge of the bed and sat for a moment, feeling a slight hangover. After breakfast, she seated herself at the computer and studied the new sign above her desk. An alcohol induced filter had made the task seem easier last night. She silently repeated the sign's message. She would not give up. With renewed determination, she planned to work all day, breaking only to eat and go jogging.

She opened her project binder and found a note from Miyako stating that the latest version of the software was ready for testing. She felt the familiar ripple of anticipation. After months of exhausting trial and error, she sensed they were close. Would this be the version that worked?

Keyboarding rapidly, she retrieved a historical database containing the Dow's performance over the last thirty years, which she routinely downloaded for testing and analysis. She set the program parameters to identify all trading signals for the past year; then, she placed her finger on the enter key. She hesitated, consumed by a mixture of excitement and apprehension.

She took a deep breath and struck the key. The disk drive murmured, accessing data for calculation, and, then, a rectangular box with a zero-line running across its midpoint appeared on the screen. A yellow line moved up and down across the screen in waves, tracking her indicator over a span of one year. The line crossed zero five times. A descending transection represented a sell signal; an ascending move signaled a buy.

She brought up a fifty-two-week chart of the Dow Jones Industrial Average and scanned the first two trading signals. Perfect. Her burgeoning enthusiasm shattered when she saw the third entry. After the program had generated a sell signal, the stock market had gone sideways for two weeks before rallying sharply. Three of the five signals had been precise, but two had failed, and one of the losses would have been substantial.

She controlled her disappointment and worked diligently on the program, manipulating data, changing parameters, hoping to find an answer. After several adjustments, she tested the indicator over a five-year period, then ten. With minor exceptions, the results were mirror images of the first test.

Over the next four hours, skepticism cut into her productivity. She slid back her chair and looked at the sign above her desk. Who was she kidding? She wanted to sweep her desk clear and give up.

"Did you test it?"

Kelly dropped her pencil and spun around. "God, Miyako. You scared me to death." She turned back to the screen and sighed.

"I guess that means no," Miyako said, easing onto a chair. "You look tired. How long have you been at this?"

Kelly shrugged. "I was so sure this time. I had this feeling." After discussing various software problems, she revealed her confrontation with Crittenden.

Anger flared in Miyako's delicate eyes. "Sue the bastard for harassment."

Kelly was taken aback by her friend's use of profanity. Gentle language, devoid of expletives or harshness, had always been a distinctive marker of Miyako's personality. "I'd never be able to prove it." She tapped her fingers on the desk, thinking ahead. "Leads would dry up and my income would suffer. I can't afford that right now."

"That's the trouble with that sort of thing. It's too bad you didn't get it on tape. Maybe you could set him up in another meeting and record it." Even in anger, Miyako looked fragile. Her delicate beauty acquired from her French-Japanese heritage did not lend itself to displays of indignation.

"I think he'd expect that now," Kelly said. She turned off the monitor and got up. "I've had it for today."

She went to her room and changed into running shorts. Kelly ran five days a week to keep in shape, but she also used physical exertion to relieve stress. She glanced in the mirror as she removed her sweats. The sight of her near-naked body reminded her of another benefit of exercise. Running temporarily eased the familiar sexual urges smoldering inside, unsatisfied.

The cumulative demands of commuting to San Francisco, developing new software, and caring for Cody had left her little time for dating during the past year. Kelly cherished heartfelt intimacy with a special man, but past experiences left her puzzled. She could walk into a conference room and make quick, accurate judgments about men in the business world; yet, she had an abysmal history of selecting romantic partners.

She thought back over a long list of mistakes, mistakes that had started with Sean Keene at age nineteen. She had been strongly attracted to Sean, an eighteen-year-old employee of the local health spa, by his lithe body and a striking combination of blond hair and incredible blue eyes, and Kelly believed she had fallen in love. Years later, she tried to persuade herself that infatuation, sex, and youth had been the primary drivers of the romance.

She had become pregnant during their fifth month of dating, and Sean disappeared shortly after she had informed him of her pregnancy. Rumors circulated that he had taken a job as a diving instructor on the east coast of Australia. The Great Barrier Reef evidently offered more than she did. She would never forgive him for abandoning her, but she was grateful for his only gift—Cody.

She had endured a difficult pregnancy without the support of a partner, but Kelly's world changed the instant she held Cody against her breast. It was a profound moment that propelled her to a new level of maturity. During those precious seconds, she had vowed to give her son a propitious future. Her goal meant years of hardship for her small family, but she was determined to avoid a life of dependency.

She opened the door and called to Miyako. "I'll be back in about forty-five minutes."

Following her usual routine, Kelly headed for the back lot to do a few stretching exercises. She rounded the corner of the house and heard a series of curses interspersed with banging noises. Her landlord often spent part of his day restoring a 1959 Cadillac convertible.

DALE BRANDON

Sparky had crammed his four-foot torso under the hood in such a way that Kelly could see only his legs. One scuffed cowboy boot rested on a kitchen stool, the other moved up and down like a pump handle.

She came alongside the car and tapped on the fender.

He backed out and swung his legs over the edge of the fender, a broad smile softened his weathered face. He wiped his hands on his trousers, adding to the ample coverage of grease. "Greetings, Kelly. You're late."

"Long night." She gazed under the hood. "How's it coming?"

"I feel like a gnat trying to eat a watermelon." He ran his hand lovingly over the fender. "I've always wanted to restore one of these babies, but I had no idea it would take so long."

"Aren't you almost finished?"

"Trans-fatty acids."

Kelly shook her head at Sparky's proclivity for subject hopping. "Trans what?"

"They're formed when vegetable oils are hydrogenated. It seems the body doesn't know what to do with them. Not good. Not good at all."

Kelly nodded as she reflected on Sparky's habit of overindulging in vitamins, herbs, and unusual health concoctions. He had often said that middle age had been the biggest surprise of his life, but his final passage would be different. He intended to fight senescence with nutrition.

He gave her an earnest look. "I want to join the team."

Kelly loved this capricious, grease-covered little person, but she felt herself hovering on the edge of exasperation. Hesitantly, she replied, "I don't understand."

"Cody thinks you need help with your system. I'm available." He raised his arms. "No charge."

Kelly knew he would pester her constantly if she said no. She also knew he had come within an eyelash of passing the qualifying test for Mensa. Besides, the final stages of development had been taxing. She extended her hand. "I accept your offer."

"Great!" He looked skyward, following an outbound 747's ascent. "We have excellent synergy."

"You think so?"

"No doubt about it," he said in an upbeat tone. "Our team has a talented leader, a brainy Eurasian damsel, and a middle-aged dwarf. We'll kick Wall Street's butt."

After thanking Sparky, she ran down Water Street and then turned onto Terrace Way. Three blocks later, she angled toward the ocean. She left the sidewalk and increased her effort to offset the sluggish pull of the sand. She headed for the shoreline, pleased there were few people in the area. The absence of tourists and fog made late spring an ideal time for running on the beach.

She moved at a steady pace, feeling the first sheen of sweat on her body. She thought about Crittenden and increased her speed, hoping pain would blot out the disturbing memory. Seagulls flapped away, squawking excitedly at her approach. After a three-minute burst, she found herself breathing hard for air and stopped. She placed her hands on her knees and attempted to lower her pulse by taking slow, deep breaths. Fatigue and the familiar smell of tide and seaweed narrowed the focus of her senses.

After recovering, she strolled to where the sand firmed, marking the maximum penetration of the waves against the shore. She stared at the breakers and thought about her trading system. It seemed as if she were in a race she could not win. Somehow, she had to get it right—and fast. She stood looking at the horizon as a succession of fear and doubt swirled on the fringes of her thoughts. She concentrated on the waves, hoping to draw strength from the puissant force of the surf as she fought off feelings of uncertainty and scrutinized her logic. What had she overlooked?

She designed her system to include two separate modules. Several minor indicators combined to form one timing device, but a pattern recognition indicator had been devised as a powerful stand-alone system. Both modules worked to a point, but they were not good enough to attract big money.

She wandered along the beach and watched a wave curl over itself as it approached the shore. She shifted her gaze beyond the breakers and focused on a flight of birds skimming inches above the undulating waves. They seemed to move as one. Inspired by the sight, she applied the concept to her software. What if she combined the two systems? Would the strength of the whole overcome the weaknesses of the parts?

She began to jog, her mind sailing over technical matters. There had to be a way to mesh the two systems. She increased her speed as her excitement transmitted itself to her legs. She streaked along the beach and felt exhilarated by the wind caressing her face and hair. She maintained her pace, moved onto the street, and raced toward home. She jumped a curb and ran across a vacant lot toward the rear of the house.

Sparky sat on his stool and saluted.

Kelly yelled, "Come on, Sparky. We've got work to do."

She burst through the front door and shouted at Miyako. "What if we couple the systems?"

Miyako put down her book.

Kelly gulped in air. "Can we do it?"

Miyako weighed the idea.

"Well?"

"I don't see any major problems."

"How about working straight through till we finish?" Before Miyako could answer, Kelly added, "I'll send out for pizza."

Miyako rolled her eyes. "Okay . . . okay."

Kelly showered and then put on jeans and a white blouse. She entered the front room in time to answer the doorbell.

Sparky stood next to a chair with an unusually high, padded seat that had obviously been designed to give him full access to working surfaces. He tugged the chair up the step. "I had to scrub the grease outta my pores."

Kelly created a mental flowchart and delegated the work effort. She would handle logic and assist Miyako in programming, Sparky would tackle data input, proofreading, and miscellaneous tasks.

After a productive three hours, Kelly turned from her computer. "Sparky, are you finished proofing that data?"

He got down from his chair. "Including urine, your body loses about seventy ounces of water a day. About thirteen ounces of that is lost through exhalation." He handed her the data sheet and disappeared into the kitchen.

Miyako, her mouth open, looked at Kelly with a bewildered expression.

Kelly tilted her head toward the kitchen. "It's a bumpy ride, but he's worth it."

Sparky returned with a tray containing three glasses of water. "The Romans knew how important a good source of water was. They had several aqueducts with a combined length of two hundred and sixty miles. The most revered aqueduct was the Aqua Marcia, which delivered excellent water. It was fifty-seven miles long. Most of that length was underground but the last seven miles was above ground on an arcade. It was an amazing engineering feat that resulted in a continuous flow of water. What they accomplished was truly incredible." He pointed toward Kelly's monitor. "You can go online and see pictures of the ruins." He drained his glass and went back to work.

The conversion took over six hours.

Full of anticipation, the trio huddled over the screen like expectant parents. The test used a five-year historical model. Two oscillating lines appeared on the screen. One indicator crossed the zero line seven times, the other eight. She compared the signals and came to a sudden, palpable conclusion: the two lines never crossed zero at the same time. Thus, no signals. Kelly's visions of success crumbled.

An hour and ten minutes later, exhausted and dispirited, they sat on the living room floor balancing slices of a veggie pizza and drinking red wine.

Halfway through the meal, Kelly abruptly put down her glass, splashing a small amount of wine on the carpet. "What if we gave the indicators a time window? Say five or ten days."

"I don't follow," Miyako said with a puzzled look.

"What kind of signals would we get if both lines crossed zero within a few days of each other?"

They hurried to the computer, leaving a half-eaten pizza on the living room floor.

Miyako entered a ten-day window.

Kelly scanned the data. "Too long. Five days, try five days."

Miyako changed the parameters and said, "You do it."

Kelly hesitated; then, she pressed the enter key.

CHAPTER 5

Martin Scanlan had heard the tape half a dozen times, but he felt compelled to listen to it again. He sat in a high-back leather chair in his sprawling office at Scanlan Equity Management with headphones covering each ear. A cord trailed down his body and coiled in his lap before snaking into a nearby desk drawer.

He found the tape shortly after his father had died. The cassette, one of over forty, had been stored in a metal box inside Phillip Scanlan's private safe. The tapes contained conversations of various staff members, obviously recorded surreptitiously, over many years. The safe also contained a schematic of the entire building, complete with tiny red crosses designating the locations of hidden microphones. His father had gone far beyond bugging his own office.

When Scanlan discovered the tapes, he finally understood how his father seemed to know everything that went on within the firm. He also knew why his father's will contained a performance clause. The suggestion had been made by Cameron Langston, an old friend of his father's, and it had been recorded on one of the tapes.

Scanlan remembered how he had sat in stunned silence during the reading of the will. A single sentence had burned itself into his memory: *If Scanlan Equity Management's performance is not consistent with historical levels over the next three years, the business shall be sold, and the proceeds shall be distributed equally among my sister and selected charities listed herein.* He shook his head in anger. The old man was surely laughing at him from his grave.

Scanlan did not have to check his calendar to know he had only eleven months left. He tracked his own mental version of the Time's Square lighted ball: descending, counting off time. It would take a miracle to recover the losses he had incurred during the last two years. The performance of the firm's managed accounts had trailed expectations, and his decisions on the house trading account had been disastrous. Excessive personal expenses, which he had charged to the corporation, contributed to the poor performance, but he did not intend to curtail his hedonistic lifestyle.

He turned on the antiquated cassette player and listened to a conversation between his father and Cameron Langston. Key words pierced Scanlan like daggers. Words like "incompetent," "egocentric," "unstable" and "sybaritic." They had always talked about him behind his back.

Next came his father's cruel joke: "I just can't believe Martin was the fastest out of half a million sperm. I guess Mother Nature fucks up occasionally just like everyone else." Laughter resounded through the headphones.

The virulent comments revealed how Phillip Scanlan had limited Martin's trading activities by keeping him occupied with administrative duties. Then, the most injurious revelation of them all; his father told Langston how they had "faded" his son by taking opposite positions on trades. The two men laughed, recounting the profits they had made in this manner.

Scanlan yanked off the headphones and glowered at a huge gilded, oil portrait of his father. Consumed by hatred, he grabbed a letter opener and bolted from his chair. He lunged at the painting and brought his hand down swiftly, ripping his father's face. Uttering a barrage of seething, guttural sounds, he raised the makeshift dagger repeatedly, slashing until tattered pieces of cloth lay open like flesh ripped from his father's body.

With shaking hands, Scanlan flung the letter opener across the room and paced. He would never have to look at the old man's face again. He stared one last time, hoping to banish forever the memory of his father's contravention in his affairs. In a final mocking gesture, one of his father's eyes dangled from disjointed threads, glaring at him. Scanlan grabbed the frame and sent it crashing to the floor. He should have destroyed the picture long ago.

Needing a drink, he pushed a button on the wall and a wooden panel slid open, exposing an elaborate wet bar. He poured and swallowed two fingers of an upscale bourbon and leaned against the counter, savoring the alcohol's tasteful burn. He replenished his glass and returned to his desk.

He sipped his drink and continued to brood over the tape. He had cleansed the room by destroying the picture, but Cameron Langston's irksome cackle clung to him like an endless echo. His hatred for the pretentious old codger soared as memories of Langston's demeaning laughter ricocheted through his mind. Clearly, Langston must pay for meddling in the composition of the will. Scanlan began to formulate a plan for revenge, a plan that would silence Cameron Langston forever. Only then would he be able to purge the memory of the tapes. He would assassinate the old crony himself, and he would do it in a most unusual manner.

He removed the cassette from the recorder and spun his chair toward his safe. The office schematic tumbled out when he withdrew a metal box. A business card clipped to the corner of the folded layout read: PIGEON SURVEILLANCE SYSTEMS. Below the name were a P.O. Box number in Pescadero and a telephone number identified as voice mail.

In recent months, Scanlan had learned much about the card's unscrupulous owner and his willingness to do anything for money. His subsequent relationship with Danny Fagan had been a fortuitous one. After discovering the power of the covert listening devices, Scanlan had hired Fagan to install additional units.

He also instructed Fagan to hide microphones in the bedrooms of his home in Hillsborough and his mountain retreat. Recording sexual encounters without his partner's knowledge gave him an incredible rush. He quickly learned how to exhort his many consorts to verbalize their needs and feelings, and he reveled at the sounds of women moaning and cooing over his sexual prowess. But the tapes Scanlan liked most were those recorded in the guests' bedrooms.

Scanlan's appetite for vicarious thrills increased dramatically. To satisfy a growing need for visual stimuli, he instructed Fagan to install miniature, hidden cameras in each bedroom. Elaborate measures, including redecoration, provided extraordinary concealment for the devices.

Though Danny Fagan had become an important resource, Scanlan did not appreciate his style or appearance. He particularly disliked Fagan's pockmarked face and the splotches of pigeon droppings covering his shoes. Nevertheless, his phenomenal expertise and secretive nature caused Scanlan to overlook these idiosyncrasies.

Scanlan slid the business card between his fingers and thought about their last contact when Fagan had informed him of Heather Coyne's death. If the woman had lived another few days, she could have destroyed him. He eased back, thankful Coyne's supervisor had been on vacation and that Heather had come directly to him about a deficit in a client's account. He had temporarily diverted $800,000 into his own trading account to cover a margin call, but he should have realized he could not hide a transfer of that size for long, especially from Heather Coyne. If his father's executor, or the authorities, had found out about the misappropriation, he might have lost everything.

His thoughts returned to unfinished business, renewing his anger. Cameron Langston's hideous laughter had invaded his dreams long enough. He planned to kill Langston himself, but he needed an accomplice to handle the grunt work. Danny Fagan's ingenious methods for disposing of bodies made him ideal for the job.

A phone call snapped Scanlan's reverie.

"Martin, it's Brian. Can you spare a few minutes?"

Brian Doane had taken over Nathan Rosenberg's desk after the top analyst's sudden departure. Scanlan agreed to see him.

Doane stepped into the office and stopped abruptly when he saw the slashed portrait.

"Don't ask," Scanlan said curtly.

Doane took a seat, fidgeted a moment and then opened a folder. "We've lost two more accounts to Rosenberg's new firm. I think we—"

"Who?"

"The Bartlet Trust and Mrs. Harrington."

"Bartlet? Jesus Christ!"

"I'm trying to get them back, but they feel strongly about Rosenberg. Loyalty and all of that."

Scanlan rose and paced the room, and then he stopped behind Doane, but said nothing. His father had done the same thing to him during a meeting with a dozen influential executives. It had been an unsettling experience.

Doane shifted uneasily in his chair.

Scanlan wanted the timid little shit to sweat a little longer.

Doane tugged at his collar.

Satisfied, Scanlan said, "We can't afford to lose any more accounts. What are you going to do about it?"

"Well . . . ah, we're working hard on bringing in some new money. The stock market is hot right now, and we have some major prospects."

"I've heard that same bullshit for six months."

Doane said nothing.

Scanlan watched him squirm, then went back to his desk and asked a question he already knew the answer to. "How's our trading performance this month?"

"We're a little behind the S&P Index."

"Unacceptable." He let the word sink in. "We've got to take some risks and bring up our numbers. I want you and the staff to put together a new strategy for the rest of this year." He leaned forward. "You have two priorities. Bring in a substantial amount of new capital and improve our trading performance." His tone turned truculent. "If you and your people can't get the job done, I'll find someone who can."

Doane dropped his folder. He picked it up and said, "I–I'll get right on it," He rose to leave, but turned back. "There is one more thing. While I was going through Rosenberg's desk, I came across a file of letters from a broker."

"So what? Brokers solicit us every day."

"I know, but this might be something we should look at."

Scanlan felt his patience slipping and was about to dismiss Doane, but the possibility of a catastrophic change to his lifestyle made him reconsider. If he did not do something to change the firm's performance, he would lose everything in a year. He motioned toward the chair. "What's so special about this broker?"

Doane, obviously still nervous, eased onto the chair and opened a folder. "Well, there are the normal letters soliciting our business, but the broker also sent three different trade recommendations over a period of several months. So far, they're all winners."

"We're in a bull market. It could have been pure luck. Besides, the time frame is too short to know if he's any good."

"There's more." Doane pulled out another sheet. "One of the trades was a short position. It's very hard to pick those in a market like this."

Scanlan leaned forward, his interest piqued.

Doane continued, "The recommendations came from a proprietary timing system the broker is working on. The final version will be ready in a couple of weeks."

"There are dozens of trading systems around. We use several ourselves."

"Yes, but this one is supposed to be a breakthrough using neural networks."

"What in the hell is a neural network?"

"It's rather complicated."

"Give me a quick overview."

Doane eased back in his chair. "The technology for neural networks was inspired by the human brain. The result is a computer model designed to simulate the behavior of biological neural networks. Some interesting progress has been made in pattern recognition."

Scanlan waved a hand. "Get to the point."

"It really comes down to this: a neural network learns from its mistakes. That means a system can give more accurate output with each repetition of a task. Many believe this kind of software could be of great value in a trading system."

It all sounded too complicated, but Scanlan's plight compelled him to consider new risks. Perhaps he should spend a few minutes with the broker. "What's this guy's name?"

"Actually, it's a woman. Her name is—"

Scanlan rolled his eyes. "Jesus, Brian. First, you say it's theoretical, and, now, you tell me the broker is a female." His tone turned boastful. "I'll bed a woman whenever I like, but I'll be damned if I'm going to bet my future on some new software designed by a tech-weenie broker wearing pantyhose."

A dumbfounded Brian Doane excused himself and left the room.

———

Scanlan left the office and drove his Mercedes S-Class to the San Francisco International Airport. He looked forward to entertaining David Merriweather, his biggest client, at his mountain home. Scanlan had arranged for two young women, Danielle and Nichole, to join them, and he had promised Nichole a substantial bonus to perform a single task—screw Merriweather's brains out.

But Danielle was his. Scanlan stepped into his charter airplane, remembering the last time he had been with her. He loved women with long legs and kinky habits and Danielle fit his needs perfectly. He joined his guests and marveled at Nichole's manipulation of Merriweather. She frequently leaned against him, offering an intimate view of her cleavage as she whispered in his ear. They were still on the ground, but she already had him under her spell.

Scanlan planned to videotape their liaison. He visualized Nichole's naked body straddling Merriweather, riding him with abandon. Excited by his anticipation, he slid a newspaper over his lap to hide a burgeoning erection.

CHAPTER 6

Kelly lifted a trembling hand from the keyboard. Had she overlooked something? The screen flickered, and she sensed she had entered a minute capsule of time that would determine her future. Fearful of the outcome, she peered at the monitor but saw only an agglomeration.

"Are you all right?" Miyako asked.

Kelly nodded.

"The format isn't great," Miyako said, "but we can change that."

"If it's worth changing."

"You're forgetting your own advice," Sparky said, pointing to the handmade sign above Kelly's computer. "You've got to believe."

"I know. It's just that so much depends on this." Kelly checked her notes. "Okay, let's take it a year at a time." The results were better than anything she had achieved so far, but she sensed something was wrong. She scanned a matrix of trades the system would have recommended over the last five years. The bull market had started six years ago and had undergone three minor corrections. The system had forecasted them, but it had also given false signals that would have created an excessive number of trades with small losses.

"We've done it!" Miyako said.

"It's good. It's very good, but it's still not right."

"My God, Kelly. The system picked every major turn."

"I know, but there are too many false signals. Too much garbage."

The enthusiasm faded from Miyako's soft, dark eyes.

"Don't worry," Kelly said. "I think it's fixable." She doodled on a scratch pad, searching for answers. "Maybe we should give each signal a strength number. Say, from one to ten. Then we ignore everything with a reading below five. I'll use a historical data base of twenty or thirty years to come up with the parameters."

"Sterling idea," Sparky declared.

"When you finish," Miyako said, "I'll program the software to place a small dialog box in one corner of the screen to show the strength number. You'll know immediately if it's a good signal."

"Perfect." Kelly glanced at her watch. Two-thirty. "We'd better get some sleep."

In bed, she considered the changes she would work on the next day. After a sleepless hour, a yearning ache deep within her pelvis shifted her thoughts to long neglected urges. An intense schedule and the duties of motherhood kept her busy during the day, but the loneliness of her bed released a tide of complaining hormones. She wanted a man next to her, giving her attention, making her feel feminine, but it couldn't be just anyone.

———

Kelly awoke feeling listless from too little sleep. She swung her legs over the edge of the bed as she recalled a disturbing dream. She could not remember the entirety of the dream but her mind replayed a vision of her lying on a blanket, under an oak tree, wrapped in the arms of Cody's father, Sean Keene. A similar dream occurred a couple of times a year and it disturbed her greatly. Why did she continue to dream about someone she despised after all these years? The dreams were bad enough, but she often found herself wondering where Sean was and what he was doing. This infuriated her. Determined to push the dream from her thoughts, she dressed, went into the kitchen, turned on the coffee maker, and then she opened the front door to collect her Sunday newspaper.

"Sparky, what are you doing here?"

He was sitting on the step staring at the sky. "This is one of those mornings when the lunar cycle allows you to see the moon during the day." He handed her the paper. "Did you know that the moon is moving away from the Earth?"

"I had no idea."

"Most people don't." He got up from the step. "Actually, it's only about an inch and a half a year, but over time it makes a difference. Prehistoric tidal patterns were much different than today because the moon was closer to the Earth. The result was higher tides and shorter days."

He walked inside. "Enough of that, let's get to work."

She glanced at the moon, paused for a moment, then she closed the door. "I really appreciate your offer to help."

"It's a good project, and I'm excited to work with you and Miyako."

"You certainly have a good attitude for someone who isn't getting paid."

"Attitude is the key to a happy life."

"I can't argue with that."

After delegating assignments to Sparky and Miyako, Kelly worked assiduously, stopping only for quick runs to the bathroom made necessary by Sparky's relentless crusade to replenish body fluids.

When she finished the revision, a foreboding mood swept over her. She hoped she had a fix for her system, but calculating strength numbers for each signal could easily lead to another dead-end. Feeling uneasy, she input the same five-year historical database and started the program. The system gave fewer recommendations. A positive sign, but Kelly had to determine which trades had been eliminated. After making a list of trades, she grabbed the previous test sheet and compared the two. She stared at the results in stunned silence. The new system had eliminated eighty percent of the false signals. This was better than she could have hoped for, and the impressive results threw her off balance. Could the system really be this good, or had she made a horrendous mistake?

Obviously, Miyako had no such fears. She hugged Kelly, her eyes shining brightly.

Sparky raised both arms the way referees do to signal a touchdown.

Kelly broke the embrace. "We can't celebrate yet. We need to do two more tests."

"Why?" Miyako said. "It works."

"We've got to check it over a longer period to be sure. Twenty years at least. Then we'll do the biggest tests of all. Would the system have given sell signals for the 1987 and the dot com crashes?"

DALE BRANDON

The room bristled with electricity as they ran the last test. Kelly worked quickly, her energy level fueled by anticipation. She compiled the results and sat motionless, her eyes locked on the numbers. Tangible proof obliterated her momentary disbelief. They had done it.

———

After Miyako and Sparky had left, Kelly collapsed on the couch. Eighteen months of doubt, fear, miscalculation, and deprivation had ended. She had completed a formidable task, but she had no idea in what direction her life would turn. Surely, things would change. Surely, it would be better for her and Cody, but life seemed to have a way of throwing a wrench in the works at the most inopportune times.

A growling stomach reminded Kelly that she had not eaten since breakfast. She gathered ingredients for a turkey sandwich and thought about Cody. She missed him and wanted to share her news. She glanced at the clock. He would return from his scouting trip in about an hour. Cody's picture on the refrigerator door changed her mind about the sandwich. She would take him out for his favorite meal—burgers at The Burger Spot.

———

Kelly rose at 4:00 A.M. Monday morning and tiptoed into Cody's room. She sidestepped a baseball mitt and a pair of jeans before bending to kiss him on the forehead. After leaving the house, she drove to the highway and thought about her future. Intensive development of the program had left little time for marketing strategies, and there were many new issues to consider. She pulled into the parking garage, thankful that Huey had survived the trip. She sat in her car, contemplating a new problem. Did she have a future at Boucher and Crittenden? Her confrontation with Emmett Crittenden severely strained her loyalty to the firm, but she could hardly strike out on her own before her system had established a positive record.

She dreamed of founding her own consulting firm or publishing a market letter, but she was still dependent on others for regular income. Her best strategy would be to land the Scanlan account and save her job. After careful documentation of real-time trading results, she could investigate a myriad of options. Only then could she afford to leave Boucher & Crittenden.

If she did manage to stay with the firm for an interim period, she had to be wary of Crittenden. She had seen him in action and knew his style. At the very least, he would try to take partial credit for her trading system, but she was not about to let him ride on her coattails. Safeguarding her system took on a sudden, chilling urgency. How would she protect the software? If it was as good as she thought, it could be worth a fortune, and unscrupulous individuals might do anything to get the program. She hurried to her desk, pushed aside a white, sealed envelope, and dialed home.

Miyako answered sleepily.

Kelly skipped the pleasantries. "How are we going to protect the system?"

"What?"

"The software. Somebody might try to steal it."

"I'm half asleep. Give me a second." After a long silence, Miyako said, "Well, we could use a password but that's not enough. There are too many sharp techies out there."

"What else?"

"Give me a minute."

47

Kelly's concern notched up as she waited. She could almost hear the wheels spinning in Miyako's head.

"The best thing for now is to copy the program onto a flash drive," Miyako said. "Then I'll erase the program from the hard drive. Even if someone has access to your computer, they won't be able to run the program. We'll use a two-step security system. The user will have to answer two questions before they can access the password screen. The questions will be something that only you would know the answers to. I'll set it up so that you have three chances to get the answers right. If you fail, the system will lock for twenty-four hours before you can try again."

"I like the idea, but I'll have to load the flash drive every time I want to run the program. That means I'll have to carry it with me."

"I don't see any other choice right now." Miyako yawned. "After I have some coffee I'll give it some more thought."

Kelly said, "I think the questions should be fake. Ask for my first pet's name but we'll put in something that has no relation to a pet. That way if they use a high-speed computer system to scan all possible pet names it won't help. How about Golden Gate Bridge for the answer?

"I like it. How about the other question?"

Kelly considered the second question and then said, "Make the second question about a number. Ask for an entry of a number between one and one million. But we won't use a number. I'll put in some personal information only I would know."

"Perfect."

"Make two copies of the software," Kelly said. "I think I'd better put one in a safe-deposit box."

"Good idea."

She replaced the receiver and noticed the letter on her desk. She opened the envelope and read the single paragraph:

Ms. Sanborn,
Pursuant to our conversation of Friday last, you
are hereby officially notified that you are being
placed on probation for a period of thirty days,
effective immediately. A review of your performance
will be made at the completion of the probationary
period, and, then, appropriate action will be taken if
deemed necessary.

Emmett Crittenden

"Thirty days?" He had told her sixty. She shook her head at his transparent tactics. He meant to gain a quick resolution by turning up the pressure, forcing her to resign or give in to his demands. Kelly wadded the letter and threw it into the wastebasket. She was not about to jump in the sack with the bastard. Bristling with anger, she bolted toward his office for a final confrontation, but she stopped half way across the floor. This wouldn't do. Mindful of the need to cool down, she turned and headed for her desk.

T. J. Halverson had apparently been observing her. He walked by and spoke in a low voice. "What's the matter, Sticks? In over your head?"

She looked him straight in the eye. "You know, Halverson. You really ought to do something about those letters on your forehead."

Unwittingly, his hand went to his head. "Letters?"

"Yes, the ones that spell prick."

A mixture of boos and laughter rang out.

Kelly returned to her desk, slumped into her chair, and stared at her quote screen, but she did not see the mercurial numbers.

Her phone rang. "Nice put-down, Kelly."

Dan Hawkins had gone through training with her. She made eye contact with him. "I just got tired of his crap."

"The guy's an idiot. Don't let him bother you."

After their conversation, she watched Dan working at his desk and wondered if his wife knew how lucky she was. It seemed as though all the good men in the world were married. She unwrapped two pieces of chocolate and popped the first one into her mouth. She leaned back and attempted to calm herself by concentrating on her trading system and her future. Things were different now. She had to believe in herself.

After further thought, she retrieved the discarded letter from the wastebasket, smoothed it out, and placed it in a folder. Emmett Crittenden might get screwed, but not in the manner he expected.

CHAPTER 7

Kelly found it impossible to follow her normal routine. Instead of making phone calls, she concentrated on the myriad of obstacles before her. Just as the market was about to close, she could no longer curb her uneasiness about protecting the software. She had to put a copy in a bank vault immediately. On her way out of the office, she heard a loud cheer. A nearby screen showed that the Dow had surged and closed at a new all-time high on extremely heavy volume. The younger brokers seemed excessively euphoric.

She arrived home and went straight to the dining room.

Miyako was standing, eating yogurt, while staring at her computer screen.

"Did you copy the software?"

"All done. I put it on a flash drive. I made three copies, checked to make sure they worked, and then erased everything on the hard drive."

"Good, I'll go to the bank today."

"The sooner, the better," Miyako said. "It scares me to death when I think about the potential value of this software." She rubbed the back of her neck. "By the way, you need a name for your system."

Surprised she had overlooked something so obvious, Kelly picked up a pad to jot down possible names.

"I've given this a good deal of thought," Miyako said, "and I have a couple of suggestions. How about Trident or Cyberstar?"

Kelly considered the names. "Trident doesn't fit, but I really like Cyberstar. There might be a trademark issue with the name, but if we call it Cyberstar Trading System that should separate it from other categories. We'll use that as a working title, but I have a hunch it will stick."

She thought about security issues while she changed clothes. She could safeguard two of the flash drives in the bank, but she would constantly need access to another. Her purse would do temporarily, but she needed to devise something less obvious—and soon.

She removed her skirt, noticed that it had begun to fray along a seam, and then tossed the garment into the corner as if to banish it from her life. If she signed the Scanlan account, she would finally be able to buy a new wardrobe. She promptly admonished herself. The operative word was "when," not "if."

She ate a quick lunch, arranged her notes, took a deep breath, and dialed Scanlan's office. At the sound of the first ring, anxiety coursed through her body, reaching an almost unbearable level. This was it. The next few minutes might be the most crucial of her career.

"Mr. Scanlan, please."

"I'm sorry, but he's out of town until Wednesday."

Kelly's heart sank. She had not prepared herself for this. She weighed her best approach. "Could you please switch me to Nathan Rosenberg?"

"He's no longer with the firm."

Another shock. She thought of Crittenden's comment about an analyst leaving Scanlan Equity Management. He had obviously been referring to Rosenberg. "Who replaced him?"

"That would be Brian Doane. I'll transfer you."

A youthful voice answered.

"Mr. Doane, my name is Kelly Sanborn. I'm a broker with Bouch—"

"I know who you are."

"Have we spoken before?"

"No. I saw your correspondence in Rosenberg's files. By the way, none of the information ever got to Mr. Scanlan."

No wonder she could not get an appointment. She forged ahead. "Then you probably know I've sent three trade recommendations to your firm. All winners. What I'm about to tell you will make those results look insignificant." She paused, hoping to build suspense. "I have just completed work on a new trading system called Cyberstar, and the historical test results are better than any I've ever seen."

She spent the next twenty minutes discussing historical market events her system would have predicted, taking special care to emphasize that her system would have forecasted the '87 crash and the start of the horrendous bear market after the dot com bubble.

Doane tried to project reticence, but Kelly sensed an underlying enthusiasm. She decided to take a huge risk, and she spoke confidently. "Because I'll be offering my services on a very selective basis, I think it's important that you understand my position. Because Scanlan Equity Management has ignored my contacts to date, my offer will not be open-ended." She drew in a deep, quiet breath.

A heavy silence traveled through the phone line, seeking, and then expanding Kelly's anxieties. Had she gone too far? She bit her bottom lip and waited.

"I'm interested, very interested," Doane finally said. "But I can't barge in on Mr. Scanlan without proper documentation. He's very demanding. I might need to meet with him a couple of times before he agrees to see you."

Doane seemed to fear his boss, but Kelly sensed that something else troubled him, something he would rather not discuss. "I'll send historical trade documentation on Monday," she said.

Savoring her partial success, she punched in Vanessa's number. "Hi. I thought I'd better check in. Everything okay?"

"Crittenden wanted to know where you were, and I told him you had an appointment with a prospective client."

"Thanks."

"You had three phone calls. Otherwise, it's been quiet."

Kelly jotted down the messages. "How did the market close?"

"The Dow was up ninety-two points half an hour before the close, but it sold off and finished up only fourteen. Still a new high, though."

"How about the internals?"

"Kind of odd, really. New highs did not expand, and advances were about even with declines. The Transportation and the Utility indexes did not follow the Dow."

Kelly thanked Vanessa and hung up. Technical indicators had been giving conflicting signals for more than three months, but the Dow kept moving into new high ground and bullish sentiment continued unabated. She considered today's market behavior and realized she had not tested Cyberstar in a real-time mode. Using historical data was the only way she could test and validate the accuracy of her system during development. She designed the software to monitor the market daily, so she might as well start now.

She found the program flash drives on Miyako's desk and inserted the first into a USB port. She started the software, downloaded current market data, and ran the system. The screen lit up. Both indicator lines had recently turned down sharply. One crossed the zero trigger line today, and the second line had turned down dramatically. It had not yet crossed zero, but its downward momentum was remarkable.

She studied the sequence of lines with a strong sense of deja vu. Where had she seen this pattern before? She put her elbow on the desk and rested her forehead in the palm of her hand. *Think, dammit, think.* Frustrated, she rose and paced the floor.

Miyako joined her in the kitchen. "I put your copy of the software in your desk drawer and—"

"I've got it!" Kelly dashed to the computer. "The crash! The '87 crash."

Her fingers flew over the keyboard, bringing up a screen of the 1987 stock market collapse. She sat in stunned silence. The pattern of the two indicator lines bore an eerie similarity to those of today's market.

Miyako moved closer. "What does it mean?"

The keyboard clicked under Kelly's fingers. "Nothing yet. Only one line has crossed zero so far. . . . But, my God." She turned on the printer and struck a key. The machine innocently copied a record of human misery—the sharp, violent collapse of the stock market in 1987. Her heart pounded as she grabbed the hard copy and then entered commands to bring up the current market. She held the printer copy next to the screen. The indicators showed an uncanny resemblance. Kelly turned to

Miyako. "I think the system is on the verge of giving a major sell signal."

"A ten rating?"

"Yes. It could be one of the strongest signals in decades." Kelly analyzed possible scenarios. "Market internals would have to make a huge turnaround over the next several days to prevent it. I don't think that's going to happen."

The possibility that her system was about to signal a massive decline in the stock market charged Kelly with energy. She rose and prowled the house, her mind on fast-forward. This might be the opportunity of a lifetime. But what if she were wrong? What if she had overlooked something? After all, Cyberstar had not proven itself in a real-world environment. Her thoughts became fragmented, and she realized she was trying to cover too much ground too quickly. She needed to step away from the problem and let things simmer in some obscure portion of her mind.

She changed into running shorts and waited for Cody to come home from school. When he arrived, she made a dash for the front door. "We're going to run early today."

Cody ran toward the rear of the house removing his backpack as he ran. He would be on his bicycle in a flash. She went out the door and broke into a trot. She turned onto the street and picked up her pace, getting a head start of about thirty yards. The routine rarely varied. After their short race, the winner always heckled the loser; then, Cody would follow her along a dirt path toward the ocean. Today she would alter their destination and go to the bank eight blocks away. She had placed two copies of the software in a sandwich bag, which she tucked inside her fanny pack.

Cody caught and passed her with ten yards to go. At the end of the street, he applied the brakes and slid the bicycle's back tire around so that he faced her. He leaned over the handlebars and broke into a wide grin.

She smiled. "I'm going to have to start calling you Speedo."

He gave a thumbs-up sign.

She set a course alongside an artichoke field and headed for the bank. It seemed unlikely that anyone knew about the flash drives, but she glanced over her shoulder frequently, searching for strangers. She suspected that this kind of vigilance would become a part of her future.

In bed that night, Kelly slipped back and forth between light sleep and consciousness. Her brain simply would not shut down. Finally, she sat up, drew up her knees, and clasped her arms around her legs. Was her system really on the verge of signaling a major turn in the market? She pondered the possibility until she became so keyed up she had to get out of bed. She slipped on a cotton robe and went to her desk. After rechecking and analyzing the data, she knew a signal was imminent. Her mind skipped from one idea to another, processing, weighing. If the second indicator line crossed zero with a ten rating she felt she needed to do something unique. Huddled at her desk in the middle of the night, she sensed the profound importance of the next few days. She could not afford to make any mistakes.

After three hours of sleep, Kelly stepped into the early morning air and nursed a coughing, sputtering car along a fog-shrouded freeway to San Francisco. Huey made it to the parking garage, but the automobile's erratic behavior alarmed her. She arrived at her desk five minutes after the market opened. Shouts from around the room caused her to check her screen. A strong economic report had sent the Dow up seventy-seven points during the first few minutes.

She spent the morning watching the market and the other brokers. Excessive enthusiasm was an important trait of market tops, and she took the office's euphoric mood as a warning signal. She had also noted the *San Francisco Chronicle's* headline story: "DOW HITS ALL-TIME HIGH." After reading the article, Kelly recalled an old Wall Street adage: Nobody rings a bell at the top. Maybe not, she thought, but prudent observers should constantly monitor trader psychology, the most reliable tocsin of all.

By eleven o'clock, the Dow had rallied 148 points; then, the market leveled off and churned within a narrow range on heavy volume. Kelly's heightened anticipation made her restive during the final hour of trading, the most critical time of the day.

Thirty-five minutes before the close, the market broke its trading range and began to decline. After a quick drop of more than ninety points, selling pressure eased and the Dow ended with a small gain. The action had been similar to the previous day; most of the advance had been lost, but the market still recorded a new closing high. More headlines, headlines that would not mention weak market internals.

Kelly had to wait thirty minutes before her data service would release today's final statistics. Between glances at the clock, she ate a piece of chocolate, doodled on a pad and fidgeted with items on her desk. At 1:20, she withdrew the program flash drive from her purse and put it into a USB port. She brought up the screen displaying the data service's menu and tabbed to the download bar. She pressed the enter key at precisely 1:30.

She leaned toward the screen, concentrating, anticipating.

"I really don't think you're going to find any new customers in that computer."

She jumped at the sound of Crittenden's voice. He had a knack for skulking around the office when his employees least expected it.

"You might as well clean out your desk and save us all a lot of trouble." His voice was louder than necessary.

She spun in her chair. "I've got thirty days, and I intend to use all of them." He started to respond, but she cut him off. "And I'm not going to let you interfere with my productivity." She turned back to her screen.

"You'll never make it, Sanborn. You're finished." Crittenden stalked off toward his office.

From an adjoining desk, Zack Nichols stared at her in disbelief.

She closed her eyes. She had too much at stake to let Crittenden get to her. After composing herself, she checked the screen and saw that the download had completed successfully. She started the program and waited. Her office computer's CPU crunched numbers slower than her quad core equipped home computer, and Kelly saw the delay as a stoppage of time. She expected a sell signal, and she wanted to act on it now.

The screen flickered.

Both indicator lines had crossed the zero line. She checked a small box in the upper right-hand corner of the screen. The numeral ten flashed like a warning light, sending a frisson of excitement through her body. Cyberstar had just given a maximum strength sell signal. She stared at the red number, momentarily paralyzed by its significance.

She needed time to think and she thought best on her feet. She removed the flash drive, turned off the monitor, and headed for the conference room. She closed the door, threw her note pad on the table, and kicked off her shoes. She paced with a sense of urgency, mulling strategies as she roamed. She stopped at the window and searched the concrete canyons as if they harbored an answer. Her gaze moved up Montgomery Street, scanning disjointed lines of people scurrying about like tiny ants carrying miniature briefcases.

She watched a man crossing the street. He stopped suddenly in the middle of the intersection, hesitated, then turned and retraced his steps. This was not a time for indecision. She decided to take the biggest risk of her life. A desperate inspiration took hold, sweeping away other thoughts. Her strategy was bold and replete with incredible risk, but it seemed her only chance. She slid onto a chair and began to write.

Loyalty dictated her first action—she would advise her customers to liquidate most of their portfolios. Her second priority would be to contact Martin Scanlan in a manner that would demand his attention. She contemplated her last strategy, apprehensive about its potential consequences. The idea went beyond radical, and it scared the hell out of her. Her plan would be deemed brilliant if it succeeded, but failure would bring complete humiliation. There would be no middle ground.

She was going to lose her job anyway, so why not take a bold approach? She hurried back to her desk and picked up the phone. She had hoped to contact all her clients within a few hours, but most of them had become so seduced by the unrelenting bull market that she had to spend extra time convincing them to lighten their positions. She pleaded with those who would not sell to at least hedge their positions by purchasing "put" options. In a declining market, the profits from these options would offset some of the losses incurred by holding stocks.

Because she finished only half of her calls, she would have to allocate time tomorrow morning for the others. At 3:30, she turned her attention to Scanlan Equity Management. She wrote several drafts of a telegram and then read the final version:

> *My proprietary software has just given a major*
> *signal on the market STOP Contact undersigned*
> *for details STOP*
> *Kelly Sanborn*

Satisfied, she went online and accessed a company's website that still offered telegram service, which Western Union no longer did. She addressed the telegram to Martin Scanlan and sent a copy to Brian Doane.

Then she phoned the *San Francisco Chronicle* and requested pricing for a display ad in the business section. The quotation stunned her. The only good news was that the newspaper would bill her. She hesitated over the cost, but she finally placed an ad measuring three columns wide by four inches high.

At the bottom of the advertisement, she listed her name, her phone number, and a disclaimer stating that the opinions expressed in the ad were solely those of the author. The last line recommended that readers contact an investment advisor before making important financial decisions. She did not mention Boucher & Crittenden. The ad read:

THE BULL IS DEAD!
SELL ALL STOCKS

A black river of doubt engulfed Kelly as she lifted her hand from the receiver. She raised her head and whispered, "My God, what have I done?"

CHAPTER 8

During his stay in the mountains, Martin Scanlan became increasingly vindictive about Cameron Langston's influence over his father's will. The performance clause suggested by Langston had become a menacing time bomb, tormenting even his dreams. On the evening Scanlan returned to San Francisco, he received a telephone call informing him of new customer defections. The news sent him stalking about his home in a state of alarm. His lifestyle required a substantial and continuous influx of funds, but he would lose everything if he did not reverse the trend.

Nearing panic, he poured bourbon into a glass with ice and went to the shooting range in his basement. The excitement of a 9mm banging away served as an outlet for stress. He emptied his Beretta at a target on the far wall, took a drink, and slammed home another magazine. Firing round after round into the target, he felt as if the gun's power had traveled up his arm and spread through his body.

His resolve replenished by alcohol and gunpowder, he vowed that nothing would stop him from gaining his rightful inheritance. He thought about the will and heard Cameron Langston's ragged cackle echo in his mind. It was time to end this shit. He laid the pistol aside, picked up the phone, and dialed the pigeon keeper.

———————

The following morning, Scanlan asked his secretary to compile a report listing changes in the customer base. He used a red marker to identify the clients that had recently left the firm. The number exceeded his expectations. He dialed his secretary. "Tell Doane, Devincenzi, and Hostetler to meet me in the conference room in fifteen minutes. No excuses."

Scanlan used the time before the meeting to check his portfolio. The Dow had again moved into new high ground, but the market's strength had done little for his own account. He had a small profit in stocks, but he had suffered heavy losses from his trades in gold futures, which were highly leveraged. Believing stock prices would go higher, he used his remaining margin to increase holdings in large tech stocks, and to purchase shares of MicroDart Security Systems, a small company rumored to have developed a breakthrough in Internet security.

After receiving his trade confirmations, he strode into the conference room and tossed the client list on the table. "At this rate, Scanlan Equity Management will be an endangered species within a year. I'll replace everyone in this building before that happens." A tense silence fell over the room as he gazed around the table.

Satisfied they were about to piss in their pants, Scanlan continued, "Last week I asked Brian to come up with a strategy to turn things around. I've read the recommendations, and I'm afraid they're just a rehash of what we've done before." He loosened his tie. "The S&P 500 is the problem. Our clients are not idiots. They know they can beat our performance by switching to index funds. Bottom line, we've got to improve our trading results. We've got to start thinking in new—"

His secretary appeared at the door. "I'm sorry to interrupt, Mr. Scanlan, but a telegram just came for you."

Surprised, he waved her in, opened the envelope, and read the brief message. He shook his head and shoved the yellow slip of paper toward Brian Doane. "You're going to get a copy so you might as well read this."

Doane scanned the telegram with a surprised expression. "Kelly Sanborn is the broker I told you about."

"I'll say one thing for her," Scanlan replied, "she has guts."

Doane said, "I received documentation on her system, but I haven't had time to study it."

Scanlan drummed his fingers on the table. A female broker perfecting a revolutionary trading system bordered on the preposterous. He started to toss the telegram into the wastebasket, but desperation made him reconsider. It wouldn't hurt to take a cursory look at the documents. He placed his elbows on the table and clasped his hand together. "Go get the package."

Doane returned with a maroon portfolio.

Scanlan thumbed through the report until he found a six-page summary of historical trades the system would have made if it had been operational. After reviewing the data, he handed the pages to Doane. "Nothing is that good. I think Miss Sanborn doctored the hell out of those results."

Elizabeth Devincenzi had slid her chair next to Doane. "If it's half as good as these figures suggest, it's still a powerful system. Why not check it out?"

Scanlan still had a problem with the concept, but he had to take risks. "All right. I want you and Brian to go through the package and give me a full report tomorrow afternoon."

"Do you want to meet with the broker?"

"Read the report; then, convince me I need to."

After the meeting, he worried about his own portfolio. What if the woman's system really was that good? A sharp sell-off would devastate his highly leveraged account. He checked the market and reviewed his charts, but he saw no sign of a pending break. He dismissed the possibility of a crash and shifted his thoughts to Cameron Langston. Scanlan opened his safe and removed the tape containing Langston's most deleterious remarks. He shoved the tape into his coat pocket and left the office in a vengeful mood.

———

Just before midnight, Scanlan poured a double shot of scotch, stepped into his garage, and raised the main door. Waiting in the dark, the combination of hatred and alcohol fueled malevolent thoughts. He slid the cassette tape back and forth between his thumb and forefinger, aware of a peculiar anticipation building within. A cargo van turned into his drive and entered the garage. Scanlan closed the door and switched on the lights.

The pigeon keeper, his pockmarked face partially concealed by a cap, opened the rear door of the van. "Your package," he said flatly.

Cameron Langston lay on his stomach, handcuffed, blindfolded, and gagged. His corpulent form rocked back and forth, testing the constraints securing him to the vehicle.

Scanlan's gaze went from Langston to a thin, disheveled man in the passenger seat. He turned to Fagan. "I thought I told you to come alone."

"I needed help to grab the old guy, and it's going to take three men to get him out of your basement when you're done. He weighs a fucking ton."

Scanlan had not thought of that, but another man's involvement made him uncomfortable. "Can you trust him?"

"Rick? Yeah, no problem. He knows I'll slit his throat if he ever crosses me."

"Did you have any problems?"

"Naw. It went pretty slick. We took a dirt road and waited in the shrubs by the fourteenth fairway. We snatched him when he went into the trees to get his ball. He's got a hell of a bad slice."

"He won't have to worry about that anymore," Scanlan said as he opened the door to his house. "Bring him in."

In the elevator, he watched the men struggle with their staggering, red-faced captive. When they reached the basement shooting range, he pointed toward two ropes hanging from the ceiling at the other end of the room. "Put him against the wall and tie a rope around each wrist."

Muffled sounds escaped Langston's taped mouth as he ran from Scanlan's voice. He crashed into the far wall and fell heavily. He rolled around on the floor, his face contorted in pain.

After the two men had secured the distraught man, Scanlan turned from his gun case and took in the scene. As instructed, they had positioned Cameron Langston squarely between two circular targets.

Perfect.

Scanlan shoved a Beretta inside his belt at the small of his back and walked toward his prey. He ripped off the blindfold, then he reached down and turned on a cassette player.

Langston's muted appeals ceased when he heard his own voice imploring Phillip Scanlan to insert a performance clause in his will to protect his good name. Recognition and fear sprang from Langston's panic-filled eyes.

Scanlan felt no compassion as Langston's fear-stricken gaze followed him, beseeching. It was time to silence the old fool forever. He took out his pistol and chambered a shell. The first bullet tore into the bull's-eye on Langston's left. The second ripped into the other target. Scanlan laughed, reveling in a feeling of great power. Then, in rapid succession, he alternately shot at each target.

He ejected the magazine, slammed in another, and then walked toward his victim and ripped the tape from Langston's mouth.

Between sobs, Langston pleaded, "Please don't do this. . . . I beg of you—"

Scanlan walked out ten feet, turned, raised his arm and aimed at the horrified man.

Langston pleaded, his voice breaking. "Dear God. . . . You . . . you can't do this. Don't—"

Scanlan lowered his arm. "Relax, Cameron. I just wanted to scare the hell out of you. I'm going to let you go."

Langston's body slumped as his tightly drawn muscles released their tension like water rushing through a punctured dike. His eyes expressed a single emotion—he was going to live.

Scanlan's arm snapped up.

A shot exploded across the room and a bullet bore a hole in Cameron Langston's forehead.

After hauling the body to the van, Scanlan checked the street. Everything appeared normal. He instructed Danny Fagan to dispose of the corpse in the same manner used for Heather Coyne's body. Scanlan loved the concept of a maturing redwood tree's roots encapsulating the victim's remains.

When the van pulled out of his driveway, Scanlan's elation floated from his body like the wafting clouds of fog skittering over the hillside. His changing emotions puzzled him. The two men who had constantly ridiculed him were gone, but he did not feel the release he had expected.

He watched the fog slowly blot out distant lights and realized that the will's performance clause had become a legacy of the dead, haunting him, threatening his future. He had to find a way out.

CHAPTER 9

On the morning her advertisement ran, Kelly purchased a *Chronicle* from a newsstand in front of her building. After tossing everything but the business section into a trashcan, she riffled through the pages until she found her ad. Reality, dressed in black ink, stared up at her. What had she been thinking when she placed the ad? Dismayed, she leaned against the building and stared into nothingness, picturing herself slinging hash in a small roadside cafe in the middle of nowhere. Surely, that was her destiny.

Certain that a torrent of ridicule awaited her upstairs, she decided to call in sick. She hurried to the parking garage and reached for the car door but stopped abruptly. The memory of an autumn day during her sophomore year in high school caused her to withdraw her hand. After quitting the basketball team, she had skipped dinner to sulk in her room. Her father came in, gave her a hug, and then he talked to her for nearly an hour about the value of a single principle: perseverance.

With her keys still dangling in her hand, Kelly focused on her late father's most important observation: if you are going to succeed, you must learn to do the hard things. Nourished by her father's wisdom, Kelly had worked diligently on her basketball skills, and she became a starter during her senior year. Today, the hard thing would be to go upstairs. She turned and headed for her office. She stepped off the elevator and reinforced her resolve by reminding herself that her software was exceptional. Exhaustive research and hundreds of historical trades had proven that. She had to believe in herself and her work.

The usual office buzz stopped the instant she passed through the double glass doors. She sensed a multitude of stares as she crossed the room. The only sound came from the ringing of a distant telephone and her heels clicking on the floor. One look at her desk brought a surge of anger. A large black ribbon adorned her monitor. Her ad and the words "REST IN PEACE" had been taped on a large bow.

She ripped off the ribbon and threw it in the trashcan. T. J. Halverson snickered. She wanted to shove his suspenders down his throat, but she was determined to take the high road. He wasn't worth a confrontation. She tried to blot out the laughter by concentrating on her screen. The market's opening drew attention away from her, but glances and whispers persisted throughout the morning.

Dan Hawkins called her at nine-thirty. "Are you okay?"

She looked across the room. "I'll make it, but thanks."

"The ad took guts. I hope things work out for you."

"I do too, Dan . . . I do too."

Kelly expected a miserable morning, but she had felt relieved when Vanessa told her Emmett Crittenden had left town on a short vacation. She had escaped the guillotine, at least for now. Vanessa also told her about a mandatory sales meeting scheduled for 2:00 P.M., and that Johnathon Rockway, a senior broker, would be the chair.

By twelve o'clock, she had received over two dozen telephone responses to her ad. Two callers had shown genuine interest in her prediction, but most had argued the bull's case for a continuing upward trend. Five had been crank calls of various flavors, including one from a derelict who wanted to perform oral sex on a bed covered with pages from a financial newspaper. One man had given her the telephone number of a psychiatrist.

Between calls, Kelly monitored the market. To her disappointment, a sharp early morning sell-off faltered, and the Dow reversed itself and closed up eighty-six points. Everything seemed to be going wrong.

At the appointed time, she took a seat in the conference room and pretended to ignore a smattering of derogatory comments by perusing her planner. Realizing her strategy had failed; she closed her book, clasped her hands together, and looked straight ahead.

A distinguished looking man with grey streaks at his temples entered the room carrying a large portfolio. He positioned his presentation material on an easel at the far end of the room and stood erect, as if to put his perfect posture on display.

Johnathon Rockway entered the room and took the podium. "Emmett is out of town, but he wanted us to go ahead with the meeting. It's not every day we get a chance to have a speaker of this caliber." He glanced toward the man on his left. "Hudson Treffinger has published the *Treffinger Letter* for the past seventeen years. As many of you know, his recommendations have made him one of the top-rated letter writers for the past three years. His market predictions have been nothing short of uncanny. He's here to give us his latest outlook."

Treffinger seemed to glide to the podium. He thanked Rockway and turned to the easel. "Every so often I come across a harbinger that turns out to be a profound indicator of the market's future course. Your fair city offered one this very morning, and it came on a silver platter. The same one that delivered breakfast." He paused, obviously toying with his puzzled audience. Then he flipped to the first page of his presentation.

Kelly stared in disbelief. She was too far away to see the actual words, but she knew the small square of newsprint in the middle of an otherwise blank page was her newspaper ad.

Everyone turned toward her.

Treffinger continued. "We're in the middle of a long-term, secular bull market. Opposing the trend, as this ad suggests, would be insane. In other words, gentlemen, don't fight the tape. I'm very bullish and my presentation will explain why. Not only that, but I have just bought heavily for my own account. Mostly highly leveraged instruments."

T. J. Halverson interrupted. "Mr. Treffinger, the author of that ad is in this very room."

"He's here?"

"*She* is here." Halverson said, gesturing toward the far end of the table. "Her name is Kelly Sanborn."

Treffinger turned to Kelly. "How long have you been in the business, Miss Sanborn?"

Kelly struggled to maintain her composure, then she looked straight at Treffinger. "A year and a half."

A soft laugh escaped Treffinger's lips. He broke eye contact and addressed the group. "Did you ever notice that when children want to appear older, they always add fractional years to their age?"

Laughter erupted around the table.

Treffinger looked directly at Kelly. "I've been in the business for twenty-eight years. Don't take this personally, but your ad smacks of rank amateurism." He paused, smiling, catering to his audience; then, he said, "Some other line of work might suit you better."

Kelly bolted from her chair. "And you, Mr. Treffinger, lack the manners of a common barnyard ass." She stormed out, leaving a room full of stunned colleagues.

There was only one word that sufficiently described her experience over the next few days—hellish. Ridicule gained momentum, fueled by a rally in the Dow Jones Industrial Average. Kelly did her best to ignore the derisive comments, but she could not ignore the market's performance. The Dow gained 148 points on Thursday. Another new high. The market churned in a narrow range Friday, but the average managed to gain 47 points on heavy volume.

Weary of her surroundings, she decided to leave early and use the weekend to recharge herself. A phone call delayed her departure.

"This is Emily. Mr. Crittenden will be back Tuesday morning at nine. He wants you in his office the instant he arrives."

Christ. The vultures could not even wait until he got back to tell him about the ad. She had to get out of the office. She grabbed her purse and heard the phone ring again. She yanked up the receiver and blurted, "What?"

"Uh, Miss Sanborn. This is Brian Doane at Scanlan Equity Management."

"Oh, Mr. Doane. I—I'm sorry. I thought it was someone else. What can I do for you?"

"Actually, I might be able to do something for you. Mr. Scanlan has reviewed the documentation on Cyberstar, and he wants to meet with you."

Kelly's heart thumped against her breastbone. She bit the inside of her cheek, admonishing herself to stay calm. "All right. . . . Okay. When?"

"Tuesday morning at eight o'clock."

My God, Scanlan wanted to see her at eight and Crittenden was going to jump down her throat at nine. She needed time to think. "Could you hold a moment while I check my calendar?"

"Sure."

She punched the hold button, her insides churning. What if Crittenden ignored her probation and fired her? She obviously had to know her employment status before meeting with Scanlan. She had to change the time. Kelly summoned her most businesslike voice. "I have commitments that morning, but I'll be happy to see him in the afternoon or on Wednesday."

"He did give me an alternative time of twelve o'clock on Tuesday."

"Perfect," Kelly said. "I'll see you then."

CHAPTER 10

Several stocks in the Dow Jones Industrial Average opened higher Monday morning, propelling the index to yet another new high. Kelly wondered if the trend would ever change. Her sell signal remained in effect, but each uptick nourished new doubts. Continued market strength would discredit her system and put her future in jeopardy.

Her incoming phone calls became a benchmark of diversity and excess. She fielded calls from a client who closed his account because of her "lousy advice," an amateur analyst who wanted to discuss "moon cycles and the market," a caustic-voiced old man who said she was "nuts," and the president of a local feminist organization.

She had also just hung up on the sexual deviant who had phoned her the first day the ad appeared. In a husky voice, he had informed her that he was "doing his thing" onto the financial pages as they spoke. Before she could yank the receiver from her ear, he had muttered something about blotting out the Dow average. She stared at the ceiling—the world is full of crazies.

As the day progressed, she became increasingly concerned about her meetings on Tuesday. She had spent much of the weekend preparing for her appointment with Martin Scanlan, but there was little she could do about Emmett Crittenden—except worry.

The telephone calls eased after the market had gone into a trading range. She was on her third cup of coffee when the receptionist phoned.

"There's a Mr. Valentine here to see you."

Kelly's eyebrows shot up. "Sparky?"

"He didn't give his first name, but he's . . . ah—"

"About four feet tall?"

"That's the one."

"Send him in." She walked toward the double doors, wondering why Sparky had come to her office. Then it struck her. Cody must be sick or hurt. Why didn't Miyako call? Maybe they were both injured. Her mind drew horrible images as she hurried across the room.

Sparky smiled. "Good morning, Kel—"

"What's wrong? Is Cody all right?"

His eyes widened. "Cody?" He hit the side of his head with his palm. "Good gravy. I should have called first." He hoisted a briefcase into the air. "I'm here on business."

"Business?"

"I want to open an account."

Kelly's shoulders slumped and she expelled a deep breath. "Thank goodness. . . . An account. Yes, of course."

She had not considered how this might look to her peers, but half way across the floor, she noticed small groups staring in her direction. She heard T. J. Halverson's coarse laugh echo across the room. She took a seat and shook her head in disgust. Sparky was more of a man than that asshole would ever be.

Sparky climbed onto a chair and straightened his legs. "I believe in your software, and I want to back that conviction with cash." He reached into his briefcase. "Here's a cashier's check for one hundred thousand dollars."

Kelly was surprised, flattered, and concerned. "Are you sure about this?"

"Absolutely. This is nonnegotiable."

"I hope you're not going to speculate with savings you may need later."

"Not at all. My career in radio was more profitable than I've let on. Besides, I own three duplex rentals in Palo Alto that are doing very well." He scooted forward. "How do I play a falling market?"

Kelly smiled, remembering Sparky's comments about his days hosting a talk show in Portland. "They can't see you on the radio," he had said. "I was very tendentious and I pissed off a lot of people. Most of them had tunnel vision. That meant more phone calls and more listeners. Actually, I made some bucks and had a great time."

She pulled out some forms for him to sign. Noting the determined look on his face, she decided to outline the alternatives and let him make the call. "There are several ways you can position yourself for a market decline. Some are average risk, others are extremely speculative."

Sparky nodded and pulled a cellophane bag from his briefcase. "Pinon nut?"

Kelly shook her head. "You can short stocks, buy put options, or trade futures."

"Explain."

"When you go short, you sell stock you don't have." Realizing that might sound odd, she added, "We borrow it for you. You sell first and buy later. If your purchase is at a lower price, you pocket the difference."

"Nifty. How about options?"

Kelly leaned back. "The first thing you need to know is that you can easily lose all of your money in options. You have the same scenario in futures."

Sparky jotted a note on his pad. "High risk, high reward."

"Precisely. I've seen options drop from one and a half to a few pennies in a single day. Conversely, I've seen them triple just as fast. The important thing is to make a good entry; then, be prepared to get out quickly if the trade goes against you." After a lengthy discussion about risk and potential strategies, Sparky signed his account forms and handed them back.

Kelly asked, "How would you like to distribute the funds?"

"Did you wash the top of that can?" he said, pointing toward the diet soda on her desk.

"Why no. I just—"

"I suspect that rats run around those big warehouses and pee all over the place. They may or may not hit some of the cans, but it seems prudent to wash the top."

Kelly grimaced and shoved the can aside.

"We'll use a troika scheme," Sparky said, shifting subjects effortlessly. "One third for put options, a third for futures, and the rest as a cash reserve."

"Considering your goals, I think that will work fine."

"Can I use the account today?"

"No," Kelly said, as she reviewed his forms. "But I'll be able to place your orders on the opening tomorrow."

Sparky got down and buttoned his blazer as if to leave, but he hesitated.

Kelly asked, "Did you have another question?"

He edged closer. "I don't think it's a problem, but I've noticed a guy hanging around the neighborhood the last few days. He took several photographs of the kids playing ball on Saturday, and he walked by the house with his camera this morning."

"Have you seen him before?"

"Nope."

"Maybe I should phone Miyako and ask her to keep Cody inside after he gets home from school."

"Actually, the guy looked pretty innocent. My gut tells me he's not up to anything nefarious, but I thought you'd like to know."

After Sparky had left, Kelly became increasingly concerned about the stranger.

———

She rose early the next morning and donned a navy-blue suit and a pale blue blouse, bargains from an upscale turnaround shop. If she had to go down in flames, she might as well do it in style. She slipped into Cody's room and sat in a chair next to his desk. Watching her son sleep always gratified her. She routinely checked on him before leaving for work, but this morning she lingered longer than usual, amazed by slumber's ability to transform a child's energy into hushed innocence.

She sat quietly in a narrow ray of light cast from the hallway, hoping that Cody's presence would bolster her resolve. When he rolled on his side and mumbled something in his sleep, she felt a pang of guilt. She had spread herself too thin over the last eighteen months. Somehow, she would make it up to him. She wiped moisture from her eyes, went to his bedside, and kissed him on the cheek. When she lifted her head, a single tear slid from her cheekbone and landed on the edge of Cody's pillow.

———————

Kelly arrived at her desk an hour before the market opened. She obtained Sparky's account number, but she wanted to make sure her sell signal remained intact before placing an order. She reached for her purse and nearly forgot the small personal alarm she had rigged inside. If anyone pulled the zipper more than half way, the dislodged pin would set off a one hundred and six decibel siren. It was not perfect, but she hoped it would do for now. She disconnected the alarm and retrieved the flash drive.

She entered her passwords, downloaded yesterday's market data, and ran the software. The indicators had slowed their descent, but they were still below the zero line. The signal remained valid. Following an agreed strategy, Kelly would spread Sparky's orders over two or three days. Dollar cost averaging would afford partial protection if the market continued higher. She wrote a ticket to buy July put options for the S&P index. Later, they would short Dow futures. The market opened slightly higher and then traded in a narrow range. The technology stocks, the recent market leaders, lagged for the second day in a row.

After the usual early morning rush, Kelly became obsessed with the clock. She was prepared for her appointment with Martin Scanlan, but she felt increasingly uneasy about her meeting with Emmett Crittenden. By nine o'clock, she had weighed and magnified every conceivable scenario until the process became counterproductive. She rubbed her temples in an effort to clear her thoughts.

When she entered Crittenden's office, he tossed her the business section of the *San Francisco Chronicle*. "That ad of yours is the most harebrained thing I've ever seen. You must have been out of your mind to do something like that."

"I didn't mention Boucher & Crittenden."

"You didn't have to. The street knows you work here, and that puts the firm in a bad light." He leaned forward, his eyes full of contempt. "You really fucked up, Sanborn. I thought we still might be able to work something out, but you've gone too far."

Kelly glared back. "I believe in my system, and I think the ad will pay off over time."

"Your system," he said, shaking his head. "You're an amateur for Christ's sake. This is a roaring bull market. Any idiot knows better than to stand in front of a runaway locomotive. You not only jumped on the track, you also held up a sign for the whole world to see."

She fought panic and started to take a seat. Somehow, she had to reason with him.

"Don't bother to sit down." A thin smile creased his lips. "You're fired."

Kelly was stunned. His words hung in the air like an affliction, spreading misery, weakening. "But, I still have two weeks of probation left."

"I expected you to say that." He opened a file and withdrew several documents. "I'm not letting you go because of the ad or your performance."

"I don't understand."

"Before I left on vacation, I asked Emily to check the references on your employment application."

Kelly lowered her eyes and searched the carpet; the same one the devious bastard was about to nail her to.

"It says here you have a degree. But lo and behold, San Francisco State claims you had not completed the requirements on the date you filed your employment application. Nobody will ever question me for firing someone who lied on their application."

She vividly remembered listing her degree on the form. It had been painful because she regularly told Cody that honesty was the core of good character. Whenever she caught someone in a lie, she put them in a category they might never escape. Now, she would pay dearly for her own lapse of dishonesty. At the time, she had felt she had no choice. It had taken seven years to get within a few units of her degree and, with time and money running out, she had taken a calculated risk out of concern for Cody.

Crittenden spoke brusquely. "You'll be escorted to your desk, then you'll be escorted out of the office."

The words ripped into Kelly's heart like daggers. She started to mention that she received her degree four months later, but she knew he did not care. She walked from his office, her breaths coming in short gasps. She stopped in the hallway and leaned against a wall. What would she tell Cody? How would she pay the bills? She never should have run the stupid ad.

Spiraling into a black hole of remorse, she repeated the advice she had often given to Cody, "You can't change what has already happened. You accept it, you learn from it, and you go forward." She knew the value of those simple words; yet, the task before her seemed impervious to such logic.

She went to the restroom and applied a wet paper towel to her neck and forehead. The cold shock against her skin narrowed the focus of her thoughts, giving her a few seconds of relief. Her respite shattered at the thought of her appointment with Martin

Scanlan. He expected to meet with a broker from Boucher & Crittenden, not someone who had just been tossed onto the street.

She rummaged through her purse, retrieved a chocolate truffle, took a large bite, and then glanced at her watch. If she did not find a solution in the next two and a half hours, she would have to cancel the appointment.

CHAPTER 11

Kelly collected her personal items from her desk and loaded them into Huey's trunk; then, she drove to the Palace of the Legion of Honor. She walked past the museum and took a footpath that skirted the adjacent golf course. After a few yards, she stopped on an incline and gazed to her right. The Golden Gate Bridge loomed in the distance. When not enshrouded in fog, the location offered a spectacular view of the majestic structure.

On her left, she could see a layer of fog blending with the open sea, eerily blotting out the horizon. Yet, the spires of the bridge stood erect in bright sunlight despite the advancing cloud of moisture. She settled on a bench and took in the scene: trees, birds, sky, and water. An atmosphere of peace and harmony surrounded her.

This view offered more than breathtaking beauty for Kelly. The setting had an inspirational quality unequalled by any she had ever known. She had come here the day after she'd scattered her father's ashes into a gentle Northern California stream that fed into the great body of water below. And, she had come here the day she'd learned that Sean Keene, the father of her child, had abandoned her for Australia.

She gazed at the ocean and let a tide of memories wash over her. She remembered standing on this very spot nearly twelve years before. She remembered caressing her belly and wondering about the fetus that lay inside her womb, nourished by the same fluids that gave life to the mother.

Desperate to shield the family from humiliation, her stepmother had urged her to have an abortion. Kelly rejected the possibility of disgrace as not being relevant in today's society. Still, she had wavered over the decision, but when she stood here with her hand on her tummy, she knew she wanted to give her child the opportunity to experience the wonders of life, both good and bad. Her stepmother had never forgiven her, but Kelly did not care. Her child was all that mattered.

Today, she came to this place to absorb its therapeutic essence once again and to ponder her future. After being terminated, she had felt jaded and was on the verge of giving up, but the cool breeze and spectacular view restored her will. Having come too far to quit now, she would keep her meeting with Martin Scanlan. She shivered from a gust of wind, smoothed her hair, and headed back up the path.

———

By the time Kelly entered the offices of Scanlan Equity Management, she had decided to give her presentation without mentioning Boucher & Crittenden. This would allow her to maintain control and keep everyone focused on her software. After all, that is what brought her here. She would announce her departure from the brokerage firm after she had evaluated their interest in Cyberstar.

A young man with a friendly smile came toward her. "Miss Sanborn, I'm Brian Doane. Welcome to SEM."

She extended her hand. "Thank you. And please call me Kelly."

"Of course." Doane escorted her through the hallways. "What do you make of the tech stocks today?"

The question caught her off guard. She had no idea what the market had done since she left the office. The technology sector had been a little weak this morning, but the drop had not been dramatic. "Frankly, I haven't been able to monitor the market for several hours. Have they turned around?"

"On the contrary. The computer and semiconductor stocks are off sharply."

"How about the Dow?"

"It was off about twenty points most of the morning, but it's starting to follow the lead of the technology stocks. It was down over a hundred points just before I came out to get you, but it looks like normal profit taking." Doane pushed through a set of heavy wooden doors.

Kelly noticed a change in Doane's demeanor when they entered the executive suite. The casual smile changed to a vigilant, anxious expression. She could almost feel the nervous energy radiating from his body.

He excused himself and spoke to a secretary who escorted them into the largest private office Kelly had ever seen. Her feet sank into thick carpet as she scanned the extensive paneling lining the room. Two sofas faced each other across an oversized coffee table. Another sofa graced the opposite wall. A lounge chair and a reading lamp fit neatly into the far corner. Original oils hung randomly on the walls. Extravagance had obviously been the designer's mandate.

Kelly's sweep of the room came to an abrupt halt when she saw Martin Scanlan. The impeccably dressed man rose from behind a desk that must have been hauled in by a brigade of workers. She had never seen a five thousand-dollar suit before, but if there were such a thing, Scanlan was surely wearing it. Perfectly tailored, it was charcoal, double-breasted, and luxurious.

Scanlan was tall with wavy brown hair and strong brown eyes beneath unusually prominent eyebrows. He approached her and extended his hand. "We're glad you could come." He motioned toward the dual couches. "Please, have a seat."

She eased onto a sofa, and the two men sat across from her. She opened her briefcase and sensed them watching her. She glanced up and caught them staring at her legs. Christ, hadn't they ever seen female limbs before? She uncrossed her legs, placed her knees together, and placed a folder on the table.

Scanlan leaned back and looked toward the window.

No one spoke.

After a long moment he said, "You're either very smart or very stupid. Which is it?"

"I'm here to discuss my trading system, Mr. Scanlan. If you'd care to participate, I'll stay. If not, I see no point in wasting each other's time." His opening remarks had offended her; yet, she could hardly believe her response. She hoped she had not gone too far.

He turned and looked at her. "I was referring to your newspaper ad and your telegram. Your techniques for gaining attention are unique. Time will tell if your prediction is right." He smiled. "Please accept my apology."

Kelly let out a breath. "Accepted."

"Brian thinks very highly of your system. I'm impressed with the numbers, but everything you've given us is based on historical data. That opens a door of doubt." He leaned forward. "It's nothing personal, but there have been many cases of individuals doctoring data to improve the theoretical performance of their system."

"Mr. Scanlan, I—"

"Let's use first names, shall we?"

"Of course, Martin." She brushed back a strand of hair. "The results invite skepticism because they're exceptional. That's perfectly normal." She studied his reaction as she spoke—nothing. She continued, "I've always believed software developers follow an unspoken rule; if your trading system isn't very good, sell it to the public." She held eye contact and spoke firmly. "Mine is not for sale."

Scanlan eased back against the sofa. "I appreciate your conviction, but I still have doubts about your data."

"I'll never allow anyone access to my software," Kelly responded, "but I can assure you these numbers are completely authentic. I'm not here to peddle a phony system that would harm both of us over the long run." She felt herself settling into a comfort zone, gaining confidence.

He studied her but did not respond.

She waited.

Finally, he said, "There is another problem. Using an outside source will increase our transaction costs."

She expected that objection. "My fees will be inconsequential when you consider the quality of the trade recommendations you'll receive from Cyberstar."

Scanlan nodded slowly. "I'm skeptical, but we are looking for something innovative. We might consider a trial relation—"

His intercom buzzed.

He ignored the summons and continued, "As I was saying, we might consider some sort of trial relationship. If your system proves itself, we could very well send you some business."

She thought about Boucher & Crittenden and shifted uneasily. She swallowed hard and said, "I have such a strong belief in my software that I've decided to establish my own consulting firm. I'm no longer associated with Boucher & Crittenden." Not exactly a lie, but she felt uncomfortable.

Scanlan's eyebrows arched. "I'm surprised you—"

A tap sounded on the door.

Scanlan sighed and called out, "Come."

His secretary appeared. "I'm sorry, but one of our traders said it couldn't wait."

Kelly's pulse quickened. She was inside the core of Scanlan Equity Management, and she loved it.

"All right, Julie. I'll take it." Scanlan excused himself, went to his desk, picked up the phone. "I'm in a meeting, Thomas. This had better be important."

Kelly focused on to the conversation.

Scanlan blurted out, "MicroDart is what?" He rushed around his desk and peered at his monitor. "Jesus Christ." His punched several keys and stared at the screen. "Brian, get over here."

Scanlan put his hand over the receiver while the two men conversed in low voices.

Kelly heard only a few scattered words, but they seemed to be discussing the tech stocks. Doane muttered something about Apple and Microsoft.

Scanlan looked across the room. "Kelly, could your step over here a moment?"

"Certainly." Stimulated by a mixture of curiosity and excitement, she approached the desk.

Scanlan told his trader he would call back, and, then, he pointed at the screen. "The technology stocks are taking a beating. Apple is down four and a half, Microsoft three, and Amazon is down over twenty. The Dow has dropped over two hundred points since you arrived. My staff thinks the market was due for a correction, and this is nothing more than profit taking. What's your opinion?"

"I stand by my earlier prediction. There's an eighty-five percent chance of a major break."

Scanlan studied his monitor. "Three months ago, the Dow dropped over four hundred in one day."

Kelly nodded.

"It soared over eight hundred points the following week. The profit taking gave shrewd investors an excellent buying opportunity. Why do you think it will be so different this time?"

"Cyberstar has given a signal equal to that of the eighty-seven crash."

Silence.

Scanlan's eyes remained riveted on the screen for a moment; then, he turned and paced the room.

Kelly checked the NYSE statistics. Declining issues led advances by a ratio of four to one—bearish numbers. Yet, the market had sold off many times over the last several years, only to come roaring back. The weak longs had sold out, and more short sellers had been suckered in. She wondered if she were the sucker this time. While observing Scanlan, it seemed that the aura of power she had noticed upon entering his office had been altered. He suddenly seemed indecisive. She thought she sensed a trace of fear that seemed to alter his body language. What in the hell was going on?

He approached her with a serious expression. "I'm going to level with you, Kelly. My personal account is heavily leveraged in tech stocks. I intended to stick it out, but you've impressed me." His gaze locked on hers and held. "Are you shoveling shit here, or is this thing for real?"

"Am I going to get paid for my advice?"

Scanlan laughed. "By God, I like you." He checked his screen. "We can't retain you for our clients until you have a proven track record, but if your advice on the techs is correct, I'll cut you a check from my own account and take you to dinner."

Sparks shot through Kelly's body. Scanlan's personal account would not sustain her, but it was a huge opening. She pictured herself framing her first dollar and hanging it on her wall. Mustering her sincerest voice, she said, "If you pay me a fee of three tenths of one percent of the total, I'll lay it out for you."

Scanlan hesitated and then said, "Done."

She looked him straight in the eye. "Everything I've told you is true. I believe my system is one of the most powerful ever developed."

He nodded but said nothing.

Kelly added, "If the market turns up, you can always get back in. You might lose a few points, but if I'm right, the loss could be catastrophic. Remember the old saying: they slide faster than they glide."

Scanlan looked at a grandfather clock across the room. The market closed in nine minutes.

Aware of the importance of his next decision, Kelly fought back a nervous tremor. Time seemed to expand as she watched him weigh her comments, and the only sounds she heard were her own breath and the dulcet ticking of the grandfather clock. Feeling conspicuous amid the silence, she went to the window and gazed out.

Five minutes before the close, Scanlan picked up the phone and punched in a number. "Thomas, it's Martin. Sell all my tech stocks. . . . That's right, everything." He hung up, walked over to Kelly, and pulled a gold-plated cardholder from his coat pocket. He removed a business card, handed it to her, and said, "It looks like we're going to find out just how good your system is. If it gives a new signal, please call me on my private number."

She slid the card into her purse. "I'll be happy to. And thank you for seeing me."

He extended his hand. "The pleasure was mine."

His handshake was warm and firm. She started to withdraw her hand, but he increased his pressure slightly, signaling his intention to maintain contact a few seconds longer. He finally slid his hand from hers in a way that allowed his fingertips to brush hers in an almost erotic manner. The gesture seemed inappropriate for the setting, but something stirred inside Kelly. She shook off the ambiguous feeling and said good-bye.

She slid behind the wheel of her car and thought about Martin Scanlan. Had he subtly come on to her, or had she read too much in the handshake? His presence and rakish good looks were appealing, but Kelly had sensed an underlying current she could not identify. A mysterious, volatile element of some sort. What would he be like on a date? Certainly not dull. She suspected future dealings with Scanlan would offer surprises.

Exhausted, she leaned back and shut her eyes. The day had produced a whirlpool of conflicting emotions that had drained her energy. She thought of the stack of bills on her kitchen table and sighed. She felt good about the fee she might receive from Scanlan, but, if the market rallied, there would be no further payments. She obviously had to plan for a worst-case scenario, and that meant she would have to get another job—and soon.

Because the market closed at one o'clock, she needed to find something that would allow her to work in the afternoon and early evening. That would give her all morning to monitor the market and solicit clients. Cody would be out of school in a few days, and she would be able to spend more time with him. The thought made her smile.

After considering the details, she wondered if she were being realistic. A part-time job would pay far less than she had earned as a broker, and she was on the edge now. Eventually, she hoped to garner substantial earnings from her consulting business, but there was a big kicker—her market predictions had to be right.

———

After Kelly had left, Martin Scanlan leaned back in his chair and stared across the room. An embryo of a new idea formed and began to expand. What if Kelly Sanborn's software really was as good as she claimed? It would not be long before he knew the answer to that question. If the software proved itself to be extremely valuable, he could certainly use her in a consultant mode, which would be profitable, but was there another option? It would be much better if he could, somehow, gain control the software.

He rose and strode about the room, considering possible scenarios. He stopped in front of his office window and realized he needed contingency plans for obtaining the software. If he decided to steal the software, how would he proceed? His thoughts shifted to the pigeon keeper.

CHAPTER 12

Kelly parked her car, rounded the corner of her house, glanced toward her doorstep, and saw two stubby legs protruding beneath the *San Francisco Chronicle*. She had forgotten Sparky.

He lowered the newspaper. "Do you always leave your clients in the dark?"

She sat, kicked off her shoes, and rubbed one foot over the other. "I'm sorry, Sparky. I've had a hell of a day, but that's no excuse for not calling you."

"I watched the business channel to see how the market closed. The Dow was off sharply. I assume that's good, but I don't even know if I have a position."

Kelly sat on the step below Sparky. "We used a third of your funds to purchase July put options on the S&P index and we shorted several contracts of Dow futures, but I wasn't able to complete your orders."

His eyebrows arched over inquisitive eyes.

Kelly's attempt at a smile came off more like a plea for mercy.

Sparky dropped his feigned expression of annoyance and said, "Something happened."

"I got fired."

He tossed the paper aside. "That asshole, Crittenberg?"

"Crittenden."

"Whatever." Sparky waved a fist in the air. "That really pisses me off." He scooted closer and said, "Did you get in a few shots of your own?"

"There really wasn't much I could say." She scratched the concrete with one of her keys. "I was escorted out of the office, so I didn't even have time to phone my clients." She sighed heavily. "It's been a tough day."

Sparky patted her on the back. "At times like this, you need to remind yourself how lucky you are."

"Lucky?"

"Absolutely. The odds against you sitting on that step are astronomical."

"I don't follow."

"Mathematics and chance." His brow furrowed. "The average ejaculation contains more than a quarter of a million sperm. We all know only one of those bad boys fertilizes the egg, but few of us understand just how incredibly extreme the odds are. It's bizarre, actually. I mean, what if your mother and father had never met? What if a different sperm won the race up the fallopian tube? What if your mother had a headache that day, or if your father had twitched a split second before ejaculating, or if the phone had rung, or—"

"I get the point."

"I don't think so." He wiggled a finger in the air. "This is the good part. Extrapolate those odds with every ancestor in your entire family tree. Out of hundreds of millions of sperm, the one with your name on it was at the precisely right place at precisely the right time." He looked skyward. "But, that's not all. The history of earth's formation played a major role. If the hundreds of thousands of asteroids had not struck the Earth in the exact order they did, life on earth might have had a completely different beginning." He picked up his ever-present water bottle and took a drink, then he continued, "There is also strong speculation that a small planet struck the earth, and that's what created the moon. If that had not happened you would not be sitting here now." He spread his arms and looked skyward. "It's like winning a thousand-number lotto."

Kelly gulped, thinking about countless generations that formed her genealogical tree.

Sparky looked her in the eye. "And then there's the most important reason of all: your son. You are very lucky, indeed."

"I can't imagine my life without Cody."

"He's a special kid." Sparky was quiet for a moment, then he said, " I think it's helpful to be thankful for something nearly every day. It can be little things or something profound, but no matter what it is I think it helps a person keep a positive attitude."

Kelly nodded. "What are you thankful for today?"

"I'm thankful that chlorophyll is green."

"Chlorophyll?"

He looked at a Camphor tree across the street. "Imagine what the world would be like if chlorophyll were black. That tree, the grass, and plants throughout the world would be black instead of green. How depressing would that be?"

"I see what you mean," Kelly replied. It seemed like an odd thing to be thankful for, but she could not fault the concept. Maintaining a positive attitude would certainly improve a person's health, happiness, and outlook on life. She looked at the tree and shook her head in amazement, thankful that such a wonderful man was part of her life. "I feel better already. Thanks."

He said, "I'm going to defer three month's rent."

"But—"

"This is not open for discussion."

She had heard that expression enough to know he was not about to alter his stance. She held his gaze. "I won't forget your help." After a comfortable silence she said, "Now, then, about your account. Our strategy was to place your orders over several days. We can still do that, but you need to call Boucher & Crittenden and instruct them to transfer your account to Dan Hawkins." Anticipating his thoughts, she added, "Don't worry. He's one of the good guys." They talked for a few minutes; then, Kelly entered the house.

From his spot on the recliner, Cody lowered a glass of lemonade. "Mom, I'm going to need new shoes for little league."

"And hello to you too."

"Oops. Hi, Mom. How was your day?"

Kelly groaned and tossed her purse on a chair. She did not want to tell him the news, but he would find out in a day or two anyway. "Let's put it this way," she said, slumping onto the couch. "I'm going to be home every day for a while."

Cody's expression changed from puzzlement to concern. He crossed the room and sat next to her. "About those shoes, I've got enough saved to pay for them. And school's almost over, so I could get a job mowing lawns to help out."

She put her arm around Cody and pulled him close. She felt comforted by the familiar scent of his hair. "Don't worry; we're going to be just fine." She held on, hoping Cody's love would sustain her through the hardships ahead.

That night, she sat up in bed, hoping the novel she had selected would offer relief from her troubles. She closed the book after six pages. Trying another tactic, she reread the personalized card she had found on her doormat after dinner. Sparky's note strengthened her resolve.

The following morning, Kelly rose at her regular hour and commenced work. She updated her database and ran Cyberstar. The previous day's market drop featured a marked deterioration of market internals. The advance/decline ratio, and up-volume versus down-volume had recorded their worst readings in over a year, and the list of new fifty-two-week highs had declined substantially.

The screen flickered and displayed Cyberstar's latest chart. As expected, the two descending lines had again turned down sharply—the sell signal remained intact. She switched on the business channel and waited for the market to open. The ticker tape running across the bottom of the screen would keep her reasonably up to date, but she needed a professional, real-time quotation system. She grumbled at the thought of shelling out badly needed funds. The TV would have to do for now.

She spent the morning working on a preliminary business plan, and glancing at the TV. The market did not act as she had expected. After an early decline, the Dow had stabilized, and then rallied briskly into the close, gaining sixty-four points.

That afternoon, she scanned the employment section of the local newspaper. Half Moon Bay was a wonderful place to live, but it was hardly a commercial center. Finding nothing that fit her needs, she laid the paper aside and penciled out a budget designed to stretch her last commission check. The rent deferment and creative manipulation of her finances would give her six weeks before she had to find another position. That was better than she had expected, and it should give her enough time to see if her system had been right.

———————

The government issued its monthly Producer Price Index at five-thirty the next morning. The contents of the report surprised the street, which created expectations for a positive opening. The early indication from futures prices indicated that the market would open about sixty points higher. However, the Dow opened nineteen points higher instead of sixty, then it hovered in a narrow range for half an hour. Kelly hoped the market's failure to respond to good news would cause disappointed investors to sell. She had seen that happen in the past, but the bull market's upward momentum might be too much to overcome.

She scanned the tape and saw that most of the tech stocks Scanlan had sold were even or slightly higher than they were when he had liquidated his position. The difference was minor, but unsettling. Martin Scanlan did not seem to be a man who doled out second chances.

Ninety minutes into the session, the market began a slow decline. After five hours, the Dow had dropped seventy-six points on moderate volume. A little after noon, the stock market headed south in a sharp selloff. At the close, the Dow had fallen 227 points. The Utility index was off only slightly, but the Transports recorded a sharp drop.

Though the market had suffered a steep decline, Kelly became increasingly anxious. She fidgeted in her chair; then, she stood and paced the room. Why was she feeling this way? While she checked the closing numbers on the TV, it occurred to her that she had every right to be nervous. The stock market would soon place a value on her system, a system that embodied part of her soul. She looked out the window and wondered if the bull market was dead or merely napping.

CHAPTER 13

For the fourth time today, Sean Keene hurried from his office, on the outskirts of Cairns, and stood beside the road leading to town. Where was the damn truck? The express carrier should have delivered his package two hours ago. Too keyed up to work, he paced the edge of the narrow road. Presently, Sean saw light reflecting off a distant vehicle. He craned his neck and saw that it was a car. Disappointed, he sat with his back against a tree and studied the large red and white sign above his office. It read:

KEENE & BISHOP
Tours & Diving Expeditions

Sean had come a long way since arriving in Australia. He and his partner, Darren Bishop, had eight offices scattered between Mackay and Cooktown. It had all begun seven years earlier with a handmade sign, a rented boat, and twelve-hour days. They struggled to purchase their first catamaran, but it turned out to be the perfect solution for expanding their business. The company grew rapidly, and now, they owned six catamarans, including the two located at their headquarters near Cairns. They achieved success by combining hard work, honesty, and a sincere desire to offer value to their customers.

Sean searched the road. No truck. He shifted his back to fit a groove in the eucalyptus tree and looked toward his office. The red and white sign advertised his financial success, but it said nothing about the sorrow that had torn away part of his soul. He shifted to one side, retrieved his wallet, and withdrew a small dog-eared photo of Kelly Sanborn. He ran his finger over her image and went through a familiar ritual of mental flagellation. Over the years, a relentless guilt had roamed inside, increasing with time. Yes, he had been only eighteen at the time, and yes, he had been extremely immature, but abandoning her had been the most selfish thing he had ever done. He gazed into the distance and thought back to the night he had left California. He still could not understand what had caused him to leave. Looking back, he realized that his physical and mental evolution had been discordant—an adolescent's mind inside a man's body.

After a lover's quarrel with Kelly, an older acquaintance had persuaded Sean to travel to Australia to experience the beach culture and to explore the Great Barrier Reef, but Sean knew he was ultimately to blame for his puerile decision. During his first two years in Australia, he had fallen into a destructive cycle of working for a couple of months, followed by three or four of hard drinking. He had been on the edge of the abyss when he managed to turn around his life.

After a particularly nasty four-day binge, he had awoken next to a trash bin, shirtless, his belly on fire, and reeking of vomit. He massaged his eyes, opened them, and stared at a rat sniffing at his crouch. An omen from hell. For the next fourteen months, he worked six days a week, saved his money, and abstained from drinking, except for those two beers on his birthday.

And now, so many years after he had left California, guilt and inquisitiveness had motivated him to hire a private detective, in San Francisco, with orders to produce a dossier on Kelly and his son. He had to know how they were getting along. Startled by a beeping horn from the express truck, he jumped up and hurried onto the road.

The driver called out. "I have only one for you today, Sean."

Sean glanced at the box in the driver's hand and said, "I'm expecting a package from California. The tracking number said it would arrive today."

"It would have, but one of our trucks broke down. It'll be here tomorrow for sure."

Sean felt a surprising level of disappointment. He took the package and said, "Thanks, Owen."

The driver leaned out and looked skyward. "Looks like a squall heading our way."

"Yeah, that's why we're in the office today."

———

The following day, Sean leaned against the same tree and waited for the express truck, which was on time. The driver beeped his horn and came to a stop. He leaned out and said, "Only one today, but it's from California."

Sean signed for the package, thanked Owen, and then he hurried toward his office. He burst inside, grabbed a knife, and opened a large pouch.

Darren Bishop tilted his chair back. "I don't know what you've been waiting for, but I'm sure as hell glad it finally got here. You've been driving me nuts."

Sean pulled out a large folder and laid it on his desk. He had been desperate to receive the material; yet, he suddenly found himself unable to look at the contents.

Darren asked, "What is it?"

No answer.

"Sean?"

Sean put both hands on the folder. "Something has been eating at my insides, and time has only made it worse."

"Every man has a secret or two tucked under his hat."

Sean nodded slowly. "I can't keep mine a secret any longer. I'm tired of living with all the shame and guilt."

Darren came over to Sean's desk. "I've seen you go off on those mental side trips lots of times, but that hasn't stopped you from being the best friend I ever had. If you want to talk, I'll listen."

Sean expelled a heavy breath. "I got a girl pregnant."

Darren chuckled and went back to his desk. "I don't see that as too big a problem as long as you support the mother and the child. Hell, it happens every day."

"Not here. In California. I had just graduated from high school when it happened. I was incredibly immature." He looked out the window. "Actually, she was almost two years older than I was."

"Is that why you came to Australia?"

"Partly. I didn't even tell her I was leaving." He grimaced and looked out the window. "I fell into a destructive cycle of surfing and drinking. I had no concept of the importance of goals and responsibility."

After a brief silence, Darren said, "I've noticed a big change in you since I first met you. You've come a long way."

"Thank God for that."

Darren said, "I guess that package has something to do with all of this."

Sean eyed the folder. "I broke ties with everyone, so I have no idea what's happened over the years. I was dying for some news so I hired a private investigator to prepare a dossier on Kelly and my son. I didn't even know whether she'd had a boy or a girl for three years." He opened the folder and inspected the cover letter. "I suspect she's married and has other children, but I just had to know how they were getting along."

"Does that thing come with pictures?"

Sean nodded, "I paid for them." He thumbed through the documents until he found a manila envelope. His hands shook as he removed a stack of five-by-seven photos. The first image was that of a boy in mid-stride, wearing a baseball cap and carrying a fielder's glove. Sean could not take his eyes off the picture.

After a moment, he removed the next photo: a close-up of the boy's face. Sean saw his own blue eyes staring back at him. And the blondish hair. My God, it was the same color as his own. He tried to push back the lump forming in his throat, but his eyes misted and blurred. He rubbed the moisture with the palm of his hand and realized he did not even know the boy's name. He flipped through the pages and found the report on his son. He saw that his son's last name was Sanborn. He could not fault Kelly for giving the boy her name.

He said the first name aloud, "Cody. My son's name is Cody. How about that?"

After studying other photos of his son, Sean pulled out a picture of Kelly. She was stunning. The eyes were the same and the hair had that same auburn tint, though it was shorter. However, the subject of the photo was a mature woman, not the teenage girl he had forsaken.

Darren stepped next to him. "May I?"

Sean nodded and laid photos of Kelly and Cody on the desk.

"I can't believe you left h—" Darren stopped abruptly. "I'm sorry. You don't need me throwing gas on the fire." He looked at the pictures and said, "The boy's got your eyes."

Words would not come. Sean could only offer a feeble nod.

He spent the next hour studying every detail in the report. He was surprised to learn that Kelly had never married and that she was a stockbroker. She had gone to night school and had eventually earned a degree, though it had taken many years. The employment record was incomplete, but it was obvious she had done everything necessary to get by. She had been a waitress at a steak house, a clerk, and an administrative assistant. Sean felt considerable respect for her efforts to improve herself. The report mentioned that she had a roommate who evidently looked after Cody while she worked in San Francisco. There was also information on a man named Sparky Valentine, who was identified as a close friend as well as her landlord.

Kelly's father had died six years ago, and her stepmother had moved to the East coast and remarried. The dossier suggested that the two women were estranged, but this did not surprise Sean. Kelly had often complained of Joan Sanborn's narrow-minded and contemptuous manner. When he had memorized every detail, he closed the dossier.

Because of the approaching storm, he left the office early and drove to a secluded location overlooking the beach. He put on a windbreaker, a baseball cap, and sat on a knoll. He picked the spot because it was not well known, and it was usually sparsely occupied. There were only two other people in sight and they were far down the beach. He looked out to sea and saw dark, billowing clouds. Twenty minutes later, the first drops of rain splattered on his cap. He sat motionless, looking straight ahead as the rain's intensity increased. He thought of his childhood and wondered how shuffling between foster homes had affected his early decisions. Maybe things would have been different if he'd had a mentor.

The rain increased and gusts of wind pushed sheets of rain toward him at angles. He sat motionless and continued to stare out to sea. The horizon blurred, and he hardly noticed the noise made by the rain pelting his windbreaker. For the next two hours, he watched the storm-heightened breakers roll over and crash onto the shore. Finally, after making a difficult decision, he rose and headed for his car.

———

The storm had eased when Sean entered his office the following day. He sat at his desk, opened the dossier, and selected the photos of Kelly and Cody. He laid them side by side and looked at them for several minutes. He closed the folder and spoke to his partner. "Would you be interested in buying my half of the company?"

Darren dropped his pen in surprise. "Why, I've never even considered such a possibility."

"Would you be interested?"

"I don't know." Darren rubbed his chin, mulling the idea. "Well, I guess I'd certainly consider it if you really want to sell. But why?"

"I'm going back to California."

CHAPTER 14

Early Friday morning, Kelly picked up a copy of the *Wall Street Journal*. A lengthy article on the market's decline focused on the sharply contrasting views of prominent analysts. The bulls captured most of the ink, explaining that the major trend was still up and the sell-off was simply another buying opportunity. Among those quoted, Hudson Treffinger announced that his current newsletter would proffer several new buy recommendations. A single bearish analyst thought the market would suffer a minor decline.

Kelly believed the eternal struggle between diverse views made the market what it was—a fickle beast dispensing opportunity to those able to supplant emotion with logic. She put the paper aside and switched on the TV.

The doorbell rang.

Sparky stood on her step holding a large carton of Greek yogurt, a plate filled with multigrain muffins, sliced fruit, and an assortment of vitamin pills. "Breakfast is served."

She had forgotten their discussion of the previous evening. Indicating a desire to absorb knowledge, Sparky had asked if he could join her today. He had offered a subtle bribe by announcing his intention to cater breakfast. Kelly selected an apricot half and invited him inside.

The Dow fell sixty-one points during the first hour. Though Sparky's options had doubled, he did not display the level of enthusiasm typical of beginners. Curious about his behavior, Kelly asked, "I thought you'd be excited by your profit."

"My papa said that one of the worst things that could happen to a man was for him to win his first bet on a horse race. I'm applying the same concept to the stock market."

"I guess he figured you'd conclude winning was easy or that you were a genius."

"Both."

"Your father was a man of exceptional wisdom."

The market rebounded over the next ninety minutes, but Kelly thought the rally lacked staying power. When the Dow was down only four points, declining issues still outnumbered advancing stocks by a ratio of more than two to one. A strong, negative divergence. With Sparky's permission, she called Dan Hawkins and shorted Dow futures for his account. Shorting would allow him to profit in a declining market.

A little after nine, the Dow began a steady sell-off, and prices declined to the lows of the day. Instead of testing the earlier support level, the market shot through the lows on tremendous volume. Between nine forty-five and ten o'clock, the Dow plunged 162 points.

The collapse accelerated as a swell of sell orders flowed in from all corners of the globe. When the Dow knifed through minus 370 points, Kelly could smell panic. Huge blocks of stocks held by prominent mutual funds flooded the trading system as everyone tried to get out the same door at the same time.

With lighting speed, the Dow hit minus 484 points, and the decline accelerated. Twenty minutes later, the Dow had tumbled 723 points on the day.

Sparky finally lost his cool. He jumped off a chair and slapped his hands together. "Holy shit. Look at that sucker drop."

Kelly advised him to stay calm, explaining that emotional extremes fostered bad decisions.

Her phone rang so frequently she had to ask Sparky to screen the callers. Yesterday, no one wanted to talk to her—today everyone did.

After taking several messages, Sparky waved the receiver at her. "It's Dan Hawkins."

Still eyeing the TV, she reached for the phone.

"It's a madhouse down here," Dan said excitedly. He yelled at someone in his office, and then said, "I thought you'd like to know that the phone on your old desk is ringing off the hook. It got so bad Crittenden had to assign Vanessa to your desk just to handle all of the calls."

Kelly pictured the scene. Nearly everyone in the office had their customers heavily committed in stocks. The younger brokers, who had never been through a bear market, were probably shell-shocked. She wondered what kind of advice they were giving their customers now. The thought caused her to worry about Dan. "How are you managing?"

"That's one of the reasons I called. I wanted to thank you."

"What for?"

"After Sparky bought the options, I gave your system a lot of thought. You believed in it so much I decided to advise my clients to lighten up on their holdings. I'm in pretty good shape."

"I'm glad it worked out that way. How about the others?"

"T. J. Halverson turned white two hundred points ago."

"It couldn't have happened to a nicer fellow."

Hawkins laughed. "We're on the same channel on that one."

"The TV showed the Dow down nearly eight hundred points," Kelly said. "What's the last on your screen?"

"That's accurate. The market hit minus eight hundred a few seconds ago. It's going to be a long weekend."

"Longer for some than others."

"You're right about that. Oh, I almost forgot. Crittenden just had your computer hauled into his office. I guess he thinks your software might still be on the hard drive. It looks like he's doing a one-eighty on your system."

"What a sleaze. There's some data on there but no program. I hope it drives him nuts." Before hanging up, she got quotes on several options, then punched numbers into her calculator and turned to Sparky. "Your account is now worth well over two hundred thousand dollars. Not bad for a few days of work."

He thought a moment and said, "I think we should take the money and run."

"Why don't we let Cyberstar decide? I'll run today's numbers after the close, then we can talk."

"Sterling idea." He headed for the door. "I haven't had champagne in years, but I think we deserve some. What's a good brand?"

"I had some Schramsberg at a luncheon a few months ago. It's marvelous."

"Done."

The phone rang.

Vanessa Pruitt spoke cheerfully. "I'm proud of you, girl. You were right on."

"It's not over yet, but I appreciate the thought."

"Channel 15 wants your phone number. Shall I give it to them?"

Kelly felt overwhelmed. A few days after losing her job, her old phone was ringing off the hook, and a TV station had sought her out. Life was often a strange and mercurial beast. "I'll talk to them, but thanks for checking with me."

Twenty minutes later, Heather Soderling from Channel 15 called. "We're doing a special on the stock market, and we'd like you to appear on the show."

Kelly's insides churned. What was she going to wear? What would she say? She immediately realized those were the wrong questions. Needing time to consider her stance, she asked for details of the show.

While listening to Heather, Kelly sensed that a TV appearance was premature. She was about to decline when Heather said, "Hudson Treffinger will be one of our guests. Perhaps you know him."

Kelly's interest soared. "Does he know I'm invited?"

"Why, no, that hadn't been decided when I talked to him."

Kelly relived Hudson Treffinger's behavior during the sales meeting at Boucher & Crittenden. He'd had the floor then, but a TV format would act as an equalizer.

She made a snap decision. "I'll be there."

CHAPTER 15

Martin Scanlan entered the main conference room and mulled a tangle of conflicting emotions. Taking Kelly Sanborn's advice had spared his personal account from a catastrophic loss, but the firm's clients had suffered heavy losses in the market. He could almost hear the time bomb in his father's will counting off the days. He took a seat at the head of the table and surveyed the haggard faces of the investment committee. The market's sudden plunge engendered a level of stress that most were incapable of concealing.

Scanlan checked a nearby computer screen. The Dow was down sharply, and the market showed no signs of stabilizing. Gripped by a sense of urgency, he addressed the staff. "We are going to skip our usual discussion of individual stocks and concentrate on our overall strategy. We'll survive if this sell-off is merely aggressive profit taking, but if this is the beginning of a bear cycle . . . we're in deep shit." He looked around the table. "I want opinions."

Elizabeth Devincenzi spoke first. "I think we've entered a bear phase. We should reduce our exposure to stocks immediately."

"In a dramatic gesture, Lewis Hostetler drew a trend line on a chart of the S&P 500. "The long-term trend is intact, and I believe the market will be higher in a few months. We shouldn't cut the allocation."

Scanlan turned toward Elizabeth. "Why the sudden change?"

"Brian and I took another look at Kelly Sanborn's documentation on Cyberstar. We think her system is very good, possibly even revolutionary."

Scanlan addressed Brian Doane who was checking a computer screen. "Do you agree with Elizabeth?"

Still looking at the monitor, Doane said, "The Dow just went through another support level." He turned toward Scanlan. "Her system gave the signal a little early, but the last three days are proof of Cyberstar's value."

"Then you accept her list of historical trades as valid?"

"I believe she's honest and very intelligent. I like the combination." Doane held up Kelly's documentation. "The potential of her system is startling."

Scanlan eased back and considered the various assessments of Kelly's software. She had impressed him during their recent meeting, and her advice on the technology stocks had spared his own account from heavy losses. His opinion of her had grown more favorable each day. He drummed his fingers on the table. If Cyberstar were the Holy Grail, there might still be time to improve the firm's performance enough to save his inheritance. If not, he could still make a fortune trading stocks on his own, but he could only do that if he controlled the software. He made a decision— get a copy of Cyberstar by any means necessary.

After a heated discussion, the committee agreed to reduce exposure to common stocks. Securities would be eliminated according to their relative strength—the weakest would go. He gave final instructions; then, he adjourned the meeting, went to his office, and peered at his computer screen. He could only think of one word to describe what he saw—chaos. Massive sell orders choked the system. He watched in awe as the market plunged to minus 1,068 points.

———

When Scanlan finally went home, he poured a drink and thought about Kelly Sanborn. He unlocked the bottom drawer in his desk, withdrew a flash drive and placed it in a USB port in his computer. He punched a few keys and watched as the screen filled with an image of Kelly entering his office. He had been wise to record their recent meeting. He studied the woman and found himself impressed with her appearance and deportment. He had not categorized her as a beautiful woman at first sight, but she seemed to have a unique synergy working for her. Her features, intelligence, and mannerisms, combined to create a striking package, and her personality had an extraordinary vitality. Lighting in a feminine frame.

He admired her skin, the fullness of her lips, and he especially liked her hair. A simple turn of her head sent clusters of auburn strands swirling through the air, colliding with one another before coming to rest in a perfect line. And those legs. They went all the way to heaven and back. He imagined his hands sliding under her skirt, seeking her feminine heat.

He turned off the computer, but his infatuation with Kelly escalated. He poured another drink and knew he had to have her. He considered the challenge, and he saw no reason he couldn't have her *and* her software. He picked up his phone and dialed the pigeon keeper.

That afternoon, Scanlan walked past the De Young Museum and descended steps leading to a small park lined with rows of well-groomed trees. He quickly spotted his contact.

Appropriately, Danny Fagan sat alone, feeding a dozen pigeons.

Scanlan waited until a boy on a skateboard went by; then, he sat on the end of the bench. "I've got an important job for you."

Fagan shoved a hand into his bag but did not look up. "These pigeons wouldn't stand a chance against my racers. Too common. Too slow." He tossed a handful of seed in a wide arc. "Breeding and diet. That's the trick." He shuffled a handful of seed in his hand. "This is a special blend."

"To hell with your pigeons," Scanlan said curtly, as he watched an elderly woman negotiate the nearby steps. "I need you to get on this right away."

Fagan's head shot up at the negative comment about pigeons. His lips quivered, but no words came out.

Scanlan handed him a piece of paper. "I want you to steal a computer at this address."

"I'm not a burglar, man. That shit's for idiots and dopers."

"I'll give you seven thousand dollars to snatch the computer. That's not bad for a few minutes of work."

Fagan tossed his empty bag on the ground. "Is it in an office?"

"Residence. I'll arrange for the occupant to attend a meeting at my office to make sure she's out of the house."

"Does she live alone?"

"I'm not sure."

"Sounds easy enough." Fagan glanced at the address. "Half Moon Bay, huh." He looked toward a flight of pigeons circling the museum's roof. "I have my eye on some champion English breeders." His head bobbed up and down. "I'll do it."

Scanlan handed him an envelope containing an address and three thousand dollars. "You'll get the rest on delivery." He waited for a young couple to pass. "Grab the computer and every CD and flash drive you can find, and don't let anything stop you."

"What if I have to get rough?"

"Do whatever it takes."

Fagan rose, shoved the envelope into his pocket, and started up the steps toward the Steinhart Aquarium. Over his shoulder he said, "Piece of cake."

CHAPTER 16

Shortly after takeoff, Sean Keene heard the landing gear retract into the belly of the Qantas Boeing 747, and he knew his life would never be the same. Watching the land give way to surf and open sea, it occurred to him that the plane had become a transitional capsule conveying him from one stage of his life to another. He already felt different. At almost the exact moment of liftoff, Sean's excitement over the trip had yielded to a feeling of apprehension.

He opened his briefcase and withdrew a notepad. He scanned the numbers and felt grateful for his relationship with his former partner. Darren Bishop had been more than fair during their negotiations for Sean's half of the business. After agreeing on a price, Darren had come up with a forty percent cash down payment, part of which had come from a bank loan. Sean would receive the balance in payments spread over the next four years.

The funds would give him time to settle in and redirect his life without having to deal with financial concerns. He had decided to spend a considerable amount of time attempting to restore a trail of long-abandoned relationships. Most of all, he wanted to befriend Kelly and spend time with his son. Was that possible? Anxiety and doubt ricocheted through his mind, but he was tired of the guilt he felt to his very core, guilt that had grown over time like an insidious cancer. Looking back, he realized that he had used work to overcome his guilt. He put in excessive hours, which helped the business, but it did nothing to squelch the ever-growing flame of guilt.

He withdrew Kelly's picture and laid it on the pad. The woman was noticeably more attractive than the girl he had forsaken. Time had been good to her, but he also saw something in her face that was new—a vigilant, seasoned look. Had he been the one who caused the change? Shaken by a feeling of remorse, he turned and stared out the window. He focused on a layer of clouds stretching to the horizon and wondered why, as a young man, he had always run away from responsibility. He reflected on how he had come into the world, abandoned by unknown parents, and shuttled from one foster home to another. He had floundered without a mentor. It seemed that society had always run away from him, and he had merely followed suit—a misguided cog in an imperfect world.

He looked down on the undulating cloud tops and realized this was the first time he had ever gone back to confront past errors. He felt good about the concept, but the thought harbored great uncertainty. What would Kelly think of him? How in the world was he going to approach her? He couldn't just knock on her door. Perhaps a phone call? Maybe he could arrange a chance meeting on the street. None of these options sounded right.

When he did meet her, he had no idea what he would say. Like himself, she obviously carried emotional scars, and nothing he could say would wipe out his betrayal. He tortured himself with guilt that had bored deep into his soul, guilt that had strengthened with each passing year, guilt that had become almost unbearable.

He glanced back at the photo, and he realized that facing Kelly would be the most difficult thing he had ever done. Presently, he replaced her picture with one of Cody. The boy had an honest face with good lines. He wondered if he would ever be able to play ball with his son. He did not deserve such a privilege, but he would give anything for the opportunity.

———

After a long flight, Sean arrived in San Francisco and checked into the Airport Hyatt. The following day, he purchased several maps, rented a car, and drove toward Half Moon Bay. He did not intend to approach Kelly for several days, but he wanted to see where she lived and learn something about the neighborhood where his son was growing up. He grew more anxious as he approached his destination. When he entered the city limits, the strain caused him to pull to the side of the road. He considered turning back, and, then, he admonished himself aloud. "This is ridiculous. I'm just going to drive by the house for Christ's sake."

He steeled himself, checked the map, and pulled onto the highway. He turned onto Water Street and checked the dossier for her address. Two more blocks. He glanced about the neighborhood, which was comprised of modest, well-kept houses. He crossed the last intersection and saw that the street ended at a vacant lot. Afraid he might be trapped in front of Kelly's house, he scrunched down in the seat and drove to the dead end. He made a U-turn, pulled to the curb, and scanned the numbers. Her address was across the street, three houses down.

He fidgeted nervously as he stared at her residence. He had not planned to watch the house today, but he found himself unable to leave. If only he could get a glimpse of Kelly and his son. He could not possibly approach them yet, but he desperately wanted to see them. Forty minutes later, a young woman with dark hair came out of the house and drove away. It wasn't long before Sean could no longer bear the wait. He started the engine and drove up the street, studying the house as he went by. He returned to the hotel and wished he had stayed longer. He *had* to get a glimpse of Kelly and his son.

———

The next day, Sean parked in the same spot and settled in for a longer stay. He brought a paperback novel, a sandwich, a bottle of spring water, and a hat to help conceal his face. He had just started the fourth chapter of his book when the dark-haired woman left the house and drove off in her car. She was slight and feminine. Sean thought she might be Eurasian. Kelly's roommate?

Not long after she had left, a man dressed in dark clothes got out of a cargo van parked on the other side of the house and walked up an adjacent driveway. Probably a neighbor. Sean rested his head on the seat back and sighed. The waiting had turned into a strange kind of torture.

Fifteen minutes later, he glanced down the street and noticed the dark-haired woman's car returning. A quick trip. He craned his neck and saw someone on the passenger side. He was not sure, but it looked like a young boy. He jerked to attention, his heart pounding against his chest.

Cody?

The passenger got out of the car as soon as it had stopped.

Sean squinted. The boy was about the right age, his hair was the right color. Realization flooded Sean's mind. *My God, that's my son.* He felt an overpowering tug on his heart. Tears blurred his vision. He wiped away the moisture and stared at his likeness.

After Cody and the woman had entered the house, Sean sat motionless, overcome by an odd mixture of anguish, joy, and awe he knew he would never experience again. He sat and simply stared at nothing for several minutes, replaying the moment he saw Cody. He had endured enough emotional shock for one day. He reached for his keys, but a high-pitched noise caused him to stop short. Was it a scream? He leaned his head out the window and listened.

Nothing.

It must have been children playing down the street. He was about to start the engine when he saw a small figure run out of the house next to Kelly's and head for her front door. Peering intently, Sean was startled when he realized it was not a boy at all. It was a dwarf—and he was running with a sense of great urgency.

Sean came fully alert. Something was wrong.

Another scream.

He bolted from the car and sprinted toward the house. The wind whipped off his hat when he jumped the curb. He drew within ten yards of the house and heard loud crashing noises. Fear flooded his thoughts. A gunshot roared from inside. Sean bounded up the steps, shouting, "No. No!"

He burst through the door and glared at the incredible scene before him. Furniture and computer components lay strewn about the floor. The boy, the dark-haired woman, and the dwarf struggled with a man wearing dark clothes and a ski mask. Cody gyrated wildly as he clung to the arm that held a gun.

The man cursed and tried to bring his weapon to bear on his attackers, but the dwarf grabbed the gunman's leg and bit his ankle. The intruder yelled out in pain; then, he hit the woman with his free hand, sending her crashing into the wall. She slumped down and did not move.

Sean dashed across the room and drove his shoulder into the man's ribs, sending bodies flying in every direction. Only the dwarf managed to maintain his grip on the assailant. Sean rolled over and saw the man crawling across the floor toward his gun, dragging the dwarf with him.

The intruder grabbed his pistol and started to spin around.

Sean sprang to his feet, took two steps, and dove through the air. The man's arm swung in an arc and his pistol crashed against the side of Sean's head. He fell heavily and rolled on his side. He shook his head and he tried to fight off a blackish cloud that had collapsed his vision to a small blurry hole. His mind screamed at him. Get up, dammit. Get up!

The dwarf bit the gunman's hand, causing him to drop the pistol.

Sean rose to a crouching position.

A boot came toward his head.

He ducked, grabbed the foot at the top of its arc and shoved upward. The intruder fell onto his back with a crash, but he was up almost instantly.

His vision clearing, Sean jumped up and drove a crunching blow to the man's chin, staggering him. Sean followed with a left to the midsection, then a right that glanced off the top the gunman's head. The blow caused the ski mask to ride up and uncover part of his face. They traded blows until Sean connected with a solid right. The gunman staggered; then, he charged across the room, cursing and tugging down on his mask. He stopped at the door and pulled a small pistol from a holster strapped to his ankle.

Cody yelled, "Mister. Look out!"

Sean turned and saw the boy toss the intruder's other gun. He caught the weapon and spun toward the door.

The gunman's arm came up. A shot echoed across the room.

The bullet tore into Sean's side and knocked him to the floor. Still holding the gun, he rolled on his stomach and fired twice. One bullet ripped into the doorframe, the other tore a hole in the attacker's backpack.

The gunman sprayed three shots into the room and disappeared.

Sean tried to get up but fell back from a sharp pain in his side. He looked around, frantically searching for Cody. The boy stood on the other side of the room, wide-eyed and shaking, as he stared at a bullet hole in his shirt collar.

The dwarf rushed toward the woman slumped on the floor and shouted. "Cody, dial 911; then, help that man. Hurry!"

CHAPTER 17

Returning from a surprisingly, uneventful meeting at Scanlan Equity Management, Kelly turned onto her street and saw an array of flashing lights in the distance. Something had happened in the next block—her block. Frightened, she leaned forward, peered intently, and saw several police cars parked at odd angles along the street. "Oh, God." Consumed by fear, she shoved down on the gas pedal as concern for Cody and Miyako blotted out all other thoughts.

She drove as fast as she dared and almost passed a police officer waving her to the side of the road. She hit the brakes and pulled over.

"Hey, Lady. You can't drive around here like that. I ought to—"

"I live over there."

The officer's expression changed. "In the house where the officers are?"

"Yes. What's wrong? Is my son all right?" Not waiting for an answer, Kelly jumped from her car and broke into a run.

"Stop!"

She ignored the cop and ducked under a long strip of yellow tape. Another policeman grabbed her arm. "Hold on, Miss. You can't cross this line."

"Yes, I can, dammit. I live here."

Still holding her arm, the officer turned and called to a man wearing a sport coat. "Lieutenant."

A man with thinning hair and a tired face approached. "Yeah, Sanchez. What've you got?"

"Lady says she lives here."

The lieutenant motioned for Kelly to step to one side. "You reside in this house?"

"Yes."

"Who else lives there?"

"My son and my roommate." She tried to read his face, but he kept a blank expression.

"It's okay, ma'am." The man nodded reassuringly. "Someone broke into the house. There have been some injuries, but your son is all right."

She ran toward the house.

"They've all been taken to the hospital."

She stopped. "But you said he was okay."

"He only has a few bruises, but our protocol requires that he be checked by a doctor. The other two sustained injuries that are more serious. A young lady. Your roommate, I think. And a man."

Kelly assumed the man must have been Sparky until she heard his voice in the distance. She turned and saw him talking with two officers. She rushed toward them.

Sparky saw her, stepped away from the men, and opened his arms.

Kelly dropped to a knee and hugged Sparky.

He whispered in her ear. "Cody's all right." He stroked her hair. "He's okay. Everything's fine."

Tears rolled from her eyes. Cody had obviously gone through a horrible experience, but he was safe. She pulled back. "Miyako?"

"I don't know how badly she's hurt, but she was unconscious when the ambulance left, and a man who helped us was shot."

Kelly's hand went to her chest. "Shots were fired?" She trembled at the thought of her son dodging bullets.

"Yeah, it was really something. We were trying to fight back and if that man hadn't come in when he did, I don't think we would have made it."

She tilted her head. "A neighbor?"

"Nope, never saw him before. He took a bullet in the side, but he seemed okay."

She grimaced.

Sparky patted her hand.

She rose and turned to the detective. "I want to see my son."

The man turned to a uniformed officer. "Take her to the hospital."

At the hospital, Kelly left the nurse behind and ran down the corridor toward Cody's room. They had informed her that he had just gotten out of emergency, and that he would be held overnight for observation. She hurried through the door.

Bandages on the side of his head did not prevent a broad smile. "Hi, Mom."

Good Lord. He had just been through a wild melee, guns and all, and he's acting like nothing happened. Still, she felt relieved.

He would not be that chipper if he were badly injured. She gave him a long hug; then, she sat in a chair and held his hand. Occasionally, she stroked the side of his face below a bandage. With Cody's safety assured, she became increasingly concerned about Miyako. She had asked about her friend's condition, but a nurse told her it was too soon to know anything.

A half hour later, Sparky entered the room. He grinned at Cody. "Hi, Pardner. Some fight, huh?" He reached into a paper bag and withdrew a large cup. "Thought you might like a chocolate milkshake. Your favorite."

Cody took the cup. "Thanks."

"Anytime, Cody." Sparky turned to Kelly. "I just got back from the emergency room. Miyako has a nasty concussion, and she's semi-conscious. Fades in and out. They wouldn't tell me much, but they're hopeful. Anyway, she'll be under intense observation, and we won't be able to see her for a while."

The news was worse than Kelly had expected. She shook her head slowly and then said, "I want to know what happened."

Sparky spread his arms in the manner he often did before a long oratory. "The whole thing was really something. We all pitched in. Actually, we had to. The guy was strong as a bull. Anyway, there were bodies flying all over the place." Sparky gave an animated, blow-by-blow replay.

Cody said. "He wore a ski mask, and he had something all over his boots. It looked like chicken dung or something like that. Really gross." He put down his cup. "The creep was trying to steal both computers. He did get away with the laptop."

Sparky shot Kelly a quick look. "The word's out about Cyberstar."

"The ad." she said. "Thank goodness we didn't have the program on the laptop."

"Yep. The whole damn town knows about you now. You're going to have to figure out a better way to secure your software." He tilted his head toward Cody. "And maybe get it out of the house."

Kelly caught his meaning. She had no idea how to deal with the problem, but she was not going to put loved ones in jeopardy. After a moment of silence, she turned toward Sparky. "What about the man who got shot? How bad is he?"

"I asked about him after checking on Miyako. Fortunately, the bullet barely nicked a rib and went out his side. The doctor said it sounds worse than it is, and he thinks he should be out of the hospital in two or three days. They'll let us see him when he gets to his room."

"We owe him so much," Kelly said.

Cody touched his bandage. "He saved our lives, Mom." Cody reached over and grabbed the shirt he wore during the shooting. He poked his finger through a bullet hole in the collar. "Look at this!"

Realization struck Kelly like a thunderbolt. Her son came within inches of being seriously injured or killed. She pulled Cody close and held him tight, not wanting to let go, as horrible images of what could have been flooded her mind.

Cody, said. "I want to thank the man too."

Kelly smiled. "We'll all go. Sort of like a thank you committee."

A nurse stuck her head in the door. "Mr. Valentine, may I see you a second?"

After speaking with the nurse, Sparky reappeared. "There's been no change in Miyako, but we can have a brief visit with the man who was shot. He's just down the hall."

Kelly looked at Cody. "Are you up to it?"

130

"Sure, I'm fine."

Sparky bent at the waist and swung his arm toward the door. "After you."

Kelly walked down the hall with her arm around Cody's shoulder. If the man had not intervened anything might have happened. She shuddered and tightened her grip.

Sparky stopped three rooms down and gestured inside.

Kelly entered the room and glanced at the first bed. Empty. A nurse tended a man in the other bed. Kelly waited until the woman moved, then she edged forward, eager to thank the stranger.

The man turned and looked at Kelly with magnificent blue eyes; eyes she had hoped she would never see again. Her knees weakened. She put her hand on the bedside table for support.

"Y—you!"

CHAPTER 18

Martin Scanlan preferred to meet Danny Fagan somewhere other than his home, but he had an urgent need to gain possession of the Kelly Sanborn's computer. His estate, in Hillsborough, had a tree-lined drive that made cars entering the sprawling compound nearly impossible to see, especially at night.

Just after dark, Scanlan watched the pigeon keeper exit his car, open the trunk, and retrieve a backpack. "You have the merchandise."

"There was a problem."

Scanlan stiffened. "Inside."

Fagan slipped a backpack strap over one shoulder and followed him to his office.

Scanlan spoke in a sharp tone. "Did you get the computer?"

"I got one of 'em, a laptop."

"How many did you see?"

"There was also a desktop, but all hell broke loose before I could get it."

"I thought you were a pro."

"I'm a pro at what I do, but I'm not a fucking burglar. I told you that."

Scanlan shook his head. "Tell me what happened. Then we need to check the laptop."

Fagan took a chair in front of the desk. "I watched the house for a while, then I went behind some bushes to a side window and looked in. I saw the computers right off. Nobody in sight. I couldn't be seen from the street, so I waited about ten minutes, then I picked the lock on the back door and went in. I shoved the laptop into my backpack, and I was unplugging the desktop when I heard footsteps from the hall." Fagan tilted his head. "I thought you said the woman who lived there would be in a meeting with you."

"She *was*."

"Well, some other woman came into the room and screamed. Then this kid came in and threw a book at me. Before I could get out the door, this little dude came from nowhere and bit me on the leg." Fagan shook his head. "It was a fucking mess, man. I had to pull a gun."

"There was shooting?"

"Yeah, and then another guy came in the front door. I hit the woman and was trying to leave when this dude crashed into me. I ran out of there and damn near got shot." Fagan shook his head.

Scanlan took note of the negative body language of the man sitting before him. Though Fagan had managed to obtain only one computer, he was still a valuable resource he could not afford to lose. He opened a drawer and retrieved a brown envelope. "Here's your money." He tossed it onto the desk. "I'm going to throw in another five hundred because of what happened."

Fagan's eyes narrowed. "That's not much for hazardous pay."

Scanlan ignored the comment and turned his attention to the laptop. "I know you're good at technical stuff. Can you find a particular software program on this computer?"

"Sure. It's a simple process." Fagan plugged in the power cord and turned on the laptop.

A password screen appeared.

Scanlan said, "Now what?"

"Piece of cake." Fagan reached into his bag, withdrew a CD, inserted it in the drive, and rebooted the computer. When a menu appeared, he clicked several times and gave a command to wipe out the password. Then he rebooted.

After the desktop screen appeared, he asked, "Okay, what are we looking for?"

"It's a stock market trading program."

"That'll be easy to find." Fagan opened the Control Panel, and then he clicked on Programs and Features. He scanned the list. "Nothing like that here." He clicked on the computer icon and opened the program files folder. He looked over each entry, occasionally opening a folder to view the contents. "Nope." He then opened the user library. "There are multiple data files, some very large, but no program."

"Are you sure?"

"Damn right I'm sure."

Scanlan eased back in his chair and shook his head. "Fuck."

Fagan said, "It might be in the other computer, but I doubt it."

"Why do you say that?"

"If it's valuable, the program might be portable. You can run a lot of programs from a USB flash drive, but you have to design them that way."

Scanlan rubbed his chin. "So, the data is there but the program can only be run from a device outside of the computer."

134

Fagan nodded. "That's how I'd do it. It protects your program and gives you portability. Hell, she could run it from anywhere."

Scanlan rose and paced the room. "She's smart." He stopped and turned toward Fagan. "I've got to get my hands on that program. I'll get back to you as soon as I figure this out." He tapped the money-filled envelope. "You didn't get what I wanted, but you can keep the money. I have to get my hands on that software, so I'll need you again. We're going to have to figure another way."

Fagan said, "Just tell me what you want done. I'll take care of the rest."

"Do you have men you can trust if we need more manpower?"

Fagan picked up the envelope and rose from his chair. "Yeah, two guys."

"Good, but I don't want them to know who you're working for. Make damn sure of that."

After Fagan left, Scanlan wandered through his house, analyzing the problem as he walked. His need for the program grew each day, and it became obvious that he had to maneuver Kelly Sanborn into a situation that guaranteed she would have the program while in a vulnerable position. He had just walked back into his office when the idea struck. He had a scheme that would isolate Kelly while she had the program in her possession. After further reflection, he knew he had a perfect plan that would not fail.

CHAPTER 19

Overwhelmed by the shock of seeing Cody's father in the hospital bed, Kelly turned and headed for the doorway. Her shoulder hit the doorjamb, and she nearly stumbled as she exited the room. She moved a few steps, and then turned and placed put her back against the wall and put a hand against her heaving chest.

It wasn't possible. It had to be someone else in that hospital bed, but she knew better. Those blue eyes belonged to only one person and that person was Sean Keene. She said the words aloud, "Cody's father." She shook her head slowly, trying to make sense of what had happened. The person she never wanted to see again had almost certainly saved her son's life and, perhaps, the lives of two others she loved.

She leaned her head against the wall as she tried to make sense of a jumble of emotions ricocheting through her mind. It seemed an impossible task.

After a moment of puzzled hesitation, Sparky and Cody exited the room to look for Kelly. They found her a few yards away against the wall. Sparky Valentine had long been known for his compassion and the moment he saw Kelly, in obvious distress, that element of his character rocketed into overdrive. He approached her and held out both hands, taking her right hand in his, concern etched across his face.

Kelly tilted her head and nodded toward Cody.

Sparky caught the signal. He turned to Cody. "I need to talk to your Mom. Go back to your room, and we'll join you in a few minutes."

Cody hesitated; then, he turned and walked down the hall, looking back several times until he entered his hospital room.

Sparky motioned toward a row of chairs a few yards away. He watched her closely and noticed her body tremble after she took a seat. He waited a few seconds, then said. "Okay, what's wrong?"

She shook her head. "You won't believe what I'm going to tell you."

"Well, you obviously know this man from somewhere."

Her heart was beating too fast. She gazed at the floor to calm herself. Finally, she said, "Yes, yes I do." She turned toward him. He...he's Cody's *father!*"

Sparky usually blurted out words in a rapid string but, upon hearing her statement, he simply stared at the opposite wall as he tried to comprehend what she had said. After a moment, he said. "The man who burst into the house and ran off the gunman is Cody's father? I thought he was in Australia."

"He went to Australia before Cody was born. I thought he was still there."

"Are you sure it's him?"

"Of course I'm sure."

Sparky could only manage two words. "Good grief." He was silent as he tried to take in the enormity of Kelly's declaration. Finally, he said. "Cody looks like his father. Actually, the more I think about it, the likeness is quite dramatic."

Kelly expelled a deep sigh. "I know, and the resemblance increases with each passing year. I try not to, but I think about it a great deal."

"That's normal. Try not to worry about it too much." As they talked, Sparky noticed that Kelly's comportment had gradually changed from shock to one of contemplation. She was obviously trying to comprehend the implications of Sean's involvement in the attack on her loved ones, an attack that could have ended tragically.

Sparky said. "What does he know about his father?"

"Very little. He only knows that he lives in another country. That's about it."

"Doesn't he ask questions?"

"He used to, but he learned that it hurts me to discuss it. We have an understanding."

"Cody is a smart kid. He was right behind you when you entered the room, and he stood at the end of the bed. He obviously got a good look at Sean. His mind may be working on that." He patted Kelly's hand. "You will probably have to tell him."

"But I don't know what kind of person his father is now. Maybe I don't want him near Cody. I have to protect my son, and I have to protect myself."

"Tell you what. Each of us is given certain gifts when we're born. One of my gifts is the ability to judge character within a very few minutes. I am seldom wrong. I'll have a talk with Sean and let you know what I think. Is that reasonable?"

"I'd rather just avoid him entirely."

"You know you can't do that. You have to at least thank him. And remember, Cody got a good look at him."

Kelly nodded. "Yes, that could be a problem. Okay, but I have strong reservations about this."

"I share your concerns." He looked down the hallway. "You go take care of Cody, and I'll pop in and have a talk with Mr. Keene."

Kelly rose, took a few steps, then turned. "After you finish, can you check on Miyako? I am really worried about her."

"Of course."

————————

When Sparky entered the room, Sean immediately sat upright.

Sparky walked over and extended his hand. "My name is Horatio Valentine, but everyone calls me Sparky. My mother named me after a character in Hamlet. In the play, Horatio epitomizes the faithful friend. I am that to Kelly and Cody and more. I love them like family. You need to understand that right away. I will protect them at all costs, and don't judge me by my size. I can be a mean motherfucker when the situation demands it."

Sean shook his hand. "That's quite an introduction. Mine will be shorter. My name is Sean Keene, and you have probably never met anyone more guilt-ridden."

"Okay, let's talk about that." Sparky climbed up on a chair. "The floor is yours."

Sparky listened intently as Sean gave a long record of events beginning with his relationship with Kelly, his subsequent departure for Australia, and his movements while in that country. He dwelled on the difference in his emotional and physical development, and the fact that he had been very immature in his teens.

Sparky was especially interested in hearing how Sean had cut his alcohol to an occasional drink and, after a time, founded a successful business. During Sean's last few sentences, Sparky noticed how emotional he was, including his moist eyes. It was obvious that Sean had paid a high price for his actions.

He considered Sean's comments, and then said. "Why didn't you come back sooner?"

"After several years had passed, I figured that door had closed. I thought I had no chance to enter their lives, but time tore a hole in my soul, year after year, until I could no longer handle the guilt, so I had to try."

Sparky nodded slowly, and then said, "Tell me about your outside interests."

"Well, I spent a lot of time on or near the ocean for obvious reasons. But my favorite interest was founding, and supporting, a baseball league for kids with my partner. I enjoyed it a great deal."

"A worthy enterprise." Sparky paused, and then said. "Cody loves baseball."

Sean nodded. "Wow, how about that."

"How many home runs did Babe Ruth hit?"

"Seven-hundred and fourteen."

Sparky smiled. "How did you know that?"

"I just read it and it stuck. That happens to me a lot."

"You and Cody share an interest." Sparky paused, allowing his comment to sink in, then he said. "Okay. Let's move on to something more serious. What is your philosophy on life?"

Sean did not hesitate. "It took me too long to form these ideals, but I have two that I now live by. One is never to lie. If you do tell a lie, you can be labeled a liar in a few seconds; a label that might take years to remove. It's simply not worth it. The second is this: always do the right thing, and I am desperately trying to do the right thing now."

Sean paused for a long moment, then reached over and retrieved his wallet. "Let me show you something." He extracted a thin pouch, opened it, and pulled out a small lock of hair. "This is Kelly's hair. She gave it to me one day after we made love."

Sparky was stunned. He reached over and gently touched the hair. "It's amazing that you kept it all this time."

"Yes, I guess I could not cut all ties."

They sat without speaking for a long moment as they both tried to understand the significance of the lock of hair.

After the silence, they covered a variety of subjects during the next twenty-minutes, and then Sparky got off the chair and headed for the door. "I'll be in touch."

He entered Cody's room and saw Kelly seated in a chair, holding Cody's hand.

She looked up, her body language apprehensive. "What happened?"

Sparky walked over and put a hand on her shoulder. "I like him."

CHAPTER 20

Martin Scanlan had a perfect strategy for stealing Kelly Sanborn's software. As soon as he put the various components together, he would call her with a proposal he knew she would accept. He picked up his phone and dialed Danny Fagan's number. "I'm ready to put my plan in action, and I'll need your help."

"Sure. What've you got?"

Meet me in the parking lot of the Palace of The Legion of Honor at three o'clock."

"I'll be there."

Scanlan arrived a few minutes late, as planned. He saw Fagan leaning against the wall that surrounded part of the parking lot, looking at the city in the distance. He spent five minutes checking the people and cars in the lot; then, he got out, walked to the wall, and stood about six feet from Fagan. After a moment, he said. "I'm going to hold a small conference at my lodge in the Sierras. Kelly Sanborn will be invited. She'll be told to prepare a presentation, so she'll have the software with her.

"There's a narrow stretch of road about thirty-five miles from my place that would be an ideal spot for what I have in mind. I know a place where you can park and not be seen until the last minute. I want you to pull your car across the road so that you completely block her from passing. You said you have two men you can rely on, correct?"

Fagan turned at the sound of pigeons on the pavement and, as he began inspecting the birds, he appeared disconnected.

Scanlan raised his voice. "Fuck those goddamn pigeons and pay attention."

Fagan turned and looked at Scanlan with an intense, hostile stare. Finally, he said, "Yeah, I have two guys, but I can get more."

Scanlan looked toward the city, somewhat startled by the vicious stare from Fagan. In a calmer voice, he said, "This is important, and I don't want any slip-ups. Have another man station his car about two hundred yards behind you. When she passes his location, I want both of you to pull your cars onto the road so she can't pass in either direction. That will box her in. Use your gun and demand her purse, her laptop, and anything electronic. And remember, your main objective is the software." Scanlan thought a moment, and then said. "Oh, and wear ski masks. We want to eliminate any chance of you being identified."

"Standard procedure."

"She may have her son with her, but don't hurt the boy. We can use him as leverage. Do whatever is necessary to get the items I mentioned, and that includes deadly force."

"That shouldn't be necessary."

"I want you to put severe pressure on her for the software. If she does not comply, tell her you'll hurt the boy. She'll fold when she hears that."

"Okay. When will this go down?"

I don't have a date yet. I'll let you know the as soon as things are set. And remember—do *whatever* it takes."

Fagan turned his attention back to the pigeons and said, "Piece of cake."

CHAPTER 21

Sparky's declaration that he liked Sean sent a shock wave through Kelly.

"You *what*?"

Sparky tilted his head toward the door.

Kelly caught his signal and realized they could not discuss this in front of Cody. They left the room and took seats down the hall.

Sparky said, "This is not the same person you knew when you were teenagers. He comes across as a likeable, high-quality individual."

"But, he—he deserted me."

"Yes, he made a terrible mistake. There's no question about that."

"He certainly did."

Sparky said. "I have something surprising to tell you. Sean has a lock of your hair in his wallet."

Kelly stiffened, eyes wide. "He *what*?"

"Actually, it's pretty cool."

"My God, this is just too much for me to handle right now."

Sparky smiled. "Kinda romantic doncha think?"

"No, I don't!" Kelly rose and took a few steps as she struggled with the whole concept. Without wanting to, she remembered giving Sean the lock of her hair on a mild summer day after they had made love. She shook her head and kicked the leg of a chair, then she sat down and rubbed her foot. After the pain eased, her thoughts went back to Sean. He had deserted her and nothing would change that. Yet, he not only still had the lock of hair, he had taken it halfway around the world and back again. Well, it didn't matter—it changed nothing.

Sensing a need for a change of subject, Sparky turned and started down the hallway. "Let's go check on Miyako."

Unwittingly, Kelly reached up and twisted several strands of hair. When she realized what she was doing, she dropped her hand and started walking so fast that Sparky had to jog to catch her.

On their way to the intensive care unit, a nurse stopped them in the hallway. "I was just coming for you with good news. Miyako is conscious and out of ICU. We just moved her to a room, and you can see her, but only for a few minutes."

Kelly sighed. "Is she going to be okay?"

"The doctors think she'll be fine. She just needs to rest and avoid stress."

Kelly thanked the nurse and turned to Sparky. "Before Miyako moved in with me she considered going back to Seattle to live with her mother. I'm going to try to persuade her to do that now. I could not bear the thought of anything else happening to her because of me. When she has recovered, she can work remotely. I'll still give her a percentage of profits based on our original agreement. What do you think?"

"It's a great idea. She'll be out of harm's way."

Kelly nodded. "Okay, I'll mention it, but I won't go into details. You can back me up on my suggestion." She looked down the hall. "What she needs now is our support. Let's do everything we can to cheer her up."

———————

Kelly felt a sense of relief as she walked back to Cody's room. Miyako's condition had improved dramatically, and she had agreed with Kelly's suggestion to move to Seattle and work on a remote basis. Her mother, who had a mobility issue, had been trying to get her to move anyway.

She entered Cody's room and found his bed empty.

A nurse tending a patient in the next bed said, "He went down the hall to visit Mr. Keene."

Sparky headed for the door. "I'll go fetch him."

Kelly started to follow Sparky but she did *not* want to go back into that room. She wondered why Cody had gone to Sean's room, but it only took a moment to realize the obvious. Sean had probably saved his life. She took a seat, crossed her legs, and stared out the window. She needed to calm down, and she knew it. Sparky would bring him back.

She waited patiently at first but, after fifteen minutes, her frustration escalated. Where were they? She rose and went down the hall. A few steps from Sean's room, she heard an animated discussion. The first thing she heard was something about the San Francisco Giant's bullpen. She stopped, listened, and heard a series of baseball terms, player's names, and laughter.

She was not about to enter the room with all the testosterone and baseball talk bouncing off the walls. Besides, she wanted to avoid any conversation with Sean. She turned and started toward

Cody's room when she stopped suddenly. It hit her like a brick. *My God. They're bonding.*

She entered Cody's room and took a seat. She needed a piece of chocolate. She rummaged through her purse but there was no chocolate. "Damn!"

She put down her purse and stared out the window.

Her cellphone rang.

"Is this Kelly Sanborn?"

"Speaking."

"This is Heather Soderling from Channel 15. We are going to air that stock market special at seven PM next Wednesday. Can we count on you?

Kelly's heart jumped. This might give her new consulting business a major boost. She gathered her thoughts and said, "I'll be there."

"Great, we are delighted to have you join the panel. Please plan on arriving no later than six PM." Heather went over some details, and they completed the call.

Kelly clicked off and started to contemplate what she needed to do to prepare when her phone rang again.

"Kelly, this is Martin Scanlan. I have great news. I'm holding an investment strategy conference at my lodge in the Sierras. If you join us, you'll meet some very important investors. It'll be held on Saturday, a week from tomorrow. I'll make you the lead presenter. How about it?"

Kelly's mind raced, but she knew she had to remain cool. "I have so much going on right now. Let me get back to you."

"This is a major opportunity for you. If you can't make it, I already have another participant who wants the lead spot. I hate to give you such short notice, but I have to have a decision today."

"Hang on a second." Kelly thought about the TV appearance and, more importantly, her son. He was fine, but she knew her small family might be a target. She could not leave him alone, not even with Sparky. However, the opportunity was huge, and she desperately needed to generate revenue. She said. "Can I bring my son?"

"Of course. We would love to have him."

She realized they might be safer in the mountains than at home under current conditions.

"Okay, I'll be there."

"Excellent. I'll send you a packet complete with a map. It's about a four-hour drive. Plan to arrive on Friday in the early afternoon. The attendees will want a full overview of your system so be sure to bring your software."

She hung up and leaned back in the chair. It was almost too much. Too many things were happening all at once. Yet, the possibilities were extraordinary. The TV show and the conference could give her new company an unprecedented opportunity.

Cody and Sparky walked into the room.

Kelly said, "I have news. Big news! I am going to be on television next Wednesday, and Cody and I are going to the Sierras for a conference on Friday."

CHAPTER 22

Sean was elated after Cody and Sparky left his room. He had accomplished his goal of meeting and talking to his son, and the emotions he felt were unlike any he had ever experienced. He could tell that Cody was a great kid. Bright, polite, and he loved baseball. A great combination, though just being a good kid was all that really mattered. As he thought about his son, he felt overwhelming love. It was a profoundly singular moment, and he knew he would never be the same again. Spending time with his son changed everything.

He spent a good twenty minutes enjoying the wonderful feelings that engulfed him, occasionally breaking into a broad smile; then, his mind switched to Kelly. She obviously held deep-seated bitterness toward him. Her body language said it all. She wanted nothing to do with him and for good reason.

It was then that the biggest question of all struck him. Would Kelly tell Cody that Sean was his father? He realized there was a startling resemblance that connected him and Cody. Kelly had certainly seen the likeness, but what about Cody? Had he noticed? What was Cody thinking? Sean's elation plummeted as he pondered these new questions. He tried to go back to the positive feelings about his son, but his guilt surfaced once again, suppressing his elation. Mostly he worried that Kelly might drive a wedge between himself and Cody. Certainly, she would not do that, but the thought lingered, and it bothered him greatly. As he thought about Kelly, he pulled out his wallet, retrieved the lock of hair, and ran his fingers over the hair as he thought about how she looked. She was even more stunning than she had been as a teenage girl.

Sean's wound turned out to be relatively minor, so the hospital released him sooner than he had expected. After spending two days in the hospital, he walked outside, and the first person he saw was Sparky Valentine.

Sparky smiled and said, "I'm your chauffeur and I'm going to take you to your accommodations. No charge."

"And where would that be?"

"I want you to stay in my guest bedroom for the time being." Sparky seemed prepared for Sean to protest. "It's a done deal. Let me explain my logic." He moved his arms as if to place emphasis on each word. "We are both worried about Kelly's and Cody's safety. Someone wants what Kelly has, and they want it badly. I think the situation is far worse than any of us realize, and I believe they're going to try again." He paused as his expression turned more serious. "I can only do so much but, with you in my house, we can go tag team on watching over them. It really makes sense. What do you say?"

"Are you sure about this?"

"You bet your boots, Red Ryder."

"But you don't really know me."

"I spent enough time with you to know you are a good person and that's all I need to know. I trust my instincts."

Sean was not going to accept the offer until he heard Sparky's reasoning. It made sense, and there was another huge benefit. He would be able to see Cody often, very often. How could he refuse? He said, "But what about Kelly? She really dislikes me."

Sparky climbed into his car. "I'll work on that."

"It may not be fixable."

"We'll see."

Sean got in the car and immediately looked at the gas and brake pedals.

Sparky noticed Sean's gaze and said, "Everyone always wants to know how I drive, and they always check the floorboard when they get in my car. I have a special seat cushion that moves me up and forward." He pointed toward the floor. "These pedal extenders work wonders. Simple and effective."

He started the car and said, "Polyphenols."

"Poly what?"

"Living with me means you'll get a lot of polyphenols in your diet. They are great for the cardiovascular system. It's best to get them from real food and not supplements. Berries and some other dark fruits have tons of polyphenols."

Sean could only nod.

Sparky said, "Among other things, I grow berries in my garden. Do you like gardening?"

"Love it. It's good for your soul."

"Great. We'll get along marvelously." Sparky checked the traffic. "Let's motate."

CHAPTER 23

After Kelly arrived home, she sat at her desk and considered her schedule. Obviously, she had many things to do. She had to formulate a strategy for the TV show and prepare for her presentation at Scanlan's lodge, but her top priority was protecting her son. She considered cancelling the two events, but her small family desperately needed an income stream. Sparky's postponement of rent payments would help a great deal, but that was temporary. She also had to meet the daily needs of food, clothing, utilities, and all of the other necessities of life. She decided to go ahead with her plans, but she would keep Cody close by at all times. The fact that school had just ended would make her task easier.

She had been unable to track the market because of recent events, so she turned on her computer and studied several charts. After the sharp declines her system forecast, the market seemed to have reached a temporary support level. She considered the consolidation normal. She fired up Cyberstar and found that all sell signals were still in place. The odds of further market declines were very high.

Next, she jotted down an outline for the TV appearance and one for the conference in the mountains. After two hours, she put her notepad aside and went into the front room to check on Cody. She had made him agree to stay inside and to go out with only her for the time being. She had stressed the need for safety. Cody understood the potential danger, and he had agreed to the conditions. Normally, he would have lodged a minor complaint, but the shooting incident had obviously altered his thinking.

She worked another three hours, and, then, she leaned back in her chair and reviewed her plans. The TV show was exciting, but the trip to the mountains meant that she and Cody could leave the area and feel secure for several days. They might even do a little exploring when the conference ended. She liked the idea.

The following morning, she stood before the front room window with a yellow pad. She often walked around the house jotting down thoughts and ideas. Just as she was about to turn away from the window, Sparky's car pulled into his driveway. She noticed that he had a passenger and thought little of it at first. She started walking back to her desk when she suddenly turned and went back to the window. There was something familiar about the passenger. She looked outside and saw Sean pulling a suitcase from the trunk of the car. What was that all about?

She stormed out of the house and headed straight for the car.

Sparky saw her coming and said, "I think you know my new house guest."

"Your *what*?"

"Sean is going to stay with me for a while."

"You can't be serious."

Sparky chuckled. "You sound like John McEnroe."

"Sparky!"

Sparky held up his hands and said, "Let's go sit on the front step. I'll explain everything."

She did not move.

Sparky sat on the step and motioned for her to join him.

Finally, she walked over, but she did not sit down. She crossed her arms and said, "I'll stand." She looked toward Sean and saw him standing next to the car, obviously waiting for them to finish their conversation.

Sparky patted the steps beside him and Kelly finally sat down, prepared to counter whatever he said. She leaned and whispered, "I hate him. I can't live next door to him."

"You don't hate him. You only think you *should* hate him. That's a big difference."

Kelly said nothing as she considered his profound statement. Sparky was often a deep thinker but, surely, in this case, he was wrong.

He spread his arms. "This is about safety for you and Cody. You have something valuable that people want and I think they will try again. I can only do so much, but with Sean here, we can both watch over you. Kind of a tag team deal. It really makes sense."

Kelly started to protest, but her thoughts took a turn. The words "safety" and "Cody" struck home. She sat silently as she tried to push emotion aside and think in a logical manner.

After a moment, Sparky said, "Kelly?"

"I'm thinking."

She really did not want to admit it, but the plan had a major benefit, and that benefit was more protection for Cody. *Nothing* mattered more. She recalled the intruder's attempt to get her software, but the most disturbing fact was that shots had been fired. If Sean had not come along when he did, anything might have happened. The thought that she might have lost her son never left her. After a moment, she said, "When this is all over, he goes."

Sparky patted her shoulder. "We'll talk about that when the time comes." He rose and called to Sean, "Bring your suitcase, and I'll show you to your room."

Kelly turned away when Sean approached the steps.

He stopped and said, "All I want to do is protect Cody . . . and you."

She did not respond, and she did not look at him. The last thing she wanted to do was to look into those incredible blue eyes. She rose and walked toward her house. She had accepted the arrangement, but that was as far as it went.

The following day, she walked out the back door to check the progress of some flowers she had recently planted when she heard voices from next door. She looked over and saw Sparky and Sean working in the vegetable garden. Sparky always put a great deal of effort into his garden, which was organic and neatly arranged. Nothing else would do.

Sean had removed his shirt and she could not help but look. They were so intent on their work that they had not seen her exit the house. She did not want to stare, but she could not help herself. Sean's physical appearance had excited her in her teens, but now he was a grown man with great muscle tone and a very healthy appearance. He exuded sex appeal. A flood of sensual memories washed over her, and she was startled by a sudden stirring excitement. This simply would not do. She turned away but, after a moment, she looked again. Disturbed by her actions, she spun around and headed back into the house, suddenly aware that she had completely forgotten the reason she had gone outside.

———

Kelly felt both excited and nervous when the day of the television show arrived. She had done her homework, but, on live TV, anything could happen. She watched the market and after a weak rally, stocks sold off and the Dow closed down 246 points. Had another leg of the decline started? She would know in a few days, but her sell signal remained intact, and she estimated the chances for another sharp decline at eighty percent.

Cody and Sparky accompanied her to the TV station. She had arranged front row seats for them as part of a small audience of about forty people. She made it clear that Sean should not attend. She arrived at the designated time and was escorted to the green room, where she was introduced to the two other panel members. She had previously met Charles Camp, the newspaper's financial editor, who greeted her warmly. The other panelist was a member of a business television network. Hudson Treffinger, founder of the *Treffinger Letter*, had yet to arrive. Though she felt prepared, she opened her portfolio and studied her notes.

Treffinger arrived very late. The producer, Karen Yee, met him in the hallway just as she started to escort the panel to their seats. Karen briefed him as they walked toward the studio. Kelly brought up the rear, pleased that Treffinger had not recognized her.

When they were seated, Kelly noticed that Treffinger paid no attention to his fellow panelists. He adjusted his necktie, smiled at the audience, and seemed extremely confident. She could tell he expected to be the star of the broadcast.

All of the audience seats were occupied, and, in one of the chairs in the back row, sat a man with a pockmarked face and a scattering of pigeon droppings on each shoe. Otherwise, his earth toned attire offered nothing unusual.

When the show began, the anchor, Robert Naworski, immediately turned to Treffinger. "Mr. Treffinger, your record over the past two years has been outstanding. Because of the recent severe selloff, I'm sure our audience would like to hear your prediction on the market."

Treffinger smiled. "Of course. It's really very simple. This selloff is what we call a flash crash, which was initiated by massive sell programs from hedge funds and other large traders. It's all about computer algorithms. The selling is nearly over, and we are witnessing an unusual buying opportunity. Viewers can get my latest recommendations in my market letter."

Naworski said, "Let's check the other panelists to see if they agree. Does anyone have a different view? How about you, Miss Sanborn?"

Treffinger immediately turned toward Kelly with a surprised expression.

Kelly, who was seated on the opposite end of the panel from Treffinger, spoke up, "As you all know, I issued a major sell signal based on my new market software. The original signal is still intact, and I expect another sharp decline any day. We are now in a bear market, and I would recommend extreme caution until the market signals otherwise."

Treffinger butted in. "Nonsense. This is just a computer driven flash crash. Nothing more."

Kelly said, "Just so the audience knows, Mr. Treffinger and I had words about the market recently during a meeting where I previously worked." Kelly looked at her yellow pad. "Here is what he said at that meeting:

"We're in the middle of a long-term, secular bull market. Opposing the trend, as this ad suggests, would be insane. In other

words, gentlemen, don't fight the tape. I've never been more bullish, and my presentation will explain why."

"Ladies and gentleman, those words were offered within a few dozen points of the top. Since then, if his clients followed his advice, they have suffered substantial losses. I have one customer, who is in the audience, who took my advice. He has a substantial profit in a short period of time." She glanced toward the audience and saw Sparky pump his fist. She continued, "It should be noted that we used extremely speculative instruments not suited for everyone."

Naworski turned and said, "Mr. Treffinger."

The color drained from Treffinger's face. "Well, it's…it's just a fluke. This is a powerful, secular uptrend, which will resume any day."

Kelly intervened, "Mr. Treffinger also said one more thing to me during that meeting. He said, "*Some other line of work might suit you better.*'"

The women in the audience, and several men, hissed and booed.

Treffinger, obviously shaken, said, "You are nothing but a rank amateur."

She fired back, "Life can be difficult when your age is higher than your IQ, Mr. Treffinger. Do hang in there." Kelly looked at the audience and saw the crowd erupt. Sparky nearly fell off his chair with excitement. With the audience firmly on her side, she was enjoying herself. Of course, her sell signal prediction was fraught with risk, risk she willingly accepted.

After the rowdy audience calmed down, Robert Naworski turned his attention to the other panelist and sought to balance participation for the rest of the show, though several women in the audience continued hostile outbursts toward Treffinger.

When the camera turned off, Kelly ignored Treffinger and headed for the audience where she greeted Cody and Sparky with hugs.

───────

Seated in the back row, the pigeon keeper had a new take on Kelly's system. If the software was as good as it appeared, it was far more valuable than he had imagined. He foresaw the potential of making tens or even hundreds of millions of dollars for whoever controlled the software. At that moment, he realized that he was being grossly underpaid for his services. He muttered two words as he stared across the room, "Chump change." That's what he was being paid and he was pissed. With his anger rising, he left the studio, mulling a combination of devious thoughts about the software and about the very attractive Kelly Sanborn.

CHAPTER 24

Two days later, the excitement was palpable inside Kelly's rental car when she turned onto the final highway that transitioned from the Sierra foothills into the majestic mountain range. A blue sky with a scattering of billowing white clouds greeted her and Cody. They followed a narrow, two-lane highway that gained altitude nearly every mile. Getting a rental had been an easy decision as it was doubtful that Huey could have made the climb.

Kelly slowed for two deer darting across the highway.

"Look at that, Mom. I've been counting and that makes six deer we've seen in the last half hour."

She smiled. "We're in a remote part of the Sierras and wildlife seems plentiful." She looked out the side window. The dirt had a faint reddish tone, and the trees often came close to the edge of the road. "It really is beautiful." She rolled down the window and breathed in air filled with the strong scent of pine trees that reminded her of childhood visits to the mountains.

Forty minutes later, they passed a sign that read:

ELEVATION 4,000

Cody noticed the sign. "How high are we going?"

"Not sure, but I think it's between five and six thousand feet. If Mr. Scanlan's map is accurate, we'll be there in less than an hour."

———————

Before Kelly and Cody left for the mountains, Sean and Sparky sat down at the dining room table. Sparky had a special chair that allowed him to use the table and gain direct eye contact with his guests. He did not mind people looking down at him at other times; it went with the territory, but he wanted to be on the same level at the table.

Sparky's face displayed an unusually pensive expression. After a moment, he said, "I'm worried about Kelly's trip to the mountains. Yes, I know they will probably be okay, but I can't shake this high level of concern I have for their safety. Whoever wants that software is not going to give up. I feel it in my bones."

Sean said, "I feel the same way and I was going to talk to you about her trip. I'm thinking I should tag along, but the problem is that she'll spot my car because of the distance. There is no way I could follow her that far and go undetected."

Sparky nodded, "It's a problem, but there is a way. Here's my plan." He leaned forward. "She told me she is renting an SUV because Huey does not do well at altitude. That old car has paid its dues, but time and mileage have taken a toll." He placed a sheet of paper in front of Sean. "I made a copy of the map she has and I've studied it carefully. Just follow her as far back as you can. You'll lose her occasionally because of traffic and stop signs. That shouldn't be a problem because we know her route. You can easily catch up, and that way she will not see your car every time she looks in the rearview mirror. You should be able to keep contact forty or fifty percent of the time." He traced her route with his finger. "The key is that she'll be safe on the major highways. The last part of the journey is on a two-lane road that is fairly remote. Even if she sees your car, she would not be suspicious because there is nowhere else to go, except for a few minor roads that mostly lead to dead ends."

Sean said, "That makes sense. She would assume I was just another driver headed to my own destination."

"Exactamundo."

"I'll leave before she does and swing in behind her when she reaches Highway Ninety-Two. I'll stay back until she reaches the turnoff to go into the mountains; then, I'll close the gap." He studied the map. "Call me when she leaves."

"I'll let you know the minute she gets in the car."

Sean considered the plan and then said, "I don't know where I'll stay, but there must be a few small motels along the road near her destination."

Sparky pointed at the map. "I marked one for you. It's a small, twelve-unit place. I've already made a reservation for you for two nights."

"Thanks. She should be okay once she reaches her destination, so I'll just make sure her travel is safe in both directions." Sean rose and headed for his room. "I'd better get ready."

Dany Fagan had told Martin Scanlan that obtaining the software from Kelly would be a piece of cake, but he knew better. He had several obstacles to overcome; the most difficult was how to temporarily stop traffic in both directions while he blocked Kelly's passage. The fact that the highway was in a remote area, with little traffic, would certainly make his task easier, but timing would be paramount. It took two days, but he developed a plan he was sure would work. Before he entered the higher mountains, where he would lose his phone signal, one of his contacts would call and advise him of Kelly's departure time, and a description of her vehicle. This would give him the approximate time of her arrival at his location.

Thirty minutes before her expected arrival, he planned to drive around a bend in the road and cut a tree with a chainsaw to block passage. Not a huge tree, but one large enough to cause a substantial delay for cars coming down the mountain. Next, he would have one of his men, Isaac Wycoff, drive behind Rick's car in a pickup overloaded with four by fours. Isaac would rig the load so that he could pull a cord to drop the unsecured tailgate and spill the unstable load onto the road; then, he would take his time picking up the load. Because Isaac looked like an NFL linebacker with a surly attitude, Fagan knew no one would interfere.

He intended for the job to end quickly, and for good reason. As soon as he put a gun to Cody's head, he knew Kelly would hand over the software and the password. That was the piece of cake part, relying on a mother to protect her son at all costs.

He punched a number into his phone to call Rick. No signal. He expected that, because of the mountains, but he wanted to make sure. He wasn't worried because he had given Rick very specific instructions, complete with a map. He had even hung a blue ribbon on a tree limb to mark the spot where Rick was supposed to stop, and a red ribbon where Isaac was to drop his load of four by fours. He liked the location because traffic in this part of the mountains was sparse, and there were no towns of any size along the highway.

He exited his van and walked to the edge of the road. Nothing in sight, but it would not be long now. He went back to the vehicle, which was the same one he had stolen weeks earlier. He preferred cargo vans because most thieves targeted cars. Furthermore, he could carry the equipment he needed for most of his jobs. He had a dozen license plates from abandoned vans and other vehicles he had obtained from junk yards, and he was not stupid like most car thieves. Those fucking idiots often broke traffic laws and drove around in stolen vehicles with tail lights out. Not Danny Fagan, he followed all the rules—a model driver. He was proud of his mind, especially his natural abilities with anything electronic. He was a quick learner.

The only thing he regretted was that he had to leave Oscar, his favorite racing pigeon, at home. However, with the payoff from this job, he would buy a prized racing bird for breeding. He dreamed of winning major racing competitions, and he intended to do exactly that with his new pigeons. He smiled at the thought.

He checked his watch; then, he drove around the bend and cut the tree as planned. He rushed back and maneuvered the van into position. There was a long stretch of straight road, which he could see easily from his position. When he saw Kelly's car, all he had to do was drive forward and block the road. His thoughts went back to what Scanlan had said, "Do whatever it takes."

CHAPTER 25

Just before Sean turned off the main highway to enter the two-lane road that led to Kelly's destination, he saw a car and a pickup pull out of a turnout and fall in behind Kelly. His desire to maintain close contact on the narrow road instantly became more difficult. He gunned the engine and pulled up as close to the pickup as possible without tailgating. As he drove, he occasionally lost visual contact with Kelly's SUV on the twisting mountain road, but there was little he could do, because the pickup tailgated the car directly behind Kelly. His initial concerns about the two vehicles subsided, and he settled in for the drive while keeping visual contact as often as possible.

After twenty minutes, he realized something about the load in the back of the pickup did not seem right. He pulled a little closer and examined the lumber. There were too many four by fours, and they were not properly secured. It was an extremely haphazard arrangement. He dropped back and considered the implications. First, the car and pickup pulled out of the turnout just after Kelly passed by; then, there was this extremely unusual load of lumber in the pickup. The more he thought about it, the more concerned he became. He decided he needed to pass the pickup so he could be closer to Kelly's SUV.

On the next straightaway, he gunned the engine and attempted to pass the pickup, but the driver sped up. Sean eased back into his lane. Odd, he thought. He waited for another straightaway and made another attempt to pass. The pickup not only sped up, but it crossed the centerline in an obvious maneuver to block Sean.

Alarm bells went off in Sean's mind. What in the hell was going on? Then it hit him. There was a solid chance that the driver of the car and the pickup were out to harm to Kelly and Cody. What better place than a remote, two-lane highway in the mountains? Gripped with fear, he searched for a strategy. The problem was that he had no idea what they intended to do or when they might act on their intentions. It might just be some jerk trying to bully him on the road, but the more he thought about the driver's actions, the more he became convinced of imminent danger.

He decided to hang back and wait for a large, sweeping curve in the road. The chance came a few minutes later. When the pickup disappeared around the curve, Sean floor boarded the gas pedal. He came around the curve at high speed and swept around the pickup on the straightway before the driver had a chance to react, although he did try to block the lane at the last second. Sean felt extremely edgy as he dropped in between the car and the pickup. He looked ahead and saw Kelly's SUV winding its way up the mountain. His position between the car and the pickup engendered an extreme level of concern.

___

Not long after Kelly had turned off on the last highway, she noticed that the car she'd seen earlier had moved closer after hanging back a considerable distance. Perhaps she was driving too slowly. She glanced at her speedometer and saw that she was driving the appropriate speed.

After a long climb, she came to a straight lane of road that widened slightly. She glanced at Cody. "It won't be long now." She looked back at the road and saw a cargo van suddenly drive out of high brush lining the road and stop, completely blocking her passage. A man jumped out of the van and signaled for her to pull to the side of the road.

"Mom. He's wearing a ski mask!"

Kelly skidded to a stop and put the car in reverse. She started to turn around when she saw the car that had been following her now blocked her exit. Terrifying thoughts flashed through her mind and she knew only one thing—*run!*

She backed up so that she was midway between the two cars to give her as much distance from the attackers as possible. She stopped, grabbed her purse, and yelled at Cody, "Get our backpacks and follow me." Thankful she wore jeans and sneakers, she ran around the car and headed into the trees. She stuffed her purse into the backpack Cody handed her, then she and Cody ran deeper into the forest—desperate to get away.

———

It had not taken long for the driver of the pickup following Sean to react after being passed. After only a few minutes, the pickup suddenly appeared very large in his rearview mirror. He sped up, but the pickup did the same until he was sandwiched between the car ahead of him and the pickup. The pickup rammed his car. Sean tugged on the wheel and narrowly avoided crashing off the road. Again, the pickup loomed large in the rearview mirror. Sean worked desperately to avoid careening out of control. Suddenly, the pickup slowed and most of the load of lumber it carried spilled onto the highway, blocking access to any travelers coming up the mountain.

Sean looked up the highway and saw the car in front of him slow down and straddled the white line. He also saw a van blocking Kelly's passage a couple of hundred yards up the road. The thug's intentions came to him in a flash. Acting on instinct, he sped up as the driver ahead maneuvered his car to block the road. Sean's sedan struck a glancing blow to the back corner of the car in front of him, spinning it off to one side.

He saw Kelly and Cody bolt from their SUV and run into the woods, each carrying a backpack. To his horror, a man wearing a ski mask pulled a gun and fired at the fleeing pair. Sean honked continuously and drove straight at the gunman. The man jumped aside and Sean rammed the rear corner of his cargo van. He came to a stop thirty yards up the road, jumped from his car, and ran toward the forest. A shot rang out and a bullet thudded into a tree on his right, another bullet clipped a branch eight inches from his head.

After twenty yards, Sean turned in the direction he had last seen Kelly and Cody, desperate to find them before the gunmen did. He tried to gauge the distance from where he had seen them and how far he had driven before he stopped his car. He angled for a spot between where they disappeared and where they might be after running straight. It was a gamble but he had no other choice.

He slashed through the brush, swatting branches aside as he ran. After about fifty yards, he changed directions slightly to lead him deeper into the woods, trying his best to intercept Kelly and

169

Cody before they got too far into the forest. After another forty yards, he burst through some brush at the edge of an old dirt road and ran into Cody, knocking him to the ground.

Kelly yelled, "Sean! My God, where did—"

Sean grabbed Cody's hand and pulled him up; then, he pushed Kelly from behind. "Run! Run faster than you ever have."

Danny Fagan was pissed. What a fucking circus. Kelly obviously had the software in her backpack; that's why she grabbed it—and the software was money. He glanced around and knew he had to hide the vehicles before he began the chase. If he left them as they were, the sheriff and the Highway Patrol would quickly arrive to investigate. There was a trailhead with a parking area about fifty yards up the road on the opposite side from where his target had disappeared. There was also a dirt road beside a small creek a few yards farther up. He yelled at Rick, "Park your car in the parking lot near the trailhead." He ran to Kelly's SUV and found the keys still in the ignition. He yelled, "Tell Isaac to hide any car that has damage and clean up the debris on the road. Tell him to stay here in case they double back. You and I'll go after them. Hurry!"

CHAPTER 26

Sean led the way up the old road until they came to a Y intersection. The dirt lane that curved left was far superior to the other road, which was narrow, rutted and looked as if it had not been used in decades. The main road continued and went around a curve. He made a snap decision. "They'll probably think we'll use the better road. We won't. Take Cody and start up the path on the right while I run down the main road and leave sign for them to see."

Kelly started to object. "But—"

"Do it! It's our only chance. I'll catch up."

He shoved her and then turned and ran down the dirt road, leaving a few fresh scuffmarks in the dirt. He ran as far as he thought safe and then he broke a small branch leading into the forest. He walked into the trees for about fifteen yards, trampling grass as he went. He knew he was running out of time. He turned and went back to the road, then he ran along the hardpan on the edge of the lane to avoid leaving tracks.

When he turned onto the old road, he looked at the mountainside ahead and did not like what he saw. He hoped to reach safety by going higher but the rugged mountain appeared impassable from his viewpoint, although he hoped there might be a gap they could use. He increased his speed and nearly fell because of the ruts in the road.

He ran a considerable distance before he spotted Kelly and Cody, and he was impressed by their physical condition. He ran up to them and said, "I think we gained some time, but we have to keep going. You two okay?"

Kelly shook her head. "We're good, but what are we going to do?"

"Run like hell. They'll eventually figure out that I left markings on the other road to throw them off."

Sean took the lead and started jogging at a steady pace. The old road wound through thick pine trees and an occasional meadow before it began to climb the mountainside. He stopped so they could catch their breath. He glanced up the rut-filled lane and saw a small, dilapidated shack in front of an abandoned mineshaft. Decaying support beams lay across the entrance of the dark tunnel. That explained the presence of the old road.

He pointed and said, "Over there. Let's go."

Cody burst ahead of them and ran to the old shack. "Cool."

Kelly said, "It might be cool but watch your step. It looks like it could fall down any minute." She knew she sounded like a mother, and she was often over protective, but Cody was the core of her existence. His safety was all that mattered.

Sean said, "I've got my cellphone. Do you have yours?"

"Yes, but the battery is low."

"It probably won't matter because I'm sure we are out of range." He pulled out his phone. "I'll try it anyway." As expected, there was no signal. He turned off his phone and went up to the old door, which was held in place by a single hinge. A lopsided deer antler hung over his head.

"I'll have a look." He entered the one room, ramshackle cabin and swatted cobwebs. The insides were spartan at best, including a dirt floor, which added to the fusty smell. He glanced up and saw that the roof consisted of corrugated tin panels. Except for a few holes, the roof seemed in reasonably good shape considering its age. The interior was a mess. A single bed, consisting of a frame and springs sat on the far end of the room. A workbench, complete with a scattering of old, rusty tools, stood against the opposite wall. The fireplace had been outfitted to handle the cooking chores as well as heat the building. A single, broken rocking chair and a small table were the only other furniture.

Kelly looked inside. "I'd like to stay here, but I know it wouldn't be safe."

Sean said, "They would eventually find us so we have to keep moving." He went outside and looked around, not liking their situation one bit. On either side of the old cabin, steep, jagged cliffs rose skyward. Could they make their way along the edge of the cliffs? After further inspection, he realized there was no way up the treacherous mass of rock. Going back down the road made no sense because they would be going toward their pursuers.

He walked around to the back of the cabin and saw an ancient game trail leading up the side of the mountain. Why would animals use that trail unless it provided a way over the top? It was worth a try. He ran back to the front door. "I may have found a way up. Before we start, what do you have in those backpacks? Any water?"

Kelly unzipped her bag. We both have a bottle of water, a trail bar, a sweatshirt, and I have some chocolate. And my software and some folders. That's about it."

Sean said, "We need to conserve water but I think we should each have a few swallows because of the distance we've run. We don't want to become dehydrated."

Cody said, "We can find water in the mountains, but it might not be safe."

Sean said, "Are you a Boy Scout?"

"Only for about a year, but I've learned a lot."

Sean looked at Cody with an appraising smile. "Great. We'll need your help."

Kelly said, "I wish we could go back down, but I know that's a bad option."

"Those guys chasing us are smart. They set things up so there would be no interference for a quite a while. We can't take a chance. Besides, there's only one way down. We need to find a safe spot and sit tight. If we lose them, we can go back down later."

Kelly put her arm around Cody. "Makes sense."

"Okay, let's go."

Without complaint, Kelly and Cody fell in behind as he started up the old trail. After a steep climb, Sean began to feel optimistic. The trail, though old and rugged, seemed to be heading for a gap on the mountainside.

———

As Kelly followed Sean and Cody up the trail, she had mixed feelings about what had happened and how she, once again, found herself thankful for Sean's help. She believed she had the will and the strength to dodge the pursuers, but they were men with guns. Having Sean along offered another mind and body to help them escape. She wondered how in the world he happened along that dirt road at that precise moment. The more she thought about it the more one name came to mind—Sparky Valentine. Had the two of them concocted a plan to watch over Cody and herself? It sounded like something Sparky would initiate.

She watched Sean on the mountain trail, climbing for a time, then stopping to check on her and Cody. She knew they were both in better condition than he might have realized. She would be thankful for his help, if they survived, but that was all. Nothing else would change. As she reminded herself of that fact, she could not help noticing how strong Sean looked as he seemed to climb with ease. There was not an ounce of fat on his lithe frame. She suppressed sensual thoughts and immediately reprimanded herself. *Stop this nonsense and climb, dammit.*

She told Sean to stop atop a ledge so they could each take a small amount of water and part of a trail bar. She knew they had to maintain strength for whatever the future might offer. She checked with Cody and knew he had more than enough stamina to continue at the same pace.

They finished their brief respite and began to climb again. She occasionally looked back, hoping she would see and hear nothing. She shuddered as she thought about what would happen if the thugs caught them.

CHAPTER 27

Sean topped a rise near the summit and stopped. A massive landslide of shale obliterated the ancient trail. Several flat stones slid down the steep slope as he watched. Some stopped near the bottom while others skidded over the edge and fell into the canyon below. The area of shale was large and excessively steep. At the bottom, there was a ledge with a few trees on the near side, but the opposite side appeared to be the edge of a cliff. Treacherous was the only word to describe what he saw. He looked around for another way to cross the mountain, but the surrounding cliffs eliminated all other possibilities.

He turned to Kelly. "This looks dangerous, but I'm going to test it." He edged onto the shale and immediately began to slide. He put out his hand to cushion his fall and banged his elbow on the flat rocks. He twisted and tried to scurry back up using his hands and feet, like a four-legged animal, but he continued to slide as more shale from above cascaded around him. Finally, he grasped an exposed root at the side of the slide and held on. He maneuvered sideways until he came to the edge and pulled himself onto the dirt, a good twelve feet below where he had started. He rubbed his elbow and climbed back to the trail.

He stood next to Kelly. "That shale is vicious. Really nasty stuff." He looked across the slide. "I don't see how we can make it. There is no way we can cross, and if someone slips, they could easily slide all the way down, probably breaking a bone or two. They might even go over the edge."

Kelly said, "We'll have to go back and take our chances."

Sean looked down the trail. "I don't like it. Those gunmen have probably discovered that we took the other road by now. We'd run into them for sure." He made eye contact with Kelly. "We wouldn't have a chance."

Cody tugged on Sean's sleeve. "I know a way, Mr. Keene."

Kelly turned to her son. "Okay, let's hear it."

Cody said, "Remember those panels on the roof of that old cabin? Well, we could use them to slide down the shale. Kind of like a toboggan."

Kelly said, "It won't work. We wouldn't be able to hold on and we'd go too fast." She looked at Sean. "What do you think?"

Sean tilted his head and thought a moment. "You know, there just might be a way. I have an idea." They moved down the old trail at a rapid pace. Just before they reached the cabin, Kelly came to a sudden stop. "Down there. There are two men on the main road."

Sean looked past the treetops and saw the men. "They figured out that we didn't use the other road, and they're coming this way. They're quite a ways below us but keep out of sight—and hurry!"

They ran the last few yards and entered the cabin. Sean ran to the old workbench, reached underneath, and pulled out an old rope. "I saw this before and we'll need it." He examined the rope. "Damn, it's in pretty bad shape."

Cody rummaged through miscellaneous junk in the corner. "Here's another one, but it's frayed."

"Bring it anyway." He grabbed an old rusty hammer and turned to Kelly. "I'm going to climb up and get a roofing panel. See what tools you can find and lay them on that shelf."

He ran outside and turned the corner. One piece of tin sheeting had fallen off and lay on the ground but it looked unusable. Another panel had come loose and was hanging above his head. He jumped and managed to grab the end and pull it down. He noticed that the panel was thin and low-grade but it would have to do. He ran back inside. "We have to bend the end of this panel for our feet and cut a hole in the other end for the rope."

Kelly pointed to the bench. "Those are the usable tools. How can we help?"

Sean turned toward the door. "Cody and I will fix the panel. Go outside and watch for those men. This is gonna be close."

Kelly ran outside with a sense of urgency.

Sean handed the hammer and an old screwdriver to Cody. "I'm going to try to bend the end of this panel. Use that screwdriver and pound a hole in the other end. Right in the middle and make it wide."

"What about the noise?"

"We've got no choice. Let's get to work."

Their tools were old but they got the job done. Just as they started outside, Kelly ran to the door. "I heard one of them yell. They're not far away."

Sean put a few of the old tools in Cody's backpack, including a small roll of wire, and a dull knife with a broken tip. "Let's go— double time!" Sean took up the rear in case the men caught them. He urged Kelly and Cody to move faster.

They reached the shale and Sean said, "Cody first. I'll go last." He cut off a piece of rope he did not trust; then, he tied the remaining two lengths together. He put the rope through the hole Cody made and secured it with a knot. He placed the tin panel on the edge of the shale and looped the rope around a small boulder. He helped Cody onto the panel; then, he leaned over and said, "When you get down to that bench, go to the left, and see if there is a way down. If there is, give us a thumbs-up. If not, give a thumbs-down."

Sean began to let out the rope and Cody's jury-rigged toboggan started its slow journey down the shale. After only a few feet, a good amount of shale began sliding but Cody held on.

Kelly moved closer to Sean. "My God, this is scaring me to death."

Sean kept lowering the rope. "Me too, but it seems to be working so far."

It took nearly four minutes, but Cody landed safely on the tree-covered bench and disappeared. After only a minute, he popped back into view and gave a thumbs-up.

Kelly let out a loud sigh.

Sean pulled the rope back up and helped Kelly maneuver onto the sled. He grabbed the rope. "Hold on tight."

He let out rope until dozens of pieces of shale slid down and hit the sled, nearly toppling Kelly off to one side. He gripped the rope and called to her, "Hold on. We need to let this stuff stabilize."

Just as he began to release rope, more shale came loose and struck the sled.

Kelly tightened her grip and held on.

When the shale stopped sliding, he slowly released more rope. After another thirty feet, she reached the bench. She got off and hugged Cody.

Sean pulled the sled back up the slope. He now faced the most difficult part because he could not lower himself in the same manner as the others. As he tried to figure out a way, he heard voices.

Hurry!

He noticed that the rope had frayed badly in a middle section, but there was nothing he could do about it now. With no time to ponder the best method to lower himself, he looped the rope around the rock, then took the rope ends in each hand and got onto the sled. He began to release rope. It was exceedingly unstable, and difficult, but he moved slowly downwards. Dozens of pieces of shale broke loose and slid down the slope.

Worried about the sled's stability, he said, "Stand back."

Twenty feet from the bottom, the frayed rope broke. His sled picked up speed and veered to the right, heading straight for the cliff. He leaned to his left so hard the sled nearly tipped over. He gained speed and braced himself for the impact he knew was coming. He slid onto the bench, crashed into a tree, bumped his head, and was tossed to the ground. He heard shouts from above. "Kelly, hide the sled while I retrieve the rope. We don't want them to know how we got here."

She followed his instructions, and, then, she and Cody helped Sean up. He stumbled and fell. Just as he got up, the two men appeared above them.

Kelly said, "Quick, they saw us."

They moved along the bench just as a gunshot rang out. A bullet zipped past Sean's ear and slammed into a tree.

They heard loud cursing from above as they searched for a way down the mountain.

Safely out of view from the gunmen, Kelly looked at the perilous declivity and said, "I don't like the looks of this. It's steep and rugged."

Sean moved next to her and looked down. "Rugged as hell, actually. This will not be easy, but at least they can't follow us now."

Kelly opened her backpack. "We'd better have a snack and a bit of water before we begin. We're going to need it."

Sean nodded and looked for a possible path down. As he searched, he thought about their situation and he liked none of it. With no way back up, they were now committed to this side of the mountain, and they were in serious trouble. They were in a naturally hostile, remote area with very little food and water.

Danny Fagan looked across the layers of shale and yelled a string of obscenities. They had fallen for an ancient trick, and they had searched in the wrong place too long. Had they not spent so much time on the other road, and in the forest, they would have caught them for sure. He looked at the shale slide. They managed to get down the shale, so he could too.

He turned to Rick. "They must have walked down, so it must be more stable than it looks. Give it a try."

Rick turned and stared at Fagan, his face full of doubt. "I don't like the looks of that slope."

"Aw, hell, Rick. A woman and a boy made it, and here you are whining."

Rick hesitated, then he stepped out onto the shale. The rocks immediately gave way and he fell and landed on his tailbone. He cried out in pain and scrambled toward the edge. Rocks around him gave way and slid down the slope, many flying over the edge of the cliff.

Fagan moved down the edge, grabbed Rick's extended hand, and pulled him off the shale.

Rick got up and bent over in pain. "Christ, man. My fucking tailbone is killing me. I think I broke something."

Fagan was not concerned about Rick's tailbone, but he was very concerned about what to do next. The shale slope was vicious, and he had no idea how his targets managed to reach the ledge below. "They didn't fly down there, Rick. Try it again."

"No way, man. That's some tricky shit. Too steep."

Fagan started to try it, but when he touched one piece of shale, it started a slide of several dozen stones. He pulled his foot back and considered his options but it only took a moment to realize he had none. "We're screwed. Let's get the hell out of here." He turned toward the trail. "We'll get them later. I'll make damn sure of that."

CHAPTER 28

They were on the other side of the mountain now, and Sean surveyed the wilderness before them. They were on the north side of a gigantic V-shaped mountain range. An unseen river, at the bottom of the gorge, had obviously shaped the majestic mountains over eons. As far as he could see, there was nothing but trees, mountains, and sky. The only living thing he saw was a single hawk soaring above the gorge below.

Kelly and Cody stood beside him, gazing at the vastness before them. Finally, Kelly said, "Magnificent and dangerous all at the same time."

Sean said, "Very dangerous." He looked to his left. "Snow melt at higher elevations cut through these mountains millions of years ago. It's amazing what the forces of nature can do over time. The changes are so slow they are unseen by man but they are continuous."

She scanned the mountains. "This area is too rugged for access by people; at least that's how it looks from here."

Cody stepped closer to the edge. "Our Scoutmaster told us that if we were ever lost we should follow creeks or rivers downstream."

Kelly put her arm around Cody's shoulder. "Okay Mr. Woodsman. That's exactly what we'll do." She turned to Sean. "It's impossible to go back so we might as well get started."

"You're right, but I am not going to sugar coat it. We're facing a very difficult challenge."

"We know that," she said. "We're wasting time. Will you lead?"

"Sure." Sean moved to his left and started down a thickly wooded declivity, but he was worried. They were in the wild without supplies or proper clothing, and he knew that finding safe water would be difficult. He was acutely aware that if anyone got sick from drinking bad water their situation would become desperate. Survival itself was at stake, but he did not want to say more than he already had. He felt he had to lead, but he knew input from everyone was vital. Cody had already proved that, a fact that made him proud.

After a short break, they resumed their trek down the mountain. During their rest, Sean gave thought to the time of day. Darkness fell quickly in the mountains and it would turn cold due to the elevation. He stopped after an hour. "It'll be dark soon, so we had better start looking for shelter. A cave would be great, but it's long odds on finding one."

Cody said, "We can make our own shelter. I know how."

Sean smiled. "Okay, keep an eye out."

They made their way lower but found no suitable shelter. Fifty minutes later, Sean came around a rocky crag and stopped. "There's a fallen tree over there. I think we can do something with that. What do you think?"

Kelly looked where he pointed and said, "That's the best we've found so far. We'll make it work."

Cody spoke up, "All we need are evergreen boughs and they're everywhere."

After they reached the tree, Sean and Cody began cutting boughs from bushes and overhanging trees. The knife was dull but it did the job. They laid boughs on the ground to form a wilderness mattress, then they cut poles to hold boughs overheard in lean-to fashion, using the fallen tree as the back.

Despite their dangerous situation, Kelly felt proud of Cody. He had pitched in enthusiastically and offered useful information. She sat down and opened her pack. "We don't have much, but it will have to do for now." She broke her only chocolate bar into thirds.

Sean said, "I don't suppose you have any matches in that pack."

"I wish I did."

Cody said, "If we find the right kind of rocks, we might be able to make a fire."

Kelly looked toward the darkening sky. "Tomorrow, I want you to keep an eye out for those rocks." She pulled out her sweatshirt and told Cody to do the same. It would be a cold night. "Sean, I'm sorry, but we only have one sweatshirt apiece."

Cody said, "When it's cold at night you have to share body heat. We can do that."

Kelly stiffened. Good grief, she had not thought about that. Well, there would be no need for that. Surely, it would not get that cold. Or would it?

"Sharing heat is a necessity," Sean said, "We'll put Cody in the middle."

She let out a slow, quiet sigh. That would work.

———

Sean woke several times during the night for a myriad of reasons, including a headache caused by his sled crashing into the tree. Animal and forest noises woke him, but the worst was the cold— cold that penetrated his bones. His denim shirt offered little protection against the elements, and he found it impossible to escape the biting wind that swept down from the mountain. He studied the forest and felt as if there were a nameless menace lurking among the numerous stygian pockets between the trees.

Unable to get warm, he rose early and rubbed his hands and arms to generate heat. When the first ray of sunshine broke over the far mountain, he strode back and forth and worried about food and water. They were in for a challenging ordeal, and he liked none of it. These mountains were rugged, remote, and dangerous. They had to get to the bottom of the gorge and fashion a raft if the river would allow safe travel. If a raft would not work, they would have to follow the river on its relentless search for a lower level. They had no idea how far they needed to travel to reach safety. Ten miles, thirty miles? The unknown bothered him greatly.

He wondered if there might be a rescue party actively searching for them, but he doubted it. He could only speculate about what the gunmen had done on the highway but they seemed to have everything well planned. If they cleaned up the road, there might not be any reason, for now, for the sheriff or other authorities to look for them. Cars parked at a trailhead looked completely normal, especially at this time of the year.

He thought about Sparky, whom he knew would sound an alarm, but it would probably take twelve to twenty-four hours for him to become worried enough to act. Moreover, even if there were a rescue party, they would not be looking on this side of the mountain. The sheer, ragged cliffs blocked all access to this side. The only way across was by the ancient path that led to the steep, shale-covered slope. Rescuers would stop there and make a quick assumption that no one could possibly cross.

Filled with concern, he bent to wake Kelly, but he suddenly stopped and just looked at her. Even under these difficult conditions, she was stunning. It wasn't just her appearance, it was much more. It was a coalescence of everything she was. The way she moved, her eyes, her skin, her hands, and her wonderful curves. And then there was her voice—feminine with a melodic tone unlike any he had ever heard. He could watch her and listen to her all day, every day.

He gently shook her shoulder.

She woke with a start. "What?" She blinked a few times, got her bearings, and put her arm around Cody.

"We need to get moving."

"Yes, of course."

A few minutes later, they set off down the mountain. After a difficult and tiring hike around a rocky crag, they stopped to rest. Kelly pulled out their two bottles and checked the water levels. "I'm afraid we only have a little left."

Sean refused the bottle extended to him. "You and Cody drink the last of it."

Cody said, "We can't trust the water in streams and creeks."

Sean looked around as he spoke. "You're right. Animal droppings or other sources of contamination might be upstream that are undetectable from below, and there is always the risk of ingesting parasites. I suspect the only reasonably safe water would be from springs gushing from rocks or other locations."

Kelly took a sip of water. "I'm really worried about that."

They resumed their trek and Sean said, "Everyone keep an eye out for a spring. If we see any likely possibilities, we'll check it out. Even if it's out of our way."

A little after noon, they stopped under a towering rock wall to rest. For the first time, they could hear the river below. With nothing to eat or drink, they simply rested and observed their surroundings.

Cody rose and said, "Why don't we check along this rock wall."

"Makes sense to me," Kelly said. "It's a pretty massive wall."

Sean put his hand on Cody's shoulder. "We'll fan out, but let's stay in visual contact."

Twenty minutes later, Sean saw Cody signal. He ran toward him and arrived just as Kelly came from another direction.

Cody pointed upward. "There's a trickle coming out of the rocks up there."

Sean turned to Kelly. Hand me those bottles. I'm going up."

He stuck the bottles in his pockets, climbed up, and found two places where water exited the rock wall. The flow was small but the water looked clean. He filled the two bottles and tossed them down. "Drink slowly but drink as much as you can. Leave a little water in the bottles for weight and then throw them back up."

They spent thirty minutes near the small spring. They rested and consumed a considerable amount of water that tasted better than they expected. They felt refreshed as they resumed their downward journey. An hour later, they stopped on a small ledge overlooking the river and were stunned by what they saw. A torrent of fast moving white water cascaded over boulders and through gorges. The snowmelt from the higher elevations was approaching its peak, sending enormous amounts of water into the streams and rivers that flowed through the iconic mountain range.

Sean had hoped they might be able to build a raft and navigate the river, but it took only a glance to know that was impossible. He fought back pessimistic thoughts as he led the way down. After moving only a few yards, he stopped, picked up a rock, and whispered, "Quiet, there are some quail over there." He moved behind a tree, then he crept forward, careful to avoid stepping on twigs.

He saw a half dozen quail pecking near a large bush. He took aim and threw the rock, which sailed past the nearest quail's head. The birds took flight, following a fast, low trajectory toward safety.

"Damn!"

Cody ran up. "Did you hit one?"

"Nope, missed him by inches."

"Maybe we should carry a few rocks for next time."

"Good idea." Disappointed, they turned and rejoined Kelly.

Another view of the raging river caused a wave of pessimism to sweep over Sean. At first, he did not want Kelly and Cody to know the full extent of his concern, but he also knew he could not, and should not, conceal reality from them. After a moment he said, "We need to talk about what we're up against." He pointed toward a group of trees. "There's a good spot."

Before they settled down, he pulled out his phone and turned it on. "No chance of a signal, but I should check every so often just in case." As expected, the mountains blocked any signals and he turned off his phone.

He said, "We're in a hell of a jam. We haven't heard or seen anything that might indicate they are searching for us. I'm sure that's because we're on the wrong side of the mountain. I had hoped to hear helicopters by now, but all we've heard is silence and, of course, the river. We need to go downstream, but it's a daunting task at best. Using a raft in that river would be suicide. So, we have to make our way along the riverbank, which as you can see, looks precarious. We'll give it a try after we rest."

Kelly said, "You really think it's that bad?"

"I do." He gazed at the mountain slope next to the river. "We can go for days without food, though it will weaken us, but our main concern is safe drinking water." He turned to Cody. "What do you know about edible plants in the Sierras?"

Cody sat upright with an eager expression. "We studied that some, so I know a little. I think our best bet is to find miner's lettuce. It's late for that at lower elevations, but we might find it up here. It's easy to spot." He grabbed a stick and drew a picture of a round leaf. "It looks like that with a stem coming right out of the middle with tiny flowers on it. And mountain Sorrel. Oh, and dandelion. You can eat most of the plant."

Kelly's face brightened. "Joining the Boy Scouts was a great idea. We'll put you in charge of finding those plants."

Sean felt a surge of pride as he watched Cody, followed by a pang of guilt. He had missed so much over the past eleven years. He said, "That'll really help, Cody, and the plants will provide us with much needed moisture." He had a touch of optimism in his voice but as he looked at the rugged mountainside, he felt another wave of apprehension. Would they survive?

CHAPTER 29

As Danny Fagan made his way down the mountain, he continued to struggle with the concept of how a man and a woman with a kid in tow managed to successfully negotiate their way down a treacherous slope filled with tons of shale that gave way at the mere touch of a person's foot. It was too steep for them to walk down. Rick had tried it and he had immediately fallen on his ass. Fagan was not about to make the same mistake; that's what Rick was for—the grunt work.

He reached the highway and observed the only thing that had gone right—Isaac had managed to hide the vehicles and clean up the mess. There were no authorities in sight, light traffic was flowing, and everything looked normal. Isaac stepped from behind his pickup, which was parked in the trailhead parking lot, and waved.

Isaac noticed Rick limping and said, "What happened to him?"

"He busted his ass on some rocks."

"Did you get the merchandise?"

"Fuck no, and I don't want to talk about it."

Fagan checked his van and decided he could drive it without drawing attention from the Highway Patrol, but he would need to switch vehicles when he returned to his compound. He had two stolen cargo vans and a car hidden in the trees on his property. He looked at the mountain and a thought struck him. He ran to his van, opened the door, and grabbed a folder. When he planned for the trip, he had obtained several maps, including a regional, county, and a topographic map. Topographical maps contain a myriad of helpful information about any area, including terrain, elevation, drainage, forest cover, roads, and populated areas.

He opened the topo map and ran a finger along the highway until he found his location. He studied the mountain range on the other side of the shale slide, and he found it to be treacherous and remote. He started to give up when he saw a narrow service road about four miles down the highway from his current location. It did not go all the way to the river, but it was the only access for at least thirty miles. Because it was nearly dark, he knew he could reach that section of the river before his targets did tomorrow, assuming they stopped to sleep, which he knew they would because of the boy.

He had packed enough provisions for several days so there was no need to find a store. He double-checked the terrain, folded the map, checked his gear, and exited the van. He yelled at Rick and Isaac, "Get over here. We can catch them."

Isaac came over, but Rick walked with a limp, bending to one side, cursing with every step.

"We'll sleep in our vehicles and get up before dawn. There's only one way they can go, and we'll be waiting."

Rick reached behind his back and massaged the muscles around his tailbone. "I can't do it, man. This pain is killing me."

Fagan started to jump all over Rick, but he realized anyone in his condition would likely hinder their efforts. He looked at Rick. "Okay, get the hell out of here."

A look of relief flashed across Rick's face; then, he turned and limped toward his car.

Fagan yelled at him, "Be careful. We don't want anybody getting stopped for traffic violations." He looked at Isaac. "We'll go down the highway to the service road and take it as far as we can. I have food, and we can sleep in my van. I've got a sleeping bag and some blankets. We'll get up before dawn and nail 'em."

The forest service road Danny Fagan saw on the map turned out to be a narrow, rutted, twisting, eroded nightmare. Once again, Fagan realized how badly underpaid he was, and he meant for that injustice to end. After a difficult ride to the end of the road, Fagan got out and scouted the area, looking for their best route to the river. They would have to negotiate a steep decline filled with rocks and trees but it was the only access in the area. He went back to the van, had a couple of beers with Isaac, and, then, he crawled into his sleeping bag.

He rose at 4 A.M., had a quick breakfast, checked his Glock, and headed toward the river, feeling confident he would soon have the software in his possession. After he stole the program, he knew he could not leave any survivors who might haunt him later. No witnesses, no problems.

Sparky Valentine waited for a phone call that never came. Kelly was supposed to have called the minute she arrived. She had left him a copy of the map showing her destination and Martin

Scanlan's private phone number at his lodge. When they were three hours overdue, Sparky called Scanlan's number.

He heard a voice after four rings. "Mr. Scanlan. My name is Valentine, and I'm a close friend of Kelly Sanborn. She was supposed to call me when she arrived, but I haven't heard from her. Is she there?"

"Why no, she isn't. She called around four and said she had changed plans. She said she had decided to cancel, so she could take her son to a resort north of here. I thought it odd, but it was her decision. Fortunately, I had someone available to take her place."

"Mr. Scanlan."

"Yes."

"You're full of shit!"

Sparky hung up, fully aware that Scanlan had probably lied. He sat for a moment, then he rose and paced the room, his face etched with concern. He went to his computer and found the phone number for the local sheriff. When they answered, he said, "I think my friend has been kidnapped—or worse."

Sparky gave the deputy all the information he had, including the brand and the color of Kelly's rented SUV. He hung up and paced the floor while his mind overflowed with concern for Kelly and Cody. Then it struck him. What about Sean? Why hadn't he called? What in the hell was going on?

Three hours later, the phone rang.

"Mr. Valentine. We sent out a car, and we notified the Highway Patrol. I'm sorry, but we have patrolled the entire length of the road you gave us, and there is no sign of her car. She might have gone somewhere else, maybe even as far as Nevada."

"Thank you for your efforts, but she would have never done that."

"We'll keep looking and call you in the morning."

Sparky hung up and stared at the wall. What could he do to help? He realized there was nothing he could do, and it filled him with anguish.

CHAPTER 30

Sean led the way along the river, which turned out to be a difficult task. They were in wild country carved by a river of considerable power, a dangerous natural wonder they quickly learned to respect. They had to climb numerous times to skirt around impassable barriers. The early going was tough but they soon came to a long stretch where they made good time. They took advantage of the terrain until the mountain came nearly to the river's edge. They stopped to rest before attempting the next section, which looked formidable.

Sean had no sooner sat on a rock when he saw a flight of squawking ravens burst from trees on the steep slope to his right. Two deer bolted from the forest and bounded away. He stood and said, "There's something up there. Probably a bear or a mountain lion, but it could be people. Let's cross to the trees near that ridge and watch."

Kelly said, "It might be those men who chased us?"

"I doubt it but we can't take any chances. Hopefully it's a friendly group, but it might be a predatory animal."

They started toward the twenty-foot high ridge when Cody said, "There are two men up there. One of them just raised a gun!"

Kelly pushed Cody and yelled, "Run! Go, Go!"

They dashed toward the ridge, which was their only possible escape route. The mountain on their right was too steep to climb and the left side consisted of a sharp drop of thick, brush covered terrain right down to the river's edge. They reached the base of the steep, dirt-covered incline, which temporally shielded them from the men up the slope.

Sean yelled, "Climb. Fast!"

Cody scampered up the ridge with little effort, followed by Kelly. Sean looked up the mountain slope, saw two men come out of the trees, and run in their direction. He powered up the incline just as three shots rang out. One bullet nicked his shirt, and the other two dug into the ground next to him. He dove head first over the top.

Sean's first thought was to run, but he knew the gunmen would be on them in a matter of minutes. Kelly had started to run when he yelled, "Wait. We have to fight back."

Kelly's expression of astonishment sent a loud message. She wanted to run, a natural instinct. She stopped. "That's crazy. We have nothing to fight them with."

"We have to fight. They'll be up that ridge and run us down, shooting all the way. We'll use what nature gives us." He took a quick look around. "Cody, start bringing rocks from that creek bed. As big as you can carry."

Kelly said, "What about those limbs over there?"

"Good idea. Grab the bigger ones and bring them over here. Get the ones with the fewest branches." Sean peeked over the edge and saw the two men running straight toward their position.

Obstacles would delay them, but he estimated they would reach the bottom of the ridge in less than a minute.

He spun around and saw Cody dropping a second load of rocks. Kelly ran toward him with several large limbs. He yelled, "More! More!" Then he ran to the dry creek bed and lifted two large rocks. He ran back and looked over the edge. The two men had just reached the bottom of the slope. Sean picked some rocks Cody had gathered and began tossing them over the edge. Then he picked up one of the larger rocks and rolled it over.

He heard curses from below. He picked up more rocks and threw them over as fast as he could. While Sean peeked over the edge, Kelly tossed limbs, big ends first, as if throwing a spear. He rolled another large rock and saw it bounce off the slope and hit the taller man's leg.

The man yelled out, "Damnit! They hit my knee."

The other man cussed after a rock thrown by Cody hit his head and sent him sprawling. They continued throwing everything they had until the two men hobbled away from the ridge. Sean watched and saw them go behind some rocks about forty yards away. "I think they're going to try again." He turned toward Cody. "Bring all the rocks you can find. Get some that are about the size of tennis balls. I can heave them a long way."

Kelly searched for more limbs suitable for tossing down the slope.

Sean watched as the smaller man studied the mountain. He knew the gunman was looking for a way to flank them, but the rugged terrain would slow them considerably, perhaps as much as two hours. He believed they would discard that option.

A few minutes later, the two men started walking toward the ridge. The smaller man lifted his pistol and fired several shots, but there was nothing to hit. He evidently hoped to use covering fire to allow them to get close. When they advanced to within fifteen yards, Sean started throwing rocks as fast as he could. One of the missiles hit the larger man in the chest, which caused him to stop and bend over. The other gunman hid behind a rock and fired more shots.

Nothing happened for several minutes; then, they saw the two men retreat. One of them yelled over his shoulder, "We're not done. We'll get you, and you're gonna fucking pay for this. You're gonna pay big time."

Kelly grabbed Sean's arm. "Let's go. Maybe we can find a place to hide."

Sean threw one last rock and turned. "Good idea but we need to put some distance between us first." He crossed the narrow creek bed that supplied the rocks and started jogging. Kelly and Cody followed close behind.

Sean processed a variety of thoughts as he ran. Foremost, he felt proud about how Kelly and Cody had handled the crisis. Neither whined, neither seemed frightened, although they surely were. They had pitched in and fought for their lives in an efficient and aggressive manner. Next, he thought about their options. Could they outrun their pursuers? They almost certainly could not because of the terrain. They would lose valuable time searching for ways around too many obstacles. Could they hide? That all depended on what the mountain had to offer and how much time they had. He decided to inspect the topography as they ran, hoping to find a solution. He slowed to go around a fallen tree; then, he stopped and scanned the mountainside, which now revealed more rocky walls and fewer trees. In the distance, the forest, again, became the predominate feature.

After a brief rest, they continued at a brisk walk. After several minutes, Cody pointed toward a rocky wall. "That looks like a small cave."

Sean looked in the direction Cody's finger pointed and saw a small, dark depression in the wall. "Let's have a look." When they were about twenty yards away, he saw a cave with an opening about five feet across, but he immediately knew it could be a death trap. It was too visible to anyone passing by. If they went into the cave, they would be discovered for sure unless it went deep into the mountain, which would only present more problems as there would be no way of knowing if it came to a dead-end. Without a flashlight, they would have to search the depths of the cave in total darkness.

He turned to Kelly. "Stay here. I'm going to check out something." He went to the rocky wall next to the cave and began to climb. He went up about thirty feet and stopped on a small ledge that was covered with rocks of all sizes. He looked up and saw another ledge about twenty feet higher. He wanted to inspect a large boulder on the upper ledge, so he moved to his right and began to climb. When he reached the upper ledge, he had a good view of the surrounding area. He looked in the direction they had come, but he saw no sign of movement. Satisfied, he turned and inspected the ledge; then, he looked down and saw that the lower ledge was directly above the cave entrance. He had an idea, a very dangerous idea.

He went back down and stood with a contemplative expression. "They said they would keep coming, and I believe them." He looked upriver, checking for signs of pursuit. "We don't have many options. The mountain is very steep here, so we can't go higher to hide. We also don't have food or water, which I am sure they have in their backpacks." He rubbed his forehead. "I already feel a bit dehydrated."

Kelly nodded. "We all do." She studied the mountain above the cave. "What do you have in mind?"

"There are two ledges above the cave. We can hide there. Or, if they go into the cave, we might be able to trap them. Several boulders are right on the edge. I think we could get them rolling and cause a landslide big enough to cover the entrance."

Kelly frowned. "Sounds like a longshot. What if it doesn't work?"

He shook his head. "I don't know; I really don't." He looked downriver. Or we can try to outrun them."

Kelly looked at the mountainside, then at the river. "You're right. I think they'd catch us. Too many obstacles."

Sean again checked for any sign of the two men. "We were lucky last time and maybe our luck will run out, but I think we should try it." He glanced up. "One more thing. If they don't go into the cave, we'll just hide up there and hope they don't find us."

"What if they're good trackers?"

"I doubt if they are, but I'll cover our tracks as best I can." After Kelly and Cody started up the rocky cliff, Sean went to the cave entrance and walked backwards, sifting a fine mist of dirt over their footprints. When he reached the rock wall he examined the dirt for any trace of footprints. Satisfied, he turned and began to climb.

Kelly was inspecting a boulder when he reached the upper ledge. "I thought you had a bad idea but, actually, I think we could get this moving. It is just hanging there waiting for a storm to erode the base and topple it."

Sean got down on his knees and inspected the edge. "I wish we had some timber to use as a lever, but you're right. It is ready to go." He rose and looked at Kelly and Cody. "This is a big decision, so we all need to understand what's at stake. First, we should hide and see what they do. If they enter the cave, I think we should try it. Otherwise, it's probably just a matter of time before they find us. That one guy won't give up. I can tell."

Cody said, "I can't be sure, but the shorter man looks like the one who broke into our house. I never saw his face, but he's the same size, and he has the same color hair."

"It figures," Sean said. He paused, considered their options, and then said, "Okay, I have a plan but give me your thoughts." They covered the possible scenarios and agreed on an action plan. Then they hid and waited.

Twenty-five minutes later, they saw the two men walking toward them. The shorter man took off his baseball cap and rubbed his head where the rock had struck him. The much larger man lagged about fifteen feet behind, moving with a noticeable limp. They were near the river and almost passed by when the man with the baseball cap pointed toward the cave. Immediately, they changed directions and started up the incline.

They stopped ten feet away, and the man with the hat said, "We need to check that cave, but first I want to have a look around." He studied the adjacent area, then he looked above the cave. "There's a ledge up there that would give a person a good view of the surrounding area. I'm going up for a look-see."

Sean whispered, "Damn, he's going to climb up. If he stops at the first ledge we have to be very quiet and hope he goes back down. If he continues toward this ledge we have to stop him." He glanced around. "Quick, gather some rocks to throw, but be very quiet." Sean gathered several large rocks; then, he glanced at Kelly and Cody. He saw fear in their eyes, but they had acted bravely during the last confrontation with the gunmen, and he expected the same response this time. Would it be enough?

Sean watched as the man began to climb.

The gunman reached the first ledge, stopped, turned, and looked downriver; then, he looked upward.

Sean ducked back and tried to give a reassuring nod to Kelly and Cody. The next few minutes might determine their fate. He waited but heard no sounds. Finally, he peeked down and saw the gunman gazing toward the distant forest.

After a moment, the man began to make his way down to the cave opening. When he reached the bottom, he said, "Let's check the cave." He pulled his gun and said, "You first, Isaac."

The larger man hesitated.

"Go on. We have guns, and they don't. I'll be right behind you. Here, take my flashlight."

The larger man walked up to the cave's entrance with a pistol in one hand and the flashlight in the other. He paused and then stepped into the cave. The man outside waited a few seconds and then said, "See anything?"

"Naw, but it's a lot bigger and deeper than I expected. Help me check it out."

When Sean saw the second man disappear, he gave the signal. He put his back against the boulder and Kelly and Cody took positions on either side and put their hands on the boulder. Sean nodded and they began to push.

Nothing.

Sean tuned to face the boulder. "Again, harder!"

Still, no movement.

They knew they were running out of time.

He turned and put his back against the boulder. "Push, guys. Hard!"

They put everything they had into the effort. Just when they were about to stop, dirt beneath the leading edge of the huge rock began to crumble. After a few seconds, the edge gave way with a sudden, violent rush. The boulder bounded down and crashed into a cluster of rocks with tremendous force. The second, smaller ledge, collapsed and rocks of all sizes careened down the slope followed by a massive volume of dirt.

They looked over the edge and saw a huge plume of dust billowing upward. Following their prearranged plan, they did not wait to see what happened. Instead, they moved along the rocky ledge, to their right, climbed down, and ran into the forest. They hid in a stand of trees and looked back.

Dust still clouded the entrance, so they could not tell if their plan had worked. They waited. After a few minutes, Sean said, "It's sealed. No, wait. There is a small hole at the top."

Just then, a hand poked through the hole followed by a head. The man seemed to stop as though he did not have enough room to escape the cave. They watched as the man continued to struggle. He wiggled back and forth for nearly ten minutes; then, his shoulders emerged followed by his body. He crawled over the rocks and lay on the dirt below. He did not move, but they could hear him cursing. Finally, he got to his knees and then, slowly, he stood.

Another hand appeared at the small hole at the top of the heap of rocks. The man's head appeared, and he yelled something at his companion. The larger man struggled but made no headway because his body was much broader than the man who had escaped. The smaller man climbed up the rocks, looked things over, and then went back down.

The gunman with his head sticking out of the hole was obviously too big to climb through the hole. He pleaded for help, but the other man just stood there. Finally, the smaller man turned and walked straight toward the trees, gun in hand, obviously leaving the other man to fend for himself in an impossible situation.

Sean whispered, "He's one mean sonofa—" He stopped short because of Cody.

"No, you're right," Kelly said, "He's a cruel sonofabitch. Might as well call it like it is."

Sean shook his head. "The man has no soul."

CHAPTER 31

When the lone gunman continued in their direction, Kelly turned and started jogging into the deep forest. They had been lucky so far, but she was not about to confront the armed thug again. Her only thought was to get Cody as far away as possible. She looked over her shoulder and saw Cody and Sean close behind. They had only gone a couple hundred yards when they heard a single gunshot. Kelly and Sean looked at each other in disbelief. They could only speculate, but they both had the same thought—the smaller gunman intended to leave no witnesses.

After three hours of alternating between walking and jogging, Kelly's concern switched from evading their pursuer to a second looming danger—survival. The more she thought about what might lie ahead, the more she worried about their safety. The mountains and forest were wilder and more rugged than anything she had ever seen. She knew she was out of her element so she decided to rely on Sean more than she would in any other situation. She knew she was more than capable in her everyday world, but this was vastly different. Sean's knowledge of the wilderness was superior to hers. Moreover, it was not just Sean she intended to rely on; she knew Cody's Boy Scout training would offer valuable wilderness knowledge.

They slowed to a walk, went to the river's edge, and stood in awe as they observed the torrent of rushing water.

After a moment Sean said, "I've been thinking about where those two men came from. The mountains seem impassable, so I can't imagine how they got this close to the river. My first thought was to double back to see if we could find the passage they must have taken, but the more I think about it, the more it worries me."

"I wondered about that too," Kelly said as she scanned the mountain. "The problem is that we don't know if he's still following us. He might be lying in wait to ambush us. We also have no idea how he got here. If we go back, we might easily get lost. I think Cody is right. We should follow the river."

They agreed to stay the course. They followed the river but, they soon had to climb to navigate around the mass of rocks and brush that lined the river. They finally came to a wide spot and took a breather.

Kelly suddenly jumped up and pointed skyward. "Over there. A plane!"

They saw a single engine airplane, heading east, high above the mountains on the far side of the river. She yanked off her sweatshirt and started waving frantically. Cody did the same, and Sean waved his shirt. The plane continued its course and slowly went out of sight.

Kelly sat down. "I guess we were too far away, but it was worth a try."

"We should see more," Sean said. "Everyone keep an eye out."

They walked for hours, struggling against the rugged terrain, which often caused them to go higher just to make headway. After a difficult climb, she felt exhausted and Cody and Sean seemed nearly as tired. She pointed toward a rocky area with an overhang. "I think we should stop for the day. That looks like a good spot with some shelter."

They turned and headed for the overhang.

Cody took off his backpack and said, "I'm going to look for food."

"We'll all look," Kelly said.

They had previously searched for pine cones, which they wanted to harvest for the nuts, but they had been disappointed. It was the wrong time of the year, and those they did inspect had either been eaten by squirrels or had insect infestations. Others contained nuts that were rancid. They found a few they could eat, but it proved an unreliable food source.

After a long search, Cody ran from a shady area and said, "Miner's lettuce! Lots of it."

Kelly retrieved a plastic bag from her backpack and joined Sean and Cody. They picked enough to fill the bag, then they went to the overhang and surveyed their gatherings.

Sean reached into the bag. "I'll be the guinea pig." After a few bites he said, "Better than I expected. Not sure how much nutrition this stuff has, but it's edible. Dig in."

The sun disappeared, it turned colder than the previous night, and piercing gusts of wind blew down from the mountaintops. They huddled together, with Cody in the middle, and they soon entered a fatigue-induced sleep.

The next morning, Kelly awoke and found Sean's arm around her and her head on his shoulder. Cody must have gotten up during the night, and he was now asleep on the other side of Sean. She started to jerk away, but she felt protected, and he was warmer than the surrounding rocks. Cody had been right; they needed to share body heat. Still, it unnerved her because she intended to always have Cody between her and Sean. After a few moments, she eased away hoping that Sean was asleep, though his breathing rhythm seemed suspicious.

———

Their journey had been an ordeal, but they had tolerated the difficulties reasonably well although dehydration was becoming a serious problem. Things changed shortly after they began the new day's travel. A scattering of ominous clouds scudded across the mountaintops, bringing with them a temperature drop of several degrees. A few gusts of wind got their attention, but that was not all. They stopped on a ledge overlooking a gorge full of torrents of angry, rushing water.

Kelly saw no way to proceed and turned to Sean. "Looks like we have to climb again."

"Yeah, I don't see any alternative. It's damn sure rough country."

As they climbed, Kelly noticed a definite drop in her stamina, a condition obviously caused by poor sleep, cold temperatures, and a lack of proper nutrition. She noticed that Cody was not his usual chipper self, and Sean remained quiet. They trudged up the mountain, fighting obstacles all the way, searching for a way around the canyon surrounding the gorge.

Kelly slipped and fell against some brush and tore her sweatshirt.

Sean helped her up. "Let's stop here and rest. You look done in."

She offered no argument as the climb had brought on a case of fatigue she felt to her core. It made her think of that old adage: there's no place like home.

Sean watched the clouds. "It looks bad. Does it storm much this time of the year?"

"Only in the mountains," Kelly said, as she looked skyward. "We do see forecasts for thunderstorms in the Sierras in June almost every year. They come and go quickly."

After resting, they found a gap that allowed them to move down the mountain, but the climb had a brutal impact on their stamina. They scrambled over obstacles, forded small creeks, and fought through heavy brush. When they neared the river, the sky had turned dark, and they felt the first drops of rain accompanied by a sudden dip in the temperature. Twenty minutes later, jagged lightning bolts flashing across the sky unleashed a cloudburst.

Sean stopped and looked around. "We have to find shelter. Keep an eye out while we walk."

They wove through the forest, not far from the river, searching as they went. A cave would be ideal, but that seemed to require luck that had evaded them so far. They came to a rocky wall and stopped. Kelly said, "Let's look for another overhang like we found last night."

Sean nodded, and they began to search. They trudged forward fighting wind, rain, and terrain. They came to a clearing and Cody jogged about twenty feet ahead.

Sean suddenly tilted his head. He thought he heard a strange noise up the mountain, but after concentrating, the only thing he heard was the sound of the trees buffeted by gusts of wind. Cody was halfway across a shallow creek when Sean looked up the mountain. He heard the roar, and he saw a mass of angry, white water surging down the creek bed.

He yelled, "Flash flood!" He dashed into the creek.

Kelly screamed, "Run, Cody. Run!"

Sean hit the creek bottom and swept Cody up with his arms. The water hit them as they started up the opposite bank. Just after Sean pushed Cody to safety, a massive wave enveloped him and carried him toward the river below. He fought his way toward the bank, but a cascade of debris knocked him backwards. He struggled and managed to reach the bank again when a large limb came at him with a rush. He ducked under water and lost his footing.

He surfaced, looked downstream, and saw a boulder embedded on the edge of the creek. If he struck the rock, he knew he would be injured. He fought with all his strength to reach the edge of the bank. A few feet from the boulder, he reached up and grabbed a limb hanging over the stream. The water whipped at him as he pulled himself up enough to reduce the pull of the raging water. He scrambled out of the water and sprawled under a tree, shivering and sucking air.

It took more than an hour for the rush of water to subside, and, then, Sean walked into the receding stream and helped Kelly. When they reached the bank she said, "I don't know how to thank you."

He whispered, "He's my son too."

She looked into his eyes with an expression of gratitude, but she said nothing.

They came to another rocky area, and Cody ran up to an oddly-shaped wall and said. "It's not a cave, but it'll work."

Kelly found the overhang better than the one they had used the previous night. It was nothing more than a jagged indent in a rock wall, but it created an alcove that offered more protection than being in the open. They settled down and ate the last of the miner's lettuce. Hopefully, that would give them enough moisture until they found safe water.

Sean tried his phone but, as expected, there was no signal.

Everyone was too tired to talk, so they huddled next to each other and tried to sleep. The rain came in sheets with the wind occasionally whipping rain in on them. There was simply no way to stay dry. After a wet and miserable night, they awoke to scattered cumulus clouds and cold conditions. Sean rose first and said, "There should be some rain water trapped in depressions on the rocks. I'm going to take a look."

Cody jumped up. "I'll go with you."

Kelly watched them go with mixed emotions. They were father and son, but only one of them knew that. What if they did not survive their ordeal? Did Cody not have the right to know Sean was his father? She struggled with the concept, uncertain how to handle such an important issue. After considering their situation, the decreasing odds of survival made the decision for her. The treacherous terrain, the lack of food and water, and the elements might very well kill them.

When they came into view, Cody ran ahead of Sean with two bottles of water and proudly displayed them. She took the bottles and motioned for her son to sit next to her. After he seated himself, she turned to him and said, "There is something very important I need to tell you." She started to speak but she had to pause twice to compose herself. She glanced at Sean, then she put her hands on Cody's shoulders. "Mr. Keene ... Mr. Keene is your father!"

CHAPTER 32

A few minutes after Danny Fagan had left the cave to chase his prey, he stopped where the rocky wall gave way to dense forest. A quick analysis told him one thing—the risk was too great. They were smarter than he had imagined, and the forest had hundreds of places prime for an ambush even for someone without a weapon. He might come around a corner and be attacked with rocks or clubs. Moreover, what if he did not catch them before dark? He would be extremely vulnerable while asleep.

He turned and headed back toward the cave. Isaac pleaded with him as he approached, but Fagan knew there was nothing he could do. The weight of the boulders prevented a single individual from attempting a rescue. So, he had done the only thing that made sense, at least to him. He climbed up the rocks, pulled out his pistol, and put a bullet in Isaac's forehead. It had been a simple matter of eliminating another risk. The odds of someone rescuing Isaac were extreme but, if it did happen, he would become an instant snitch. A bullet solved that problem.

After a difficult climb, he reached the gap in the mountain, walked up to his van, pulled off his cap, wiped dried blood from the knot on his head, and said aloud, "Fuck this shit. I know where she lives. I'll get her later." It was time to get mean and nasty, and he intended to do just that, but he also knew he had to be patient. He pondered another possibility as he started the van. Kelly Sanborn might never be seen again. His scrutiny of the topographic map revealed a wilderness full of danger, especially for those without provisions. He would have to wait and see, but he would not stop planning. He lit a cigarette, popped a beer, turned the van, and started down the rut-filled service road, talking to himself as he dodged dozens of potholes.

While he drove, his mind went into overdrive, rapidly processing thoughts and ideas. He still could not understand how his target managed to descend such a steep, shale-filled slope. It seemed impossible. If a person got off too far to one side, they might slide right off the cliff. How could they have done it? And the cave. They were smarter than he had given them credit for. Finally, he let it go. There was no use busting his ass on something in the past.

He reached the highway, turned, and began the drive down the mountain. When he entered the foothills, he turned on the radio and checked the news. One item caught his attention—the stock market had suffered several days of panic selling that had wiped out huge amounts of capital from nervous stockholders around the world. The Dow had plummeted over two thousand points in three days.

Visions of dollar signs sprang up in Fagan's mind. He had first begun to think about the possibilities of Kelly's software while he watched her in the television studio. Suddenly, the potential of her system took on a new clarity. It was worth a fortune and Scanlan had been paying him peanuts. He passed a truck and yelled, "This shit's gonna end."

He rounded a curve, and a new idea took hold and expanded. He would demand a piece of the action. If Scanlan did not comply, he had a backup plan that would not only put him in possession of the software, but he might be able to nab Kelly Sanborn at the same time. The thought intensified his motivation. His idea was in its infancy, but it would not take long to formulate a strategy that would not fail. Planning came naturally to him and he was good at it, damn good. Details were always the key.

If things went well, he could use the money he expected to earn from Kelly's software to clear some trees and build a new house at his compound. Then he could clean out the old double-wide and convert it into a world-class breeding facility for racing pigeons. The new arrangement would house future champions. He liked his new idea; he liked it a lot. He was going to put an end to people looking down on him. Money would not only buy him respect, but also it would propel him into a new and exciting future. His thoughts shifted and displayed lewd images of Kelly Sanborn as he drove into California's central valley. Why not have it all?

———

Sparky Valentine was an upbeat sort of guy, and he knew it. However, when things went badly, he became a pacer and a water guzzler. Bottle in hand, he walked the floor the morning after his call to the authorities, waiting impatiently for news. At ten-thirty, he received a call, but there was still no sign of Kelly or her car.

Sparky listened and then said, "She's been kidnapped."

"Do you have something concrete to go on?"

Sparky went into a lengthy explanation of recent events, pushing hard for a more intensive search. The Sheriff's deputy said they would make a note of his concerns and keep looking. It was not enough, and he felt he had to do something. He hung up and paced the floor for a few minutes; then, he went to his bedroom and threw a few things into a duffle bag. He put a case of water into his car, went to the kitchen, put some walnuts, fruit, and vitamins in a bag; then, he studied the map Kelly had given him. Fifteen minutes later, he pulled out of his driveway and headed for the Sierras.

CHAPTER 33

Cody sat in silence for a long moment, obviously struggling to comprehend what he had just heard. Then, in a swift move, he ran to Sean and threw his arms around his father. Neither said anything as they clung to each other. The tears running down their faces exposed the extreme emotions shared by father and son.

Despite her feelings about Sean, Kelly felt a tremendous tug at her heart as she watched them. Cody deserved to know his father, especially since Sean probably saved his life on two occasions. Moreover, she knew they had made a positive connection when they had first met.

Sean had his arm around Cody when he finally looked toward Kelly, his face expressing gratitude. She turned sideways and wiped her eyes.

Overcome with emotion, Cody said nothing, but he did not move from his father's side. They moved to a rock and sat next to each other. Sean spoke in a low voice, and Kelly only caught an occasional word, but she knew it was their first father-to-son conversation, and it was profound. After a time, they sat in silence, obviously trying to comprehend the dramatic, life-altering event.

———————

Sean felt an intense emotional jolt when he heard Kelly's unexpected declaration. He told Cody he was sorry for being out of his life for so long. He turned and looked directly into his son's eyes. "I love you, and I always will."

Cody hugged him and seemed reluctant to let go.

Finally, they walked over to Kelly. He said, "Thank you." Nothing more than those simple, heartfelt words.

She nodded but said nothing.

After a few moments, Sean looked at the sky. "It's cold, we're wet, and we need a fire. I've done some camping, and I've watched some survival films, but I've never had to start a fire with the tools nature gives us. Cody, you've obviously had some training in the scouts. Let's put our heads together and figure this out."

Cody said, "I know two ways. One is a lot easier than the other, but they are both tricky, especially if you haven't done it before." His voice turned eager. "The best way would be to use flint and the back of that old knife to ignite sparks. We won't find any flint here, but quartz will do, and there should be lots of it in these mountains."

Sean started walking and spoke over his shoulder. "The river. Let's go."

They reached the river, but they had no access to the bank. Sean started through the trees, following the watercourse, talking as he went. "What we want is an area on the bank that is accessible and has a lot of rocks."

They finally came to a bend in the river that had a small sand bar filled with rocks of all sizes. Sean looked down. "Quartz is usually whitish or pinkish white." They conducted a thorough search but, finding no quartz, they continued downstream. After walking a few yards, they heard an airplane, but they could not locate it in the sky. It sounded like it went over the mountains behind them. They had seen several commercial airliners over the last two days, but they were too high to signal.

At midday, they had to climb higher to avoid a rugged, inaccessible riverbank. Sean became acutely aware of his deteriorating physical condition. He felt pain in his muscles and he was badly fatigued. If they managed to start a fire, he would try trapping small animals. He realized they needed to forage more aggressively, searching for anything to eat, including plants, grubs, and roots. He knew they should have done this sooner, but he was intent on going downriver to find safety. The need for survival now surpassed all other needs.

They descended and came to a sloping area near the river. Before them, they saw the largest creek they had encountered so far. The rain-filled stream rushed by and plunged into the river at high speed. It took only a glance to know it was too wide and too swift to cross safely.

Sean started up the slope. "We've got to find a way across, then we'll rest."

It was the first time he'd heard groans. He turned and saw his beleaguered companions struggling to keep up. Cody, especially, seemed to have slowed considerably. Sean knew boys his age needed rest and good nutrition for their growing bodies. He had been game, but the ordeal had taken a toll on his son. Sean stopped to let everyone rest, then they resumed climbing.

Just as he was about to stop for another break, he saw a huge deadfall across the stream that went from bank to bank. It had a mass of gnarly branches sticking out in all directions, but he thought they might be able to cross. He stopped and surveyed the log. The top end of the tree was the part that lay across the stream. Because of this, the branches were smaller. Still, they created severe obstacles, and he doubted he could cut the limbs with the old, dull knife. Upon closer inspection, he found the deadfall to be recent, probably felled by wind in the last few weeks. A thought struck him. Wood that new might be pliable enough to break under pressure, at least the thinner branches.

The knife he found in the miner's shack was old and rusted, but it had been a high-quality blade when new. He knew the value of the tool and he decided to try to sharpen the knife before starting the task before him. He searched and found three stones, each a little smoother than the other. He started a back and forth motion on the coarsest stone first, then he moved to the next, and finally to the smoothest rock. It took over thirty minutes, but when he finished the knife's edge was in far better shape than before.

He climbed to the first branches. He used the knife to cut a groove on one side, then he tugged and the branch broke off at the notch. Heartened, he began working in earnest. Forty-five minutes later, he stopped and checked the log. It had been a difficult job, but he had been able to break enough branches to allow passage to the other side. He had broken off a few of the limbs in a manner that left them about the same height as ski poles. They could use them as handles as they moved across the log. His right hand ached and bled in two places, but it had been the only way.

Kelly said, "Your hand is a mess. Come over to the water's edge." She reached into Cody's backpack, grabbed a pair of athletic socks, and dipped one into the water. She delicately cleaned his hands with the wet sock, then she wrapped his hand with the dry sock. "Don't let that slip off."

Sean was so surprised he could only mutter a quiet thank you. He went back to the deadfall and climbed up on the log. He pulled Cody up and helped him cross, then he went back for Kelly. He made eye contact and held out his hand. "It's tricky. Let me help you."

She hesitated and then took his hand and climbed onto the log. She started to let go of his hand, but he held tight as they inched along the log. When they reached the thicker, unbroken branches, she withdrew her hand and maneuvered to the end of the log. He helped her down, then they went to the riverbank and searched for quartz. Again, they found none, but thirty yards downriver Cody waved. "Found one. It's a nice size."

Sean ran to Cody. "Good job." He examined the stone. "What next?"

"We need to break this into smaller parts. It's pretty easy to break. Just throw it against these bigger rocks."

On Sean's fourth toss, the rock broke into three pieces.

"Okay, what else do we need?"

"That's the hard part. We need a tinder nest, and then we need something small and dry to create an ember when we strike the quartz. We can use the under part of bark from an old, fallen tree for the nest. I know how to strip it off with a knife and then we need to break it down."

Sean smiled proudly at his son. "You're the boss. Lead the way."

Cody perked up. "Let's go find a dead tree."

The first deadfall would not do, but the second one had shaggy, broken bark. Sean asked, "How about this one?"

"That's exactly what we want. Oh, and we'll need some kindling."

"I'll take care of that part," Kelly said. "You two make the nest."

Sean pulled off some bark and began peeling thin, ragged pieces from the driest parts.

When he had enough, Cody said, "We need to rub it back and forth to break down the fibers. And we need to save the fine bits that fall, so we'll need a smooth, dry area to work over. Hopefully, the fine material will form embers when we strike the quartz with the back of the knife."

Sean moved to a flat rock. "I'm guessing we'll make a nest with the fibers and, then, put the dry bits inside."

"Yep, it'll be kinda like a bird's nest. We'll make a hole and drop the stuff in. You just keep striking the quartz until the sparks create embers, then you blow softly into the nest. As soon as we get smoke, you have to blow harder. We'll make a teepee with Mom's kindling. If we get a fire we just shove it under the kindling."

"How do you know all of this?"

"I'm working on a merit badge in forestry."

"Thought so. Okay, let's get started."

Kelly overheard and started building a teepee with the kindling she had gathered. "It'll be ready when you two finish."

Sean placed the quartz close to the nest and picked up the knife.

Cody inspected the rock. "Strike with the back of the knife on the sharpest edge you can find. If this one doesn't work, we'll try the others."

Sean struck the rock repeatedly, sending forth a series of tiny sparks but no embers appeared. He kept at it and, then, he adjusted the nest and switched rocks. He began again, this time more vigorously. Still, no embers. He turned to Cody. "Am I doing this right?"

"Yes, but sometimes it takes a long time. It's just a tricky deal."

Sean switched rocks and started again.

"Dad, we've got an ember!"

Sean was so startled by hearing his new title he delayed action and the tiny glow from the embers went out.

Cody said, "Dad, you've got to blow when you first see the embers."

Sean started again and he soon had new embers. He immediately started blowing into the small hole.

Cody said, "Not so hard. Blow gently until you get some smoke."

After a minute, smoke started coming out of the side of the nest. The small amount of smoke quickly grew in volume.

"Okay, Dad. Blow really hard."

In less than a minute, flames erupted inside the nest. Sean rotated the nest, which caused the fire to spread, then he moved it to the kindling teepee and gently pushed the flaming mass inside.

Kelly stacked larger pieces of dry wood next to the teepee. She smiled and said, "Great job, you two. We'll be warm tonight."

"And about time," Sean said. "I froze my butt off last night."

Kelly said, "You only have that one shirt so I've been worried about that."

Sean leaned over and whispered, "I didn't know you cared."

Without answering, Kelly tended the fire and, then, she looked off into the wilderness.

During the next hour, they moved the fire to a spot a short distant from a rock wall. That way they could sleep by the wall and get warmth from both the fire and the reflected heat coming off the wall. They foraged and found a small amount of miner's lettuce and a bit of mountain sorrel. For the first time during their ordeal, they had a little food, and they had warmth.

Sean fell asleep, worrying about what obstacles awaited them.

CHAPTER 34

When Kelly awoke the following morning, the first thing she thought of was Sean's remark about her caring. She certainly did not care in the way he intended. The three of them were a team on a desperate mission that involved the most important thing of all—survival. They had to support one another. It was that simple. Leave it to a man to interpret her comments in an altogether different way. Furthermore, she was not about to look into those same blue eyes that had previously gotten her into trouble. She went back in time and realized that trouble was the wrong word. If it had not been for Sean, Cody would never have been born, and Cody was everything to her.

After the others got up, they foraged for food but found none. They did find some storm water in a rock depression, but it was not enough. They drank what little there was and began another day's journey. Kelly felt increasingly weak as she walked, the cumulative effect of extreme exertion without proper nutrition. She became acutely aware of the danger of dehydration, and she worried about finding safe water.

They made reasonable progress in the morning, but they all needed to rest more than usual in the afternoon. The ordeal, and time, were taking a serious toll. They made camp early and were able to start another fire, which was the only cheerful thing they experienced the whole day. Exhausted, they went to sleep without their normal evening chatter. Weakness and fatigue were taking an increasing toll on their bodies. Just before Kelly dozed off, she had only one thought: she had to get Cody to safety. She fell asleep and had a series of terrible dreams that woke her several times during a very cold night.

The next morning, they foraged with the same results as the previous day. They found nothing to eat, but they located a small amount of water trapped in a rock depression. The storm had been hard on them, but it proved to be a blessing because of the water it left behind.

An hour into their walk, Cody stopped next to a young pine tree. "Mom, Dad, I forgot. We can eat the inner bark of pine trees."

Kelly tilted her head, doubting what she had heard. "Are you sure?"

"Yes. I forgot. I'm sorry."

Sean put his arm around Cody. "It's okay. We've depended on you for a lot so far, and you've been a big help. Show us what to do."

Cody put his hand on the tree. "You need to cut a strip about four inches wide and maybe a foot long. We cut a groove all around and then remove the bark. Then we peel thin strips off the back and eat it. The part we want is between the bark and the wood." He removed his hand from the tree. "Oh, one more thing. We only want to do one strip per tree. Otherwise, the tree might not survive. One spot will heal, and there will just be a scar next year."

Hunger overcame any concerns about taste. They found several young trees and ate as much as they thought reasonable. They did not want to overeat because they had no idea what the inner bark might do to their systems. It would be a bad time to get sick. However, overconsumption would have been difficult as it was a tedious business.

After resting, Kelly led the way and Sean took up the rear. They felt certain their pursuer had given up, at least for now, but Sean decided he would act as rearguard on most days. He did not want to take chances, and he would not assume anything.

An hour later, Cody walked in front, looking for food as he often did. He came to a narrow space between a crevice and a thick stand of trees. He edged by the trees and suddenly yelled, "Bear!"

He turned so quickly he lost his balance and fell into the fissure.

Kelly started to scream, but she knew she had to maintain control. She looked down and saw that Cody had gotten up, and he seemed unhurt. Next, she looked toward the bear. The creature rose on its two hind feet and stared at her.

Sean moved next to her.

Cody called from the crevice. "Black bears usually don't charge so I shouldn't have turned so fast. Stand still and don't make any sudden moves."

Kelly had no experience at this sort of thing, so she heeded Cody's advice.

The standoff seemed to go on forever. The bear did not move and continued to stare at them. Kelly looked into the crevice and saw Cody trying to climb out but the sides were too steep. She looked back at the bear. Suddenly, the bear dropped to the ground and turned away. The creature moved several yards in the opposite direction; then, it turned, looked back, and grunted. Finally, the bear disappeared into the trees. Kelly and Sean stood still for a moment to make sure the bear was gone.

Kelly looked into the crevice, which appeared to be about twelve feet deep. "Are you hurt?"

"I twisted my ankle, but it's not too bad."

She turned to Sean. "How are we going to get him out of there?"

Sean rubbed his chin. "We'll figure something out."

Kelly said, "Why not make a ladder out of the limbs from downed trees?"

"We should be able to do that. I think the bear is gone but watch for him while I look around." Sean turned and went back the way they had come.

Ten minutes later, he reappeared dragging a large limb. He dropped it near the crevice and went back for more. It took some searching, but he managed to gather material suitable for a makeshift ladder; then, he began cutting branches to form steps.

After a good deal of difficulty, Sean lowered two poles with improvised steps. "Climb up as far as you can, then we'll drop your Mom's sweatshirt down for you grab. I'll pull you up from there."

Cody fell back on the first try but his second effort brought him within reach of the sweatshirt. Sean pulled him high enough so that he could grip his hand; then, he pulled him out of the ravine.

Cody looked toward where the bear had been. "He left?"

Kelly put her arms around his shoulder. "We did a stare down; then, he took off."

Sean said, "I'll bet he's never seen people before. I think he was just curious."

Cody brushed off his pants and said, "Black bears don't attack nearly as often as people think they do. At least, that's what they told us in scouts."

Sean asked, "How's your ankle? If it's not too bad, it's best to walk it off. If it's really serious, I'll carry you."

"Let me give it a try." Cody walked back and forth a few times and then said, "I'm okay. I just might be a little slower than usual."

They waited ten minutes to make sure the bear had left the area; then, they skirted the stand of trees and continued their journey. With little water and no food, they had to stop to rest often. By midafternoon, they had no choice but to stop and forage for anything edible. They found a little miner's lettuce, they dug up some roots; then, they stopped and ate what little they had. Finally, they trudged on, slowed considerably by hunger, thirst, fatigue, and weakness.

During a rest stop, they agreed they needed to take more risks for acquiring water. Desperation made their decision an easy one, so they agreed that Sean would go upstream on any small creek they encountered to fill the bottles. That source had been reliable once, but they knew their luck might change if they used water that had been tainted by an animal carcass, animal droppings, or naturally occurring, harmful bacteria. They would only try the river as a last resort. The possibility of getting sick seemed better than serious, life-threating dehydration.

Weak and weary, they found a good campsite and stopped for the day. Kelly and Cody foraged for food while Sean followed a small creek up the mountain to fill the bottles. They gathered back at their camp and shared the meager results of their efforts, which consisted of inner bark from pine trees, a few roots, and creek water. After their meal, they huddled together and slept in dreamless exhaustion.

The next morning, Sean refilled the water bottles; then, Kelly took the lead and followed the river. Their weak energy levels slowed their progress to a pitiful level. She took note of how everyone looked, and it worried her more than at any time during their ordeal. How much longer could they hold on?

After four hours of intermittent walking, Kelly fought her way through heavy brush, stopped, and put her hands on her hips. "More trouble, guys. Lots of it."

Sean and Cody came through the brush and looked at the mountainside before them. A huge landslide of debris and jagged rocks blocked access to the river.

Sean said, "It looks recent. I bet that thunderstorm weakened that slope and caused the slide." He looked up slope. "We need rest, but we can't afford to stop. I'm going up and see if there is any way we can safely cross."

Cody said, "Mom, can I go?"

"No, I think you should rest."

"Aw, Mom."

Sean put his hand on Cody's shoulder. "I can use another pair of eyes."

Kelly looked at the landslide. "Okay, but you two be careful." She sat down and watched father and son struggle against the mass of rock and dirt. An hour and a half later, she saw them come around some boulders and walk toward her. "What did you find?"

Sean pointed up the mountain. "You won't believe it. Follow us."

She tried to get more information, but they would not divulge their secret. Was it good news? After a difficult climb, they entered the only stand of trees that survived the slide. When they reached the other side of the trees, Kelly stopped and stared. Before her was a crude, ancient Indian ruin.

Sean stopped next to the rock wall. "This isn't like the ruins in the southwestern desert. As you can see, it is just a mass of stones piled against a natural recess in the rock wall. It's in really good shape considering how much time has passed. We can shelter here tonight but there's more. Follow me."

Kelly soon found herself inching along an ancient pathway that led above the slide. She stopped half way across and said, "This is amazing. I can almost feel the presence of the Native Americans who created this trail. I'll bet we are the only ones to use this path since they abandoned it so long ago." She looked down the mountain. "Does this trail lead to the river?"

Cody said, "We think so, Mom. We didn't follow it all the way but it seems to drop down on the other side of this rocky area."

"We'll find out tomorrow," Sean said. "Let's go back and get some rest."

They entered the ruin and found a few bits of pottery shard in one corner, and a piece of stone that had been worked to form a crude cutting instrument. After a short rest, they foraged and found several pinecones with edible nuts. They finished the last of their water and talked until sunset, then they turned in for the night, each processing visions of sharing the same space that unknown Indians had over the centuries. They went to sleep with hopeful hearts, praying that the old trail would take them over the slide and down to the river.

———

Kelly awoke a little before sunrise. She started to go back to sleep, but she noticed that Cody was unusually warm. Alarmed, she put her hand to his forehead and immediately knew he had a fever. She shook Sean. "Wake up. Cody has a fever." Sean came fully awake. "A fever? Are you sure?"

"Put your hand on his forehead."

He withdrew his hand and said, "You're right, but it doesn't seem too bad."

"I agree, but it's in the early stage so it could get much worse." She pulled Cody close. "I'm really worried."

"I wonder what caused it."

"There's no way of knowing, but he's young and he hasn't been getting proper nutrition. I suspect his immune system is weak due to the stress."

"It could be the water," Sean said.

"I thought of that but we drank the same water."

"Maybe our age and immune systems protected us. Hard to know, really." He rose and said, "Let's wait until he wakes up and, then, we'll see how he feels, but I don't think we should travel today."

"Will you build a fire?"

"Sure, but we don't want it too close to Cody. He's hot enough already."

Kelly held Cody close as she watched Sean gather the materials for the fire. Building a fire had become second nature to Sean, and he soon had a kindling teepee burning. He broke limbs and put the smaller pieces on the fire. After he had a small blaze going, he added larger limbs.

Kelly said, "He's waking up." She waited until he was fully awake and then said, "How do you feel?"

"I feel sick." He coughed and said, "My stomach hurts."

Sean walked over and stroked his hair. "No travel today. We'll take care of you."

Kelly knew they desperately needed to keep moving down the mountain, but Cody's condition changed everything.

Sean said, "I think we have to assume it's the water, and that he got sick because of the stress and lack of food." He picked up the two bottles and poured out what little water remained. "You take care of Cody. I'm going to search all over this mountain until I find a spring. I may be gone quite awhile." He put on Kelly's backpack and said, "I'll also look for food."

Sean went back in the direction they had come until he found a rocky area he remembered and, then, he turned and began to climb. He searched as he went, but he found no evidence of a spring. After climbing for half an hour, he went back in the direction of the Indian dwelling, but he was much higher. He suspected the Indian's built their shelter near water, but time may have depleted that source. After an hour, fatigue forced him to stop under a tree to rest. He knew he was expending much-needed energy, but he had no choice. He had to find good water for Cody, and he would stop at nothing short of his goal.

As he rested, he considered their dilemma and knew their situation had gone from critical to desperate. He was the strongest of the three, and he was determined to expend every bit of energy left in his body to help them survive. He thought of food, looked around, and decided to forage nearby. He rose and walked toward an open area and inspected the plentiful young growth he found. Several small plants showed promise so he got down on his knees, pulled out his knife, and dug for roots. He had no idea what plant

233

he had found, but the roots were more tender than others they had previously used. He worked on one plant; then, he moved to another. After thirty minutes, his backpack contained a considerable number of roots. He could only hope they were edible but, at this point, they had to take chances.

He tested the roots and found them easier to eat than he had expected. After consuming an amount he thought was safe, he renewed his search for water. He struggled over a craggy section of rock and stopped to rest. He had a great view of the mountain on the other side of the river, but he could also see the mountains downrange. It was a beautiful sight, but it reminded him of how small and remote his party of three was. Mother Earth was, indeed, spectacular, but she could also be deadly.

He was about to resume his search when he thought he heard something. He tilted his head and listened. Nothing. After a moment, he heard it again. A faint buzzing noise. He concentrated his vision in the direction of the noise and said, "Bees!" He saw two bees heading toward a rock wall. Another quickly followed.

He rose and walked in the direction the bees had taken. He started across a rocky area when he suddenly stopped. He tilted his head and heard what he thought was the faint sound of water cascading over rock. He hurried toward the sound, but he was blocked by a rocky spur. He went lower until he found a way around the outcropping. He worked higher and discovered a small rivulet of water coming down from the rocks. He climbed and found a small spring. Several bees lined the edge of the water.

He sat down, used the water to clean the bottles, and then he drank as much as he thought safe. He waited, and then he drank more. He could almost feel his tissues sucking up the much-needed water.

Feeling refreshed, Sean filled the bottles and started down the mountain. Twenty minutes later, he entered an area covered with thick brush. He swatted branches aside and suddenly stopped. He heard thrashing sounds that were too loud to be anything but a large animal. He snapped fully alert, every nerve at attention as he remembered the encounter with the bear. He hoped it might be a deer but a series of grunts told him otherwise; there was a bear foraging nearby.

He looked at the nearby trees and felt relieved that he was down wind of the bear. He stood still and hoped the bear would move on, but he worried that the animal might come in his direction. After a moment, the sounds stopped.

He waited.

After ten minutes, he started to move to one side but he heard the bear moving and it seemed to be coming in his direction. He turned and climbed as quietly as he could. After a short climb, he turned west. He could no longer hear the bear, but he was now in unfamiliar terrain and it worried him. He trudged along for nearly an hour until he came to a massive granite wall. After a thorough inspection, he knew his passage was blocked. He turned and retraced his steps, then he went lower for several minutes. He had no idea where he was and he began to worry about his delay in getting safe water to Cody.

He climbed onto a rock and tried to get his bearings. He scanned the area, but it took only a moment to realize the obvious—he was lost. If he had gone too far west he would have passed the Indian cave. He decided to go toward the river and look for a landmark he recognized. Travel was extremely difficult and it worried him greatly. He stared at the mountain on the other side of the river and thought about Cody. He had failed his son for eleven years, and he could not bear the thought of failing him again. He had to find his way back.

He climbed down from the rock and plodded on. The rugged terrain would not allow travel in a straight line, which only increased his fatigue. After half an hour, weakness forced him to rest. Sweat rolled off his forehead and he desperately wanted a drink of water, but Cody needed it more. He waited ten minutes, then he continued down the mountain. He soon realized that nothing about his surroundings was familiar. He must have passed the cave. He turned and moved upriver.

He was near panic when he rounded a rock formation and saw the landslide that had previously blocked their passage. A wave of relief flowed over him as he knew where he was. He began to climb. Thirty minutes later, he passed through the stand of trees near the slide and saw the Indian ruin.

Kelly was standing outside searching the mountain. He walked up and nearly fell. He held up the two bottles and said, "Spring fed."

Kelly said, "Thank God. I was really worried."

"I got lost."

"You look exhausted."

Sean nodded and entered the ruin. He saw that Cody was awake, but he looked very tired. "How is he?"

"About the same, but I think that's a good omen. If he had something really bad, he'd be getting worse by the hour."

He handed her a bottle. "Let him have a few sips to see if he can keep it down. I also have some edible roots, but we won't give them to him now. They're not exactly easy on the stomach."

The day seemed to move in slow motion. Kelly tended to Cody while Sean foraged for more food. When he returned, they had some miner's lettuce to add to the roots. Sean refused water because he had consumed a considerable amount at the spring. Kelly took a little water, but they gave most of it to Cody in small doses.

The next morning, they checked Cody and found only a slight fever. He felt weak, but they had to continue following the river down the mountain. Kelly handled the two backpacks and Sean carried Cody in piggyback fashion. Sean moved easily at first, but as the morning wore on, he felt an increasing burden. He nearly fell while rounding some rocks and had to pause before resuming. They made slow progress and stopped a little after noon.

Sean helped Cody settle under a tree and said, "How are you feeling?"

"Better, but I'm still pretty tired."

Kelly checked his forehead. "It looks like he may have had one of those twenty-four-hour bugs. His temperature is almost normal."

They rested, drank the rest of the water, and ate some of the foraged food.

At midday, they set off with Sean in the lead. They walked slowly and stopped often to avoid stressing Cody. The pathway was surprisingly good at first, then it became more treacherous where time and weather had taken a toll on the mountain slope. On the other side of the slide, the trail descended steeply and entered a thick forest. They came across a tiny creek, and Sean went upstream as far as he could and filled the bottles. They drank the water, then he went back upstream and refilled the bottles.

When travel became easier, Kelly led the way. When they were not far from the river, she rounded a bend, stopped, and pointed. "This looks really bad."

Sean moved next to her and surveyed the scene before them. A tranquil portion of the river, complete with a sandy bank on their side, was directly in front of them. A huge gorge with steep walls lay beyond that. Just over a hundred yards from where they stood, the river plunged over a mass of rocks and powered down a steep canyon. They inspected the cliff for an access point and did not like what they saw. The mountain loomed up with a mass of jagged rocks that looked impassable.

Sean started for the cliff. "I'm going to take a look."

Kelly watched Cody follow him, marveling at their interaction that seemed so natural.

Father and son took a closer look at the steep, saw-toothed wall and knew there was no way up. Disheartened, they went back to the ledge to join Kelly.

She stood looking at the river, a pensive expression on her face.

Sean said, "There's no way up."

She did not answer for a moment; then, she said, "I thought so, but I have an idea. We can start fires now, right?"

Sean nodded. "We still have some quartz in Cody's backpack and we could probably find more."

Kelly pointed, "See that sandy area? Why don't we start a fire down there and make an SOS on that little beach? There haven't been too many airplanes, but there have been a few."

"Great idea," Sean said. "That's the first decent sized beach we've had access to." He studied the riverbank. "We could write the SOS in the sand, but there's a better way. We can use boughs from trees and bushes to make the signal. I could trim them with the knife. That would stand out better."

Cody said, "We need two fires. That way we can attract more attention, and we won't have to worry about one going out."

"Good idea," Kelly said. "Let's go down and get started."

Sean and Cody hurried down to the beach and began picking the best spot for the SOS signal and the fire. Though weak and exhausted, Kelly could not help but smile at their enthusiasm and camaraderie.

When they stood on the small beach, they decided to do what they did best. Kelly would gather kindling, Cody would bring as many branches as possible, searching mostly for dry limbs on the ground, and Sean would cut and trim boughs from trees and larger bushes. Kelly finished her task and used a stick to mark where they would put the fires and the SOS signal.

Cody dragged in some bigger branches. "Mom, there's plenty of old wood about fifty yards up that slope."

She asked, "How are you feeling?"

"Better, but I'll need to rest when we finish."

Sean brought another load of boughs and dropped them on the beach. "I think we have enough. Let's see what we can do."

In less than an hour, they stood together and checked their work. Kelly said, "Good job, guys. Let's start that fire."

After Sean and Cody had two fires going, they used the trimmed boughs and made the signal, then they sat under a tree and waited. They wondered about their odds of success but there was simply no way of knowing. By late afternoon, all was quiet—too quiet.

"Mom," Cody said, "I'm really thirsty. I'd like to drink some water from the river, but I know it's dangerous."

Kelly looked at Sean. "What do you think?"

"If we don't get water soon we'll be in bad shape for sure, but I don't want to chance the river. I'm going back to that small creek we crossed this morning. The water seemed okay so I'll fill the bottles there." Sean spoke over his shoulder as he walked away. "I'll be awhile so keep a sharp eye out."

Nearly two hours later, Sean returned with two bottles of water. "I went all the way up to where the creek came over some rocks. I doubt that animals could taint it that high, but you never know."

Kelly said, "Let's drink half now and save the rest for later."

Sean handed her a bottle. "Makes sense, but I can always go back."

The rest of the day went by with only the sound of one airplane in the distance, but they never spotted the aircraft. That evening they ate what little they had foraged, which consisted of a few edible pine nuts, some mountain sorrel, and creek water. They turned in for the night, dealing with a combination of exhaustion and a new feeling of weakening resolve.

The next day, feeling debilitated, they went through the same routine. Kelly and Cody kept the two fires going while Sean went to fill the water bottles and forage for food. Thankfully, they felt no ill effects from the creek water, at least so far. Sean returned with water, some roots, and a little miner's lettuce.

The day dragged on in near silence under a bright sky. There was no wind, they were weak and tired, and no one felt like talking. They had settled in, expecting a long day, when Kelly jumped up. "Do you hear that hum?"

Sean rose and listened. After a moment he said, "It's a plane, but I can't see it yet."

Cody pointed and yelled. "Over there!"

They looked and saw a single engine plane going east above the mountains on the opposite side of the river. Quickly, they put green leaves and boughs on the fire to raise more smoke. The plane continued its flight path and went out of sight.

Kelly saw the dejection on Cody and Sean's faces. "It's okay, guys. There'll be another one."

A few minutes later, Cody pointed up the canyon. The plane they had seen had turned and descended, following the river toward them. They all started waving their shirts. As the plane neared their position, the pilot rocked its wings back and forth, and then continued down the canyon.

The jumping and hugging that followed was charged with extreme emotion that transformed them from the depths of hopelessness to a joyous high in a heartbeat of time. After a few moments of out-of-character dance moves, Kelly walked over to Cody and hugged him, her face changing expressions as tears ran down her cheeks. Her son would soon reach safety, and nothing else mattered.

———

Fifty-five minutes later, they heard the distinctive sound of helicopter blades churning through the air as they made their distinctive whup, whup sound. Presently, the rescue helicopter positioned itself above them, and then a crewmember descended on a hoist cable. They lifted Cody first and then Kelly. As she lifted off the ground, she looked down at Sean and could not help but notice that, even after their ordeal, and, with a good start on a beard, he was roguishly handsome. It bothered her that those old feelings had re-emerged, especially at a time like this. This would not do. She looked skyward and kept her attention on the helicopter.

When Sean was safely aboard, they flew to a hospital in Sonora for evaluation and any necessary treatment. While receiving IV liquids, Kelly turned on her phone and it rang within five minutes.

She answered.

She heard Sparky's excited voice, "Kelly! Oh, my God. Are you safe? Cody? Sean?"

"We're all okay, Sparky. We were just airlifted to a hospital in Sonora."

"Hold on a sec."

She heard Sparky shuffling papers.

A moment later he blurted out, "I'm in a motel about an hour away. Stay put; I want to hear everything."

"Don't worry; we probably won't be released for a few hours. Besides, we don't have a car."

CHAPTER 35

When Danny Fagan returned to his compound, he hoped for one thing. For him to be able to acquire Kelly Sanborn's priceless software, she had to return from her dangerous journey into the wilderness, and he had serious doubts about her chances. No roads accessed the wilderness area until far downriver, a distance too far for anyone not properly provisioned for such a difficult trek. There was nothing he could do but wait.

Over the next several days, he checked the news often, but there were no reports about Kelly Sanborn. He was about to give up hope when he saw a news flash on TV. Kelly Sanborn, her son, and a companion had been rescued by helicopter and were now in the hospital for observation.

Fagan picked up his landline phone and dialed Martin Scanlan. "I need to talk to you, and it has to be tonight." Before Scanlan could say anything, Fagan added. "I'll be there in two hours." He was not supposed to go to Martin Scanlan's home without specific instructions, but Fagan's anger had increased to a level that he no longer gave a fuck about adhering to orders. He hung up, went to his work shed, and put several items into his cargo van. Because of the high probability of numerous cameras in upscale Hillsborough, he used a stolen van with plates obtained from a junkyard.

He stopped for a burger and a double order of fries. Dirty jobs always called for grease on the stomach, and he meant to be prepared in case events turned in that direction. A little after ten o'clock, he pulled into Scanlan's driveway. Scanlan stood on the porch, hands on hips, obviously not a happy man. Tough shit.

Fagan brushed by Scanlan, ignoring his comments about never coming to the house. He went inside, turned and said, "This thing is huge, and you're paying me crap. I want a piece of the action."

Obviously taken aback, Scanlan was silent for a moment. Finally, he said, "Okay, I'll pay you a little more *if* we get the merchandise."

"Not good enough. I've seen how much the stock market tanked. That software called it perfectly, and I can extrapolate out in time. The software has the potential of making huge money. You know it, and I know it."

"It does seem to hold some promise."

"Don't bullshit me, man. It may not be the Holy Grail, but it's damn close. "Fagan's voice notched up. "It's worth a fortune, and you know it."

"You get the software, and I'll bump your pay."

Fagan's anger rose each time Scanlan opened his mouth. "You don't seem to understand. This is not a negotiation. I'll handle the software on a partnership basis. You just front the money."

Scanlan walked over to a wet bar and poured a drink from an open bottle, obviously not his first of the evening. "It's not going to work that way. Besides, you'll probably spend it on those fucking pigeons."

Fagan's dislike of Scanlan hardened to an evil hatred in the blink of an eye. The veins in his forehead pulsed with fury as his anger intensified. He reached behind his back, pulled out a Taser, pointed it at Scanlan, and pulled the trigger.

Scanlan dropped like a rock.

Fagan put on gloves, pulled a zip tie from his pocket, rolled Scanlan over and secured his hands behind his back. He went to his van, grabbed a small bag, and hurried back inside. He placed a hood over Scanlan's head; then, he dragged the shaking body to the elevator that descended to the shooting range housed in the basement.

When the elevator stopped, Scanlan started screaming.

Fagan ignored him, went back to the main floor and entered the garage. He found a small ladder, carried it to the elevator, and then he pushed the down button. In the middle of the shooting range, he climbed up the ladder and threw two ropes over a beam. He moved a chair to the center of the room, climbed up and cut one rope, which had a noose on the end. Satisfied with his makeshift gibbet, he grabbed the other rope, which had a large loop, and wrapped it around Scanlan's body under his arms. He then pulled hard on the looped rope and hoisted Scanlan into the air.

Scanlan yelled, "My, God. What are you doing?"

Fagan said nothing.

"We can work this out. I'll give you a percentage."

Fagan laughed. "I'm looking for one-hundred percent, asshole. You going to cough up that much?"

Fagan maneuvered Scanlan and told him that if he did not stand on the chair, he would be tased again.

"Wait, you can't—you can't do this. I'll give you anything you want. My God. Don't do this. This . . . this is inhumane."

DALE BRANDON

"You've looked down on me, and you said some bad shit about my pigeons, man. You shouldn't have done that."

Fagan removed the hood and slapped a piece of duct tape over Scanlan's mouth.

Scanlan jerked and uttered muffled sounds of agony.

Fagan cut the second rope he had used to hoist Scanlan, leaving only the rope with the noose around Scanlan's neck.

"This is for Oscar." He kicked the chair out from under Scanlan.

He went to the elevator, rode it to the main floor, checked for loose ends; then, he hurried to his van and drove away, careful to obey all traffic laws. It would have been easier to have put a bullet into Scanlan's head, but he wanted the condescending bastard to suffer.

He headed home, mulling a strategy to not only to acquire the software, but also to get Kelly Sanborn as well. He relished the thought of controlling her and her trading system in his remote compound. A grand slam.

246

CHAPTER 36

Kelly heard a commotion and knew Sparky was in the hospital hallway. Who else would make a ruckus like that? A few seconds later, he walked in followed by a Sheriff's Deputy and a Highway Patrol officer. His animated conversation with the two officers ceased the moment he saw Kelly. He quickened his step and went to her side. He hit the infusion pole and had to grab it to stabilize the IV bag.

"Sorry, I am just excited to see you're all safe." He saw Cody in the next bed and waved. "Hi, pardner."

He took Kelly's hand. "I want to hear all about it, but I think the gendarmes want to talk to you first." He looked around. "Where's Sean?"

"I think he's in the next room."

Sparky took a seat in the corner, obviously intent on hearing everything.

They brought Sean into the room and, over the next forty-five minutes, Kelly and Sean gave the officers a complete rundown, including a description of the two assailants. The officers were particularly interested in what happened at the cave. At the end of the interview, Kelly learned that the authorities contacted the rental companies and that her SUV and Sean's car had been located and towed.

After the officers left, Kelly gave Sparky additional details, knowing that she had no other choice. No summary for him, he demanded a blow-by-blow account.

When she finished, Sparky said, "Tell me more about the storm. It sounds like it may have saved your life by providing a new source of water."

"It did but it also drenched us. It was cold, but the lightning was spectacular."

Sparky spread his arms and said, "Eight million."

Sean tilted his head and looked at Kelly with an odd expression.

She said, "Okay, Sparky. Eight million what?"

"Lighting strikes the earth about eight million times a day. That's almost three billion a year."

Cody sat up. "Wow, I never would have guessed that much."

Kelly got back on subject. "The three of us worked together, but the two men were magnificent.

Cody beamed.

They talked for another hour and agreed that Sparky would drive them home. He started for the door, but turned and said, "By the way. I do a security check on your house a few times a day. I just walk around the outside to make sure there are no break-ins. You know that phone you had installed for your new business. Well, I could hear it ringing off the hook every time I went by one side of the house. Looks like you're in demand."

They left the hospital and were surprised to find TV vans and reporters waiting outside. They agreed to a short, group interview. The press spent most of their time with Kelly, but they also wanted to learn how Cody's Boy Scout training had contributed to their survival. Kelly stopped the interviews after fifteen minutes and they climbed into Sparky's car.

———

The first day home was a day of rest contrasted with an increased sense of vigilance. It was an odd mix, but they knew they had to be alert. Kelly agreed to have Sparky and Sean visit often, for security reasons, but she told Sparky that he had to accompany Sean whenever he came to the house. Their ordeal had not changed her feelings about Sean; at least, that is what she kept telling herself.

She had obtained the phone number of the airplane pilot who spotted them on the riverbank. She called and thanked him profusely. The pilot said that he and his wife were flying to Salt Lake City to visit his mother and that he just happened to look down at the right time—pure luck. Before hanging up, she told him they all wanted to meet him when his schedule permitted, and she mentioned that her son would love to see his airplane.

A little before noon, while sipping a cup of tea, she heard pounding on the door. Sparky yelled something as he alternately knocked and rang the bell. She opened the door and Sparky and Sean rushed in.

Sparky waved his arms dramatically. "Have you heard the news?"

"No, I'm resting today. No work, no news. Everything can wait until tomorrow. I even turned off the ringer on my business phone."

"Huge news. Martin Scanlan has been murdered!"

"Oh, my God." She stood motionless, stunned.

Sean said, "And that's not all. The guy you debated on television filed for bankruptcy."

"Hudson Treffinger?"

"Yep, he's wiped out."

Kelly struggled to process the information. She reached into a bowl and retrieved a chocolate truffle. "I need to sit down."

"We all do," Sparky said. "I like the part about your TV buddy. The pompous SOB deserved it." He climbed onto a chair. "Evidently, he was leveraged to the hilt."

After the two declarations, everyone sat quietly for a moment, each pondering the news in their own way. Finally, Kelly said, "You know, I have been wondering about something, and this just adds to my thoughts. Martin Scanlan *knew* I was coming up that mountain highway, and he knew when. At first, it seemed improbable that he had played a part in the ambush—too farfetched, but the more I think about it the more it makes sense."

Sean said, "It all fits, actually. If you disappeared, no one would suspect him. There would be no reason to especially since he had a lot of people at that conference."

Sparky held up a finger. "You're onto something, guys. That cat was dirty. He wanted your software."

"That's possible," Kelly said. "But what about the guy who broke into our house and chased us in the mountains? How does he fit in?"

"They must have been working together," Sean said.

Kelly said, "I guess Scanlan might have hired the guy."

Sparky shook his head. "It's not like there's a Rent a Thug Store on every corner. It seems like an odd mix to me."

"You may be right," Kelly said. "But I don't see any other explanation." She paused as she considered the possibilities and then said, "Okay, let's suppose the guy was hired. Does that mean he'll stop because his paycheck has been eliminated?"

"That would be the logical assumption," Sean said, "but we need to be careful. Because of Scanlan's death, I'd put the odds of this ending now at seventy-five percent, but what about the other twenty-five percent? There's too much at stake so we have to assume a worst-case scenario. And we know one thing about that gunman: he's evil right down to his core."

Sparky nodded. "He's right. We have to keep our guard up." He looked at Sean. "Do you have any experience with guns?"

"Well, I shot some as a teenager, but that was a long time ago."

Sparky pounced. "Evidently, that's not all you shot when you were a teenager."

"Sparky!"

"Sorry, Kelly. I couldn't help myself."

She shook her head and looked out the window. Sparky, as usual, had a quick mind.

Sparky grimaced at his faux pas and then said, "I saw a man gunned down during a street robbery about twenty years ago. I went out and bought a pistol the very next day. Since then, I've been going to a shooting range three or four times a year just to stay sharp. I've acquired four guns over the years. Top-notch stuff. I think Sean should have a weapon, and I'd be happy to supply a pistol and take him to the range. It wouldn't take long to get comfortable and reasonably proficient." He looked at Kelly. "That offer extends to you. What do you think?"

She realized she was about to venture into a new world she had no desire to visit. Yet, he was right. They had to be prepared for whatever might happen, and she had to protect Cody at any cost. "Okay, Sparky. You supply the guns and show us how to use them, but I don't want you two going off to the range without us. We're going with you."

They set a date to visit the shooting range and then Sean asked, "Where's Cody?"

"I told him we were staying in all day so he's in his room reading. I've never seen him so tired. But don't worry, he'll be his usual chipper self tomorrow. He's a resilient kid."

"I'm going to buy a new car today," Sean said. "Can he come along?"

Kelly hesitated, not sure how to respond, and then she said, "We need to rest today. If you wait until tomorrow, the four of us will go. We agreed to work as a team for a while. Safety first."

Sean smiled, "Sort of like a family outing."

Kelly wondered if she had made a mistake. Had he taken her comment the wrong way? She countered in a firm voice, "No. Safety in numbers. Nothing more."

CHAPTER 37

The following morning, Kelly made a phone call and turned on her computer. She opened Skype and sent a request to Miyako. Within seconds, Miyako appeared on the screen with a big smile. Kelly said, "You look good. How do you feel?"

"I'm doing really well, better than I expected. I don't have to go back to the doctor for three months."

"That's wonderful. I was worried."

"Thanks, but everything is good. My mother is delighted I moved up here. She's having mobility problems so I'm going to stay and help her."

"I want you to. You can work remotely when needed, and I'll stick to our agreement as I promised." Kelly spent the next twenty-five minutes answering questions about their ordeal in the mountains; then, she signed off and leaned back in her chair. Her conversation removed one burden of worry as it appeared Miyako would suffer no long-term effects.

It was time to go to work. She had previously published a simple, one-page website, which included an overview of her services and contact information. She intended to expand the site as time permitted. She pushed a button on the wired business phone that turned on the ringer. Four minutes later, the phone rang.

"Kelly, this is Emmett Crittenden. First, I want to apologize for my behavior."

She said nothing.

"We want you back at Boucher and Crittenden. We are prepared to offer you a huge increase in pay and a private office with your own secretary. We'll give you time to settle in, and then, we'll start a massive promotion about you and your software. It'll be really special."

Again, she said nothing. Leave the bastard hanging.

"Kelly, are you there?"

"Yes, I'm here. I have a three-word answer for you, Emmett. Go fuck yourself." She hung up and smiled. Her response was completely out of character and cruder than anything she had ever told anyone, but it seemed more than appropriate. After all, he received the response he deserved.

She checked the S&P and found that the market's plunge had temporarily halted in a weak support zone. She inserted her flash drive and ran Cyberstar. As expected, the market's sell signal remained intact, although the software suggested that the market had probably entered a short-term consolidation zone. She ran some numbers and estimated the probability of further declines at seventy-five percent.

Next, she worked on a business plan, noting that she would need more working capital over the next few months than she had expected. There would be a rough patch, but she fully expected substantial revenue growth after the initial startup. She had expected a check from Martin Scanlan, but it had not been in the stack of mail after her return. Now, with his death, she might never receive the much-needed income. How was she going to get by?

She went online to check the market and realized she had not used her software for anything but the stock market. Futures trading offered dozens of opportunities in a wide array of trading vehicles including metals, energy, agriculture products, and currencies. She ran Cyberstar on selected futures contracts and discovered that the software had given a buy signal on gold three days after it had given the sell signal on the stock market. Shortly after the signal, gold rallied and a solid uptrend followed. This was not surprising as gold historically rallied when stocks plunged. Still, it was further validation for Cyberstar.

She ran other futures contracts and found that crude oil appeared to be on the verge of giving a buy signal. Oil had been in a bear market for two years and the chart pattern revealed a double bottom with weakening downside momentum indicators. Oil futures had plenty of room for a solid advance. She wanted to act if the software gave a signal but, how could she?

She had put in two hours when the doorbell rang. She knew it was probably Sparky because he and Sean had set up a schedule to check on her and Cody several times a day. She opened the door, and he handed her four large, ripe apricots.

He stepped inside. "Organic, very good stuff."

She took the fruit.

"It's been double washed. Fruits and vegetables with deep, vivid colors are extremely beneficial for your health. You should eat some every day."

"Thanks, we could have used these in the mountains."

"I think you did pretty well considering you had no provisions when you started." He walked in and took a seat. "Actually, I'm here on a serious mission." He made eye contact. "Don't be offended, but I couldn't help but notice a big change in you since you left the hospital. You've been sneaking glances at Sean, and I'm not talking about an occasional peek. I have a strong feeling something happened between you two in the mountains."

"Good grief, Sparky. Nothing happened, nothing at all. We worked together to survive. We were a team, but that was all."

"So why are you sneaking peeks at him every chance you get?"

She broke eye contact and said, "I'm not sneaking peeks at anyone."

"Kelly, you have always been an extremely honest person. That's one of the reasons I like you so much. But you are telling a little fib now."

"He . . . he's around all of the time now, so I guess a person will look occasionally." My God, she thought. How weak was that? Sparky is too sharp for such an answer.

"You're going to stick with that?"

"Well, I admire how he interacts with Cody. They've developed a special bond, so I take notice of things like that."

"That's not all you're taking notice of."

"Sparky! Are you going to badger me about this?"

"Nope, just making observations. I think something pretty interesting is going on in that wonderful head of yours."

She lifted her chin and said nothing.

"Did you know he has five by seven pictures of you and Cody on the dresser in his bedroom?

"Well, we went through a rough time together. That explains the pictures."

"I'm not so sure about that. He also has that lock of your hair pinned to the mirror frame above your picture."

This last bit of information tugged at her heart in a way that made a suitable response impossible. She remained silent, deep in thought.

Sparky seemed to sense a change in her comportment and said, "I've got a question for you. Do you think about him when you first wake up?"

She spun a ring on her finger. "Um, no. Of course not. No, I don't."

"Yes, you do. I can tell." He rose and said, "I'll leave you alone to ponder your thoughts."

She knew there was no way to avoid what might come next, so she folded her arms and waited to hear what this marvelous little man had to say.

He said, "Infatuation goes to sleep at night. Love does not. I think you're falling in love."

She sat speechless for a long moment, unable to respond. Then she said, "He deserted me, Sparky. I can never forget that. Too much damage, too much time."

"Looking backwards won't solve anything."

They sat in silence, each processing words and feelings.

Sparky said, "I'll leave you with one last thought." He held eye contact. "The road to happiness goes through forgiveness." He headed for the door. "You need to make that journey."

She sat still for several minutes, staring out the window, seeing nothing, while she evaluated what Sparky had said. The phone rang, and she turned off the ringer. She needed to give herself a break from thoughts of Sean. She turned on her favorite FM station, eased back in her chair, and tried to relax. She closed her eyes and concentrated on the music. When the third song started, she jumped up and switched off the radio. How was it possible that Elton John's "Blue Eyes" came on at that precise moment? It was all too much.

Sparky's profound comments had unsettled her so much that she changed her schedule. Instead of working, she spent time with Cody; then, she dusted and vacuumed the entire house. Next, she organized one side of the garage. She was avoiding the issue, and she knew it. The problem was that Sparky was wise, intuitive, and she had always trusted his counsel.

At three o'clock, Sparky and Sean showed up at her front door as previously arranged. They had scheduled a visit to a car dealer followed by an early dinner out. They felt safer with each passing hour, but they had agreed there was still a possibility of danger. Martin Scanlan might not be the only person seeking to steal the software. They also worried that the dangerous threat voiced by the man chasing them in the mountains might come true. They intended to stick together for any trips away from the house, at least for now.

Sparky walked in and said, "Have you given some thought to what I said this morning?"

"No, no I haven't."

Sparky did not press the issue. He said, "Sean and I have a proposition for you."

She tilted her head and wondered what they had planned.

Sean said, "We believe in your software, and we also know you're tight on funds. We want to help."

"What do you have in mind?"

Sparky said, "We want to supply funding for a small percentage of your company. That way you won't have to worry about paying your bills, and you can concentrate on your business. We want a fair arrangement for all parties but especially for you. After all, you're the one who did all of the work."

Sean said, "We're both prepared to give you one hundred thousand dollars for seven percent each. That way you'll still own eighty-six percent of the business, but that's not all. Instead of buying one car today, we'll buy two. You pick out what you want, and you can drive it home. And you need new computers—fast computers with large, multiple monitors. We'll take care of the cost of these items, and they won't be deducted from the two hundred thousand seed money."

"This last part is up to you," Sparky said, "but we think you should consider putting roughly thirty percent of the funds into an online trading account and use your software to trade when you get signals. You're the boss so that is only a suggestion."

Stunned by the offer she found no words. Finally, she said, "Gentlemen, I don't know what to say."

"That's easy," Sparky said. "Say yes."

She jumped up and ran toward the hallway. "I can't wait to tell Cody we're getting a new car. He'll be thrilled!"

Sean and Sparky smiled at each other and shook hands. It was a good day, especially for Kelly and Cody.

CHAPTER 38

After purchasing identical SUVs, except for the color, Sean and Sparky followed Kelly home. As soon as the car stopped, Cody began an inspection that included every nook and cranny of the new SUV, paying special attention to how the rear seats folded down to increase the cargo space. When Cody finished, he ran to Kelly, grabbed her hand, and then gave her a guided tour of the car's special features.

Sean watched with a fatherly glow that included feelings he had never experienced before. He realized there was a gratifying depth to fatherhood he never imagined. After watching Cody, he glanced at Kelly. Everything was progressing better than he had expected except for his relationship with her, although he felt something had happened in the mountains. The problem was that if something did happen, Kelly had not dropped her guard. He caught her looking at him several times and that pleased him, especially since he felt sure the looks were quite different from those he noticed before the ordeal in the mountains.

He was in love with Kelly, and he had been contemplating a plan designed to crumble her defenses, which he suspected disguised her true feelings. While he watched her and Cody inspecting their new car, he decided to take a risk, but he needed help. He walked over to Sparky, who was sitting on his usual spot on the front step, and sat down.

"Sparky, I need your help."

"I take it this involves Kelly."

"You're a wise man." He glanced toward Kelly. "Here's what I want to do." He outlined the plan as Sparky alternated between smiles and nods.

Sparky took a long swig of water and said, "Very unique. If that doesn't do the trick, nothing will. Tell me what you want me to do."

"Okay, here's what we need. First, we need good weather: absolutely no fog. I also need you to make the invitation without her knowing I'm involved, and I need you and Cody to drive her to the location. She may protest, but I've seen you in action. I know you can persuade her to go.

"I'll work with you, and I'll give you a suggestion. Place a small bowl on the table with some chocolate truffles. You'll score major points with that."

———

Sparky was nearly as excited as Sean when the day arrived. It took some serious arm-twisting, but the fact that Cody was going along saved the day. Kelly protested when she learned she would have to get up before dawn, but that was not his only obstacle. He had to use all his available skills to make her agree to dress as if she were going out to dinner at such an unusual hour, and he had to overcome another protest. Why did she need to take a warm coat?

Three days later, they had a perfect weather forecast. Sparky knocked on her front door forty-five minutes before sunrise. Kelly looked stunning, but he said nothing because he did not trust himself to keep the destination secret.

A few blocks from home, she said, "We're not headed toward town, so I haven't the faintest idea what you're up to."

He said nothing.

She said, "Where's Sean?"

"Oh, he's still in bed. We drank a little wine last night."

Twenty minutes later, with the pinkish horizon giving way to the first rays from the sun, he pulled into a parking area near the beach.

She leaned to one side, stared into the partial darkness, and said, "What is that?"

Without saying a word, Sparky got out of his car, went to the other side and opened the door. "That," he said, "is a horse drawn carriage."

She stopped in mid-step. "Sparky!"

Cody chimed in. "What a great looking horse."

"Don't worry about us," Sparky said. "I have whole wheat bagels, water, fruit, and a magnetic chessboard."

Cody said, "We'll be fine, Mom."

Sparky said, "Remember that journey I said you needed to take. Well, now is the time but it's up to you. You are the only one who can make the decision."

As the light began to flow onto the beach, Kelly saw Sean, standing, looking in her direction, dressed in black-tie. She saw a small white trailer and a waiter standing next to a table covered with white linen. A single rose in a bud vase and a bottle of champagne added a touch of elegance to the table.

She hesitated for a long moment; then, she took the hand offered by the carriage driver, climbed up, and sat down. How could she refuse?

As the carriage moved away, Sparky said, "He's in love with you."

———

The sunrise breakfast lasted an hour and a half, and the weather was perfect with only a slight ocean breeze. When Kelly returned home, she sat in a chair in total silence, reliving her incredible experience at the beach. After the first few minutes, without realizing it, she had let her guard down, and they became comfortable. A glass of champagne altered their mood, and they had more fun than she thought possible. Sean entertained her, but he did not touch her, not even her hand. He seemed to have decided previously to refrain from pressure of any kind. He remained a gentleman, in a dashing way, and he made her laugh frequently. She couldn't wait to see the pictures the waiter had taken. Sitting in her chair, she knew the carriage ride and the incredible breakfast had been etched into her memory forever.

She had learned something about Sean in the mountains; he was a completely different person than the boy she knew in her teens. She remembered that, even as a teen, he had been an exceptional kisser, seemingly a natural-born ability, because he had been too young to have much experience. Time must have made him even better, and he still had that lock of hair she had given him so many years ago. She felt a rush of excitement, which expanded, despite her effort to remain on an even keel. She told herself that she needed her mind to be her guide, not her heart. She wondered whether she could. After he took her home, he did not attempt to kiss her; he politely excused himself and left.

————————

Even though they all thought they were probably safe because of Martin Scanlan's death, they could not be sure. To insure their safety, they developed a security routine they had used since arriving home from the mountains. Several times a day, Sean and Sparky would rotate visits for protective reasons. Today, however, Sparky made all the visits. Why was that, she wondered? After the attention Sean had given her that morning, he disappeared. Was he just giving her time and space, or was he purposely wanting her to wonder about his absence? She had no way of knowing, but each time the doorbell rang, she rushed to the door.

On the last scheduled daily visit, she opened the door and Sean stepped inside.

She felt a surge of energy and struggled for words. Why was she so nervous?

After making sure everything was okay, he started to leave.

She said, "Where are you going?"

"Back to Sparky's house."

"No, you're not. You're spending the night."

He stopped and turned. "I wasn't expecting that."

"Neither was I."

He looked at her in a way she had never seen before.

He took a step toward her and said, "You have never looked as beautiful as you do at this very moment. Your hair, your skin, your eyes. I want to hold you and never let go." He paused and said, "I love you."

The words hung suspended in the space between them and then, in a single stroke, her last defenses collapsed, and she felt a sudden flush of desire course through her body.

He closed the distance between them; then, he took her hands in his and leaned forward.

Their kiss was long and soft as they lost themselves in a warm, sensual world.

CHAPTER 39

If Danny Fagan controlled his anger, he was a patient man. Experience and observation had taught him that haste led to mistakes and, in his business, he could not afford to make mistakes. Take the extra time to plan and to work smart—it was the only way.

Although he intended to follow his rules, he had made one mistake. Rage had blinded him when he killed Martin Scanlan, which caused him to act before he collected monies due. Because of that, he took on two security camera jobs to boost his income. That was okay because he wanted Kelly Sanborn to relax; he wanted her to think she was safe because Scanlan was dead. He had guessed that she had made the connection between Scanlan and the attempted kidnapping in the mountains.

He also needed to spend time on the final phase of his prepper cave. He had recently finished the thick, concrete wall over the entrance and he just needed to secure the metal door. The other items on his checklist were minor, mostly stocking the cave with provisions, adjusting the lighting, and installing cameras. He expected to finish in three days; then, he felt he would ready for whatever this lopsided world might throw in his direction. Moreover, he had other nefarious ideas for the use of his cave. He smiled at the thought.

Everyone has habits and patterns, and he intended to stalk Kelly Sanborn and find her weakness. He would use multiple vehicles so that she did not see the same car or van and become suspicious. He intended to rotate with Rick to reduce the odds of detection while he searched for Kelly's vulnerabilities.

———————

Four days later, Fagan finished his prepper cave, completed a contract job, and then he arranged a meeting with Rick. He wanted another cargo van for his plan to snatch Kelly and her software. A little after midnight, he met Rick on Skyline Boulevard; then, they drove to highway 17, which they followed down the mountain. They stole a van in San Jose, changed the plates, and then drove back to Skyline Boulevard where they separated. As usual, they both wore gloves whenever they touched or drove a stolen vehicle.

The next day, Fagan initiated his action plan. He put fake signs on the van's doors, then he drove to Half Moon Bay, turned on Water Street, and cruised by Kelly's house. He noted the new SUV in the driveway and wondered how she could afford a new car. Her software must already be paying dividends. He reached the dead-end, turned, and stopped. He was far enough away to go undetected but, with binoculars, he could easily watch any activity at the house.

For the next several days, he alternated with Rick and discovered a troubling pattern; Kelly Sanborn never went anywhere alone. One or two men accompanied her and her son every time she left the house. Furthermore, all the trips were local, another surprise. He went back to his compound and arranged for Rick to continue the surveillance.

It did not take him long to realize he needed to change plans. He decided to target Kelly's weakest point—her son.

CHAPTER 40

Because of her new relationship with Sean, Kelly decided to keep her business phone on voicemail for a few days. Things had changed, and she no longer needed to worry about paying the bills, but the main reason for her decision was Sean. She had fallen deeply in love, and she was enjoying life like never before. The house overflowed with joy and smiling faces, especially from Cody, who obviously loved being part of a complete family unit. She did not want to dilute such a special time in her life. Some things are just too precious, and they come too infrequently—she wanted to grab them, pull them close, and hold on.

However, she needed to manage her position in crude oil futures. She had gone long on several contracts, and she needed to follow that market closely for the first few days. On the second day, oil broke a downtrend line and rallied more than two dollars a barrel, which was a sizeable move because of the leverage inherent in futures. She placed a "good till canceled" (GTC) stop order to lock in her profit. She wanted to protect her position, because oil was a volatile market that traded 24/7 around the world. The stops allowed her to sleep without worrying about overnight news that might trigger large price swings.

She checked her messages a few times a day and responded as needed, but she took special note of a call from New York. Chase Logan, the founder of the Triple Tier Partners hedge fund, left an urgent message requesting a call back on one of his private lines.

She picked up the phone and dialed his number.

"Mr. Logan, this is Kelly Sanborn, returning your call."

"Oh, yes. Hold on a moment."

After four minutes, Kelly decided to wait exactly one more minute before hanging up.

The phone clicked. "Kelly, we're interested in buying your software and we'd like you to fly to New York tomorrow to discuss the details."

"Thank you for your interest, but I can't come to New York, especially on such short notice."

"Where are you located?"

"Half Moon Bay. That's about thirty miles south of San Francisco."

"Normally, I would make you come here but I have to go to LA next week so I could meet you at a hotel near the airport."

"Actually, I'm not looking to sell the software."

"We'd be doing you a big favor. Let's pick a day."

Kelly did not like Logan's style, but it would not hurt to hear what he had to say. She said, "Until further notice, my office is in my home. If you want to discuss the software you will have to come here. Otherwise, I'm not interested."

"That's rather odd."

"I have some issues I'm dealing with so that's the best I can do."

He checked his calendar and said, "Thursday is the only day that will work for me. Will that fit your schedule?"

"What time?"

"Four o'clock."

She gave him the address, hung up, and wondered if she had done the right thing. He came across as abrasive, but she could tell he was busy. He may have just been having a stressful day. She had not really thought about a sale, but a hedge fund might throw a ton of money at her. Why not entertain his offer? She had nothing to lose.

She leaned back and considered their options for the meeting. They had previously decided that Sparky would act as her part-time business manager, and Sean would handle security and act as an adviser. His impressive performance during their recent visit to a shooting range made his new position an easy choice. Hopefully, the decision to remain vigilant was an overreaction and not really necessary. Yet, they knew better than to assume anything, especially given the relentless nature of the gunman who chased them in the mountains. They did not know the man's connection with Scanlan, but they had seen his malevolent behavior and that was enough to engender caution.

She thought about Logan meeting Sparky for the first time and smiled. He would almost certainly misjudge Sparky's intellectual prowess. Sparky was often what cowboys of the old west called "salty," but he had a heart of gold—an eclectic mix.

She met with Sparky and Sean Thursday morning to set parameters for their meeting with Chase Logan. They arranged a table and brought in extra chairs for the meeting. Kelly and Sparky would sit at the table with Logan, and Sean would be in the room, but he would sit off to the side as an observer. He would be a few feet away if they needed his counsel.

They agreed that the software would only be sold under extreme circumstances, which meant an offer that was simply too good to refuse. They also set a minimum base amount necessary for producing a sale.

———

Chase Logan's limousine arrived fifty minutes late. He exited the car and extended his hand to a tall blonde who had dressed as if she expected to walk down a runway in front of dozens of cameras. The stiletto heels looked completely out of place for the location. Logan glanced at the neighborhood in a dismissive manner, then he shook hands with Kelly but he offered no apology for his late arrival.

She escorted him into the house and made the introductions.

The blonde stayed outside smoking a cigarette.

After they were seated, Kelly introduced Mr. Valentine as her business manager.

Logan said, "This is your business manager?"

Kelly ignored his tone and said, "Shall we begin?"

Logan said, "I don't have much time, so I want to get to the offer as soon as we can, but, first, I need to know how the software works."

She opened her purse and pulled out a flash drive. "The program is resident on this USB storage device." She opened a folder and removed several sheets of paper. "Here are some screenshots." She slid one across the table. "This is the day we received the sell signal. You'll notice the two lines crossing zero. That triggered the signal. It requires very little hands-on after that. You just do what the software tells you to do." She slid two more sheets across the table. "These are other signals the software gave.

You can see that a gold position would have resulted in a large profit. The oil signal is new, but it shows a nice gain so far."

Logan studied the screenshots.

Kelly continued, "In the off chance you purchase the software, we'll give you the code and detailed instructions on how to run the program. We'll follow that up with six months of technical support."

"Sounds pretty simple."

Kelly said, "Running the program is simple; writing the code was not."

He opened a portfolio and pulled out a sheet of paper. He jotted down a number and slid the paper across the table.

She glanced at the figure and felt slighted by the offer of $400,000. She looked at Sparky and knew he felt the same. She said, "You do realize that if you had owned this software a few weeks ago, you could have made a hundred times that amount in a matter of days."

Logan started to answer, but Sparky cut him off. "Mr. Logan, we didn't just fall off a turnip truck. If you can't extend a fair offer, this meeting is adjourned."

Logan's eyes narrowed. "Okay, I'll double the offer."

Kelly said, "First, you put me on hold for five minutes, then, you wanted me in New York with a one-day notice, next, you arrived here fifty minutes late with no apology, and then you acted in a rude and condescending manner. Your behavior is extremely rude and unacceptable. Good day, Mr. Logan."

Logan rose and said, "This whole thing is a fucking amateur hour, and you're a bunch of idiots."

Sparky said, "Telephone pole."

Logan said, "What the hell does that mean?"

DALE BRANDON

Sparky climbed off his chair and said, "It means why you don't take a flying fuck at a telephone pole."

Logan lunged and shoved Sparky so hard he hit his head on the wall and fell in a heap.

A heartbeat after Sparky hit the floor, Sean bolted from his chair and slammed a right cross to Logan's face. Chase Logan landed on his back and brought a hand to his face. Copious amounts of blood spurted from his nose and splattered his expensive suit.

Logan rose in a wobbly manner and yelled, "You're gonna pay for this"

Sean shoved him toward the door and said, "Get out. Now!"

Logan staggered out the front door and fell over the blonde sitting on the step, knocking them both to the ground.

She saw his face and started laughing.

He slapped her.

Sean rushed forward and helped the woman to her feet. He looked at Logan and said, "Get out of here, or I'm going to beat you to a pulp."

Logan put a handkerchief over his nose, rushed past his chauffeur, and got into the back seat. He glared out the window.

Sparky give him the finger.

———

Chase Logan canceled his L.A. trip and headed for the town's medical clinic. After treatment for a broken nose, he climbed into his car, pulled out his phone, and called a contact in New York. "This is Chase. I want you to send two men to Half Moon Bay, California in a few days. I'll give you more details later, but I want them to break into a house, in the middle of the night, and grab a

274

flash drive and a computer. Tell them to do whatever is necessary to get that drive. I also want them to make the guy in the house wish he had never been born. One more thing—make damn sure they break his fucking nose."

CHAPTER 41

Kelly was not about to let the confrontation with Chase Logan alter the extraordinary atmosphere that had enveloped her household. The addition of Sean added an important element that had been missing. She now had a friend and a lover, Cody had a father figure to rely on, and the presence of Sean enriched their daily lives more than she could have imagined. She felt grateful for Sparky's wisdom that guided her toward the path of forgiveness, and she promised herself she would not go back in time. She understood that opening old wounds produced hurtful and counterproductive thoughts. Forgiveness was hard, but it opened an amazing new world.

She especially loved to wake in the morning, lie on her side, and look into Sean's eyes before the start of a new day. She became very adept at convincing him to stay in bed longer than he had planned. They had to use good judgement when making love, but the fact that Cody's bedroom was two doors away made this easier. They slept so close to each other that they often made love in the middle of the night. Neither party complained.

Because of her struggles over the past two years, her experience in the mountains, and the changes at home, she decided to delay her new business venture for more than a few days. They needed rest, and they wanted to spend time enjoying their new family relationships. She would continue to monitor her position in crude oil futures but other business could wait.

She left her desk and went into the kitchen to unload the dishwasher. She stopped at the window and looked toward Sparky's backyard. Sean and Cody had gone over to help Sparky with his garden, but obviously they had other ideas. Gardening tools had been pushed aside, they had formed a triangle, and they were playing catch. What warmed Kelly's heart was the obvious camaraderie they shared. They were laughing, joking, and having a great time. She smiled as she experienced a level of joy unknown to her before this moment.

Four days later, an intense dream awakened Kelly a little after three AM. She got up and went to the bathroom. Just as she was about to head back to bed, she thought she heard a car slow and stop. Because there was almost never any late-night activity on her dead-end street, she went to the front room and peered out. She saw two men, dressed in dark clothes, exit the car, and start toward the side of her house.

She rushed into the bedroom and shook Sean. "Wake up! There are two men going around to the back of the house."

Sean bolted out of bed. "Quick. Get your gun and bring Cody in here. Call 911, then get in the closet and have him sit in the corner. If they get past me, shoot the bastards."

She opened the drawer on her nightstand, retrieved her pistol, and ran out of the room.

Sean reached under the bed, grabbed his Glock, and chambered a shell. He headed for the kitchen and looked outside. Nothing. He crouched behind the island in the middle of the room and looked toward the back door.

He waited.

A few minutes went by and, then, he heard a noise at the door that sounded like someone picking the lock. The intruders made very little noise as they opened the back door. Sean saw nothing for a moment; then, the first gunman eased into the utility room that led to the kitchen. A second man followed. Both were visible due to the faint light cast from a night light above the washing machine.

Sean held his gun with both hands on top of the counter, his finger on the trigger.

Pistol in hand, the first man entered the kitchen.

Sean yelled, "Drop it or I'll shoot." Muzzle flashes lit up the room and four bullets whizzed over Sean's head and slammed into the wall. He fired three shots at the center of the man's chest; then, he slid two feet to his right. The gunman collapsed.

The second man dropped behind the washing machine and fired toward the location of Sean's pistol flashes.

Sean sent two shots just above the washer that struck a wall.

They traded several shots and then the gunman crawled out the door. He fired two shots into the kitchen and disappeared.

Sean rose cautiously, and then he moved toward the back door, gun at the ready. He peered outside and saw nothing. He stepped out.

He heard two pistol shots followed by the roar of a shotgun.

He ran to the corner, stopped, and looked toward the front yard. Two houses away, a street light illuminated the yard enough for him to see a man lying on the ground screaming and grabbing his groin.

Sparky yelled, "At the corner of the house. Is that you, Sean?"

"Yeah, it's me"

"Sparky said, "Everyone all right?"

"Yes, they're safe."

Sparky took a few steps into the yard. "I really nailed that sucker. I didn't want to kill him so I gave him some buckshot right in the balls."

"Ouch. No wonder he's gone fetal."

"He put a couple of bullet holes in my door so I put some buckshot in his privates."

Sean winced at the thought; then, he went around the corner and walked carefully toward the man on the ground, who was curled in a ball, moaning. Sean picked up the thug's gun and stood guard over him. He said, "Kelly called 911. The other guy caught at least two in the middle of the chest. I think he's out of it."

Sparky walked toward the man on the ground. He pointed his shotgun at him and said, "I use a twenty gauge because it's easier for me to handle." He patted the barrel. "But with buckshot at close range, it does the job just fine."

"So I noticed."

"I'll watch this guy," Sparky said, "Go make sure the other one is out of commission."

Sean eased into the utility room, then he bent and checked the gunman's carotid artery. No pulse. He went to the bedroom door and yelled, "Don't shoot. It's me."

Kelly rushed out of the closet and threw her arms around him. "Thank God, you're all right." After the embrace, she stepped back and said, "What happened outside?"

He briefed her, and, then, he opened the closet door and helped Cody. The boy's eyes were wide and he said nothing.

Kelly wrapped her arms around Cody. "It's okay. It's all over."

Sean went outside and checked on the downed gunman, who had not changed his position. A few seconds later, two police cars roared down the street. He put his gun on the hood of the car so he would not look like a threat, then he waved them over.

Soon, four police cars and a technician's vehicle lined the street, and the officers stayed for six hours. Police tape sealed off the area. During his conversation with a detective, Sean revealed details of the altercation with Chase Logan. He speculated that the two gunmen might be from the east coast. The police were noncommittal, but they hinted that if the two men were from out of state, they would have the local police interview Mr. Logan. Sean doubted if the authorities could incriminate Logan, but he liked the idea of putting the miscreant on edge.

———————

Over the next several days, everyone went through two extensive interviews, although Cody had only one conversation with the authorities. The investigation verified that the two gunmen had broken into the house and initiated the gunfire. Additionally, the serial numbers on the intruder's pistols had been obliterated and both of the gunmen had criminal records, including assault with a deadly weapon. Sean and Sparky had acted in self-defense.

The break-in and subsequent gun battle made the front page of several newspapers, and TV crews stationed themselves outside of both houses eager to gain live interviews. The chaos was so bad that they packed for a short trip and left in the middle of the night in Sean's SUV. They headed north to the wine country and stayed at a secluded inn for four days. They rented a suite so they could be together.

The day before they were to return home, they held a meeting to discuss future strategies. Kelly spoke first, "My first priority is safety. Nothing else matters."

"We all agree on that," Sean said. "The issue is whether we hide or go home?"

Sparky said, "With two unsuccessful attempts I suspect it'll be quiet going forward. I think we should return home and just be vigilant. If things look shaky we can always change plans."

"Kelly said, "I suppose it would be best to carry on but I'm worried about Cody."

"Sean said, "We could send you and Cody to another state for a while."

"Kelly shook her head, "No, I want all of us to stay together."

Sparky took a drink of water and said, "I vote for going home."

"I agree," Sean said, "but I want Kelly to decide."

After further discussion, she agreed they should return home. They would ignore the press and hold off on her business except for planning. She went to bed, but it took over an hour for her to fall asleep. She kept going back to what the gunman in the mountains had said, "You're gonna fucking pay for this. You're gonna pay big time."

When Danny Fagan read the newspaper, he knew he had to change the timeline for his plans. Patience was important, but the shootout changed everything. Would Kelly go into hiding? If she did, he would still find her—it would just be a matter of time. He decided that he and Rick would continue the stakeout of the house. To avoid being spotted, they would rotate vehicle colors for each trip.

He hoped to find a pattern that would provide an opportunity to snatch her son, and he was anxious to begin the process. If things went as planned, he would obtain the priceless software but that was not all—he also wanted to inflict as much pain as possible. He relived the pummeling they gave him with rocks and cursed the slow-healing lesion on his head. He picked up his phone and dialed Rick.

CHAPTER 42

On their way home from the supermarket, Kelly looked out the rear window. "I can't prove it, but I have this creepy feeling we're being followed."

Sean checked the rearview mirror. "I watch for that every time we go anywhere, but I've never seen anything to cause concern. I saw a car and a van that looked suspicious over the last few days, but they both turned off after a few blocks." He looked back at the road. "Keep an eye out."

The following days provided more of the same. She kept looking at the cars behind them, but every time she thought they were followed, the vehicle turned off. Still, she felt something was wrong. Sparky joined them for the next two trips so they could have more eyes. They returned home after shopping, and Kelly called a meeting.

They gathered in her living room and she said, "I don't know how, but I'm sure we're being followed."

Sean said, "We've checked and checked, but I haven't seen anything."

Sparky said, "I'm with Kelly. There's something going on. I can feel it."

"Okay," Sean said, "let's suppose someone is following us. How would he do it without us knowing?"

"I've been thinking about that." Kelly said. "They would have to use multiple cars."

"I thought of that," Sean said, "but it would be tricky to pull off."

Sparky took a slug of water. "These guys aren't dummies. It can be done."

They discussed several scenarios and decided they had to assume they were being followed. Furthermore, it was probably the gunman from the mountains, and they needed to take his actions very seriously.

"We could go to the police," Kelly said, "but what would we tell them? That we *think* we're being followed. That's not good enough, especially for a small-town police force with limited resources."

"Yeah," Sparky said, "Those thugs would spot the police a mile away, even if they used unmarked cars."

"Suppose we use the same tactic on them," Sean said. "If we see someone, we'll use multiple cars and follow them. With a little luck, we might be able to put an end to all of this."

Kelly said, "It's worth a try, but we need to plan this very carefully."

"I have an idea," Sean said, "We'll have you and Cody drive somewhere safe and Sparky and I will hang back and try to spot them. If we can identify a car, we'll tag team them as far as it is safe. We might not be able to follow them too far, but it would be a first step. The next time we could go farther."

"Kelly nodded, "We really need to do something. Why not give it a try?"

They spent the next hour reviewing every possible scenario. They decided their best option was to have Kelly and Cody drive to the library and stay there until Sean called her, even if it meant hours of waiting. Eventually, the person following her would tire and leave. If Sean and Sparky saw a suspicious vehicle, they would put their plan into action.

The following day, Sparky left early and drove to a predetermined parking area that offered a good view of the library entrance. After Kelly left, Sean held back a block and followed her as planned. It did not take long for him to spot a car following Kelly. About four blocks from the library, the car turned off and a white cargo van moved into position behind her SUV.

The van parked a half block from the library entrance, but no one exited the vehicle. Sean pulled into a parking spot that allowed him to see both Sparky's car and the van.

He waited.

An hour and fifty minutes later, the van pulled away from the curb.

Sean grabbed his phone and called Sparky. "Okay, it's show time. I'll follow him first; then, I'll call you and you can take over. Follow him as far you feel it is safe to do so, then call me, and we'll switch again."

"Okay, but let's play it conservatively. I don't want him to get suspicious."

"I agree," Sean said. "Easy does it."

Sean expected the van to go toward the more populated areas to the north or east but, to his surprise, the driver turned onto Highway 1 and headed south. This changed everything because the only major intersection between them and Santa Cruz was

Highway 84, which was also known as La Honda Road. Otherwise, the two-lane road followed the ocean in a very rural setting.

Several minutes after they left town, he called Sparky. "I didn't expect this. You had better move up and I'll drop back. When we reach La Honda Road, we'll switch again even if he continues south on Highway 1."

After Sparky passed his SUV, Sean wondered about the van's destination. If he took La Honda, he could go to Skyline Boulevard and then go in any one of three directions, each leading to major populated areas, including Silicon Valley. Any of those routes would add extreme complications to their plan.

Sean's phone rang and Sparky said, "There's no reason for you to move up until we get to La Honda, which is about six miles from here. When he gets there, he has only two options. He can turn east or continue south toward Santa Cruz. There are a few, scattered turnoffs, but I only know of one that goes over the mountain. Of course, he could live somewhere in the area. Hard to say."

"Okay, but don't follow too closely."

When Sean saw the van pass the Highway 84 exit, he passed Sparky and kept the van in sight. Sparky called and told him that there was only one road ahead that made sense other than continuing south to Santa Cruz, and that was the road to the small town of Pescadero. When the van reached Pescadero Creek Road, the van's left turn blinker came on.

Sean called Sparky. "He's going to turn but if we follow him, he'll spot us for sure. Let's just continue south for a couple of miles, and I'll pull over."

Sean stopped at a turnout that gave him a view of the ocean, grabbed his map, and got out of his SUV. Sparky pulled up, and

Sean walked to the passenger side and opened the door. He climbed in and opened his map. "What do you know about Pescadero and that road he took?"

"Pescadero is small, maybe seven or eight hundred people." He put his finger on the map. "It's only a mile or two off the highway. Pescadero Creek Road goes by the town, and, then, it continues up the mountain. There are a lot of twists and turns. A lot of folks live up there on side roads among the trees. It eventually reaches Skyline Boulevard." He traced Skyline on the map. "As you can see, if he goes all the way up, we're pretty much out of luck. He could turn left and go to San Francisco or turn right and go to Santa Cruz or San Jose. He could also take several roads and go down the mountain to the Silicon Valley. We'd have a hell of a time trailing him without being noticed."

Sean folded the map. "Well, we know more than we did this morning. At least we have a starting point." He looked up the highway to make sure the van had not doubled back. It looked clear. He climbed out of Sparky's car. "Let's go home."

———

While Danny Fagan had watched the library, he read the current edition of a prominent pigeon-racing magazine. The recent sale of a top racer to a businessman in China for $400,000 surprised him. Racing pigeons went from fifty dollars and up, but this sale was unprecedented. He would pursue his goal of producing top breeders, but he would never pay that kind of money, unless, of course, he got his hands on Kelly Sanborn's software. Even then, it made no sense to pay anywhere near that much. He would simply buy some top breeders, at a fair price, and raise his own. One way or another, he intended to dominate pigeon racing.

He spent so much time assessing the news of the sale that he had momentarily dropped his guard during his drive home. A few miles from his turnoff at Pescadero Creek Road, he gave his full attention to cars following him. He noticed an SUV he thought he might have seen earlier, but he could not be sure. He should have paid more attention. Still, there were almost no exit options on this route, and there were always sightseers traveling Highway 1 for the scenic views.

He turned on Pescadero Creek Road, slowed down, and kept his eyes on the rearview mirror. When the SUV continued south on Highway 1, he said, "Probably a fuckin' tourist." He cruised past Pescadero and continued the drive toward home. After two miles, he pulled over and watched the road for twenty minutes. He saw nothing suspicious.

He went home, entered a shed, and grabbed a bag of high-end feed for his birds. He opened the first of several pigeon lofts and spoke to the birds in a low, melodic voice. Next, he gave special attention to Oscar. He stroked the bird and spoke as if he were carrying on a conversation with a person. When he finished, he stood outside in deep thought.

Since he could not find a pattern that would allow him to snatch Kelly, he decided to put an alternate plan into action. He went inside and turned on his computer. He placed orders for several Boy Scout items he had previously researched, and he paid extra for two-day shipping. Then, he ordered magnetic letters for his cargo van.

The day his orders arrived, he drove to Pescadero to get in range of a cell phone tower. He pulled out a disposable phone and dialed Kelly Sanborn's home number, which he had previously obtained from Martin Scanlan. When she answered, he used his best voice and said, "Miss Sanborn, this is Charles Hamilton. I am the regional director for the Boy Scouts of America. We were very pleased to learn that your son, Cody, played an important part in your survival in the mountains. Because of his extraordinary performance, we would like to honor him with a special award at our new regional office in San Mateo. We'll take care of everything including transportation for you and your son."

Kelly said, "What a nice surprise." She thought back to Cody's performance in the mountains. "His knowledge was key to our survival. We never would have gotten a fire started without him, and he was a big help in finding edible food. I'm sure he'd be delighted to receive the award."

"You must be very proud."

"Yes, yes we are. Do you have a date for the presentation?"

"We're thinking about Monday. Could I pick you up at ten o'clock?"

"Hold on a sec. I need to check my calendar." She glanced at her desk and said, "Yes, that will be fine."

"Great. We'll see you then. Oh, one more thing. Be sure he wears his uniform. We're going to take pictures."

Fagan hung up and smiled at his performance. He especially liked the comment about taking pictures, which would appeal to any mother. He knew the average mother would imagine a photo of her son in his uniform. Also, he knew she would be less likely to be suspicious at a moment like that. It was a nice touch.

He dialed Rick and said, "I need you all day on Monday, and bring your cousin. Tell him he'll make five hundred bucks for a five-minute job, and he doesn't have to do anything illegal. As usual, make damn sure you don't mention my name."

"Sounds easy enough."

"I want you to be at my place by seven AM. I'll lay it all out for you when you get here, but we're gonna snatch one or two people. Hopefully, we'll just grab the woman but we may need the kid. We can always use him for leverage. Bring ski masks and gloves." He knew he needed to dangle a carrot for Rick. "If things go right, you'll never have to work again."

CHAPTER 43

Kelly felt a surge of mother's pride as she thought about Cody having his picture taken at the ceremony, and this would not be a token award. After all, he had offered lifesaving information on more than one occasion during their ordeal. She had every right to be proud. Monday morning, they were excited about the award ceremony. Cody seemed a little nervous, but she knew that was only temporary. A few minutes before ten o'clock, she went into the bedroom to put on earrings. Sean was in the bathroom.

Cody yelled from the front room, "Mom, he's early. Can I go out to the Boy Scout van?"

"Sure, we'll be right there." She brushed her hair back and started to put on the second earring when she suddenly stopped. She looked in the mirror, her eyes wide. "*Van?*"

She rushed to the window, looked out, and saw a van with a Boy Scout emblem on the door and the words Boy Scouts of America on the side. She had been alarmed for nothing. She opened the front door and saw a masked man jump from the rear door of the cargo van and grab Cody.

She yelled as loud as she could, "Sean. They've got Cody!" She ran outside, but the van sped up the narrow road. Distraught, she turned toward the house and saw Sean running toward her.

He tossed her his cell phone. "Get in the car and call 911."

He ran into the house, grabbed his gun, and rushed outside to his car. He started the engine and raced up the street. A half block from the corner, a pickup pulled across the street to make a U-turn. Sean yelled, "What the hell. This street is too narrow for that."

He honked.

The driver began a series of slow, back-and-forth maneuvers to complete his U-turn.

Sean pulled up close to the pickup, rolled down the window and yelled. "Get that thing out of my way." The driver ignored him. Sean repeatedly honked the horn.

The driver got out of his truck and raised the hood.

Sean got out and ran to the pickup. "This is an emergency! Get that thing moving."

The driver said, "Aw, hell, man. I've been having trouble with this old truck."

Suddenly, Sean knew the stalled truck was more than it appeared. The street was simply too narrow for anyone to try such a maneuver. He ran to the SUV and got in. He looked to the side hoping he could drive onto the sidewalk but a tree blocked his path on one side and a fence blocked the other side. He pounded on the horn.

Nothing.

He got out, ran up to the man, pulled out his gun, and pointed it at the man's leg. "Get that piece of shit moving or I'm going blow your knee all to hell."

The man's expression changed to fear. He slammed down the hood and jumped into his truck. Amazingly, the engine turned over on the first try. The man backed up once and made the turn.

Sean said, "Write down his license plate." As soon as he uttered those words, he realized it was useless. A layer of dry mud covered the plates. "Dammit!"

He turned to Kelly. "Did you see which way the van turned?"

"He . . . he turned right."

Sean raced up the street and made a quick turn. He gunned it passed several cars but there was no sign of a sand-colored van. "They know we'd call 911, so they won't stay on this main road."

"If they hurt Cody, I'll . . ."

"Call the cops and tell them which way they went." He wanted to keep Kelly busy because he knew she was under severe stress. "We'll take some turnoffs and just keep looking. Keep your eyes open." He glanced at her. "Look up and down every street."

He drove through a strip mall, and, then, he checked the back of the building. Nothing. He pulled back on the street and continued down the main road. After a few blocks, he came to a small commercial area that included a few warehouses. He turned and drove down several streets. "See anything?"

"Sean, I'm scared to death."

He took her hand in his. "Keep looking. That's all we can do."

He turned into a rundown area and drove past a vacant building. He started to go back to the main road, but he came to a stop, turned around, and drove behind the empty building. A hundred feet ahead of him was a sand-colored van with Boy Scout emblems on the doors. He slid to a stop, grabbed his gun, jumped out, and ran to the side of the van. He held the pistol in his right hand and yanked open the door with his left.

Empty.

"Damn!"

He yelled, "Call the police."

She made the call and walked up to Sean. "My God, what have I done?" She shook her head as tears welled up. "I should have been suspicious."

He held her close and caressed her hair. "You had no way of knowing."

She knew he was right, but it made no difference. They had Cody and nothing else mattered. She clung to Sean and said, "What are we going to do?"

"We . . . we'll find him . . . somehow."

The police told Kelly to stay where they were.

They clung to each other behind the vacant building and waited.

———

Eleven miles south, Danny Fagan drove a white cargo van with a temporary sign on the side that read: A1 Plumbing. The van, which looked like a typical service vehicle headed for its next job, adhered to the speed limit as it cruised down Highway 1. In the back of the van, Cody's hands and feet were secured with duct tape and his eyes were covered with a blindfold. Rick watched him while Fagan drove.

Fagan felt good about how well his plan went down. He wanted Kelly's software *and* he wanted her. The boy was his ticket to ride. He lit a cigarette and smiled. He was on his way.

CHAPTER 44

Kelly and Sean followed the police car to the station and went inside. The police released them after a one-hour interview. The authorities tried to be upbeat, but they both knew the days ahead were full of extreme danger for Cody. They drove home in a car filled with sadness. Sean held Kelly's hand, but they said little as they both tried to sort through their emotions in their own way. A police car followed them home and parked outside. The knowledge that the house would be under surveillance for several days offered no comfort because the worst possible damage had already been done—Cody had been kidnapped.

Everyone expected a phone call from the kidnapper within forty-eight hours. The police wanted to monitor calls from inside the house, but Kelly had declined because she knew the person who had Cody would expect that. She spent the day with her phone within reach but no call came. She went to bed a little after midnight, but she only slept for two hours. Frightened and exhausted, she rose at five o'clock and went into the kitchen to make coffee. She was standing by the coffee maker when Sean came into the room. He walked up behind her, put his arms around her, and held her close. Neither spoke.

The doorbell rang.

Sean looked outside to make sure the police cruiser was still there, then he opened the door.

Sparky walked in with a platter of food. "I couldn't sleep and I saw your lights, so I brought breakfast and support." He walked into the kitchen and held Kelly's hand. "Anything I have is yours. If I can help in any way, all you have to do is ask." He put down a tray containing whole-wheat muffins, blueberries, low fat yogurt, and vitamin C tablets. "I'm here for the duration."

After the coffee was ready, they all sat at the table and ate a quiet breakfast. Throughout the morning, a somber mood hung over the room. The phone rang a little after ten and Kelly grabbed her cell. She clicked off after a few seconds. "Telemarketer."

Sean rose and paced.

Sparky stared out the window.

The phone rang again at eleven-twenty. Kelly answered.

"Listen very carefully. Don't say anything until I finish."

Kelly put the phone on speaker.

He spoke in a deep, gravelly voice. "If you don't follow instructions, you will never see your son again. If you inform the police of this call, you will never see your son again. If the police are there, tell them to leave or you will never see your son again. Do you understand?"

"Y—yes."

"Are you alone?"

"Cody's father is here."

"I had someone check the house. I know there's a police car out front."

"I wouldn't let them in because I knew you'd expect that."

"I have someone watching, so I'm aware of that also." He paused a few seconds. "Okay, here's how this is going to work. I'll trade your son for the software. There's only one decision you can make. It's very important that you understand what I am about to say. Your son is sealed in a secluded location with a two-day supply of water. If anything happens to me, he'll never be found, and he will die a horrible death."

Kelly exhaled. "You—you can't . . ."

"Shut up and listen.

"Search all you want but no one could ever find him. Again, you must understand this."

"How . . . how do I know I can trust you?"

"You don't. But you have only one option. All I want is the software so the trade is an easy choice. I want you to bring a laptop with the software loaded and a flash drive that contains a second copy. Write down all passwords and any other security information I'll need to run the software. Do you understand?"

She knew there was only one answer, but she glanced at Sean for his reaction.

He nodded.

"Alright, what do you want me to do?"

"At ten o'clock tomorrow, leave your house and drive to the intersection of Highway 92 and Skyline Boulevard. Turn south on Skyline and drive exactly four point two miles. You'll see a dirt road on your right. Take that road and drive until you see a van. It will be parked about two hundred yards from Skyline. You are to walk to the back of the van and put the laptop, the flash drive, and the passwords on the ground. Then walk back to your car and face away from the van until I have driven out of sight. After we make sure there are no cops in the area, another vehicle will come down the dirt road with your son. Get into the car, and you'll be driven about a mile farther down the dirt road. You and your son will get out, and you can walk back to your car. That'll give us time to leave the area."

"But I . . ."

"I told you to shut up and listen. I'll have spotters looking for the cops along the highway and they'll also be checking for any surveillance from the air. That means helicopters, drones, and any planes loitering in the area. The most important thing you need to remember is that if the police are involved, in any way, the chances of you ever seeing your son again will drop to zero. And his death will not be pretty. Do you understand?"

"Y—yes."

"One more thing. I'm very tech savvy. I know you can install software that will track the location of the laptop. I'll check for that before I leave. If I find a suspicious device or tracking software, your son is as good as dead."

He hung up.

She clicked off and teared up. The thought of losing Cody was incomprehensible. He was a vital part of her life, and she loved him profoundly. She shuddered at the thought of losing her son. Three heartbroken souls sat in silence as they each considered the peril that enveloped Cody.

Sean went to Kelly and pulled her close.

She said nothing.

Sparky remained uncharacteristically silent.

After a moment, Sean removed his arms and said, "I don't like this. I don't like it at all. What if he takes the software and then reneges on his promise to deliver Cody?"

Sparky put down his water bottle and said, "It's a bad setup, but it's our only option."

Sean looked out the window. "We saw him abandon that man in the cave, and I'm sure that's just the tip of the iceberg." He shook his head. "He's deep-down evil."

Kelly wiped her eyes, looked down, and put a hand to her forehead. "I believe what he said about calling the police. We just can't take that chance."

Sean nodded. "He's smart. He even knew about the tracking software."

Sparky said, "We've got to be smarter."

Kelly looked up. "That's not as easy as it sounds."

Sean paced and then stopped. "What if Sparky and I take two cars and drive up Skyline from the *other* direction? We could stop out of sight and, then, try to follow the van when he leaves. If they actually deliver Cody, you can call us and we'd stop following and turn around."

Sparky said, "He'd spot us."

"We'd hang way back and use the tag team method we used on Highway 1. If he goes back toward Pescadero Creek Road, either we'll locate him or we'll have a general idea where he lives. And remember, if he delivers Cody, it won't matter." He looked at Kelly. "It's just that I don't trust the bastard."

She sat without speaking for a moment and then said, "I can't buy into that right now. I need some time to think. Let's get together this afternoon for a final decision." As the day wore on, her thoughts shifted from overwhelming concern to anger. The evil bastard had no right to disrupt their lives the way he had. Cody was just an innocent boy who suddenly faced severe danger and possibly death. She wanted to strangle the sonofabitch who kidnapped her son. If only she could.

CHAPTER 45

At nine o'clock the following morning, Sean and Sparky took separate vehicles and headed for Skyline Boulevard. Kelly would leave at ten as instructed. They found a favorable spot about a half mile up the road from the turnoff Kelly would take. They checked for suspicious vehicles, and, then, they waited. As previously agreed, they intended to tag team the van in case Cody was not released. Hopefully, she would call and tell them everything was all right, and they would not have to follow the van. They all knew their plan involved extreme risk, but they had no other options.

At ten thirty-four, they saw Kelly's SUV turn onto the dirt road. Sean sat upright and his breathing came rapidly as his stress level rocketed up several notches. He looked in the rear-view mirror and saw Sparky waiting in his car, then he gripped the wheel and waited.

Eighteen minutes later, a white van exited the dirt road and turned on Skyline Boulevard. Sean waited for a phone call, but it did not come. Reluctantly, he started the engine and started to pull onto the road when he saw a second white van leave the dirt road and pull in behind the first van.

"Shit!" What the hell's going on? Were Kelly and Cody still on the dirt road or were they in one of the vans? It struck him immediately. The kidnapper's intended to create confusion by using two vans, and it had worked. Sean slowed and considered the possibilities. Kelly did not call so something was terribly wrong. If he drove down the dirt road, and they were not there, he and Sparky would never find them. If he followed the two vans, which one had Kelly and Cody? He called Sparky. "We're screwed."

"We have to split up." Sparky said in a strained tone. "One of us has to follow the vans and the other goes down the dirt road."

"You're right." Sean paused as his mind raced. "Okay, you take the dirt road and call me if you find them. The problem now is that they'll spot me for sure."

"I don't see any other choice."

When Sparky started to turn on the dirt road, Sean pulled closer to the distant vans. He stayed back as far as he could and hoped for a phone call informing him that Sparky had found Kelly and Cody. After several minutes, the phone rang.

Sparky said, "Her car is here but there's no one in sight."

"Damn." He tightened his grip on the wheel and shook his head. "Okay, try to catch up with me."

After three miles, one of the vans turned off on Wible Road. Sean looked in the rearview mirror, but he did not see Sparky's car. He looked back on the road and knew he had to follow one of the vans—but which one? Because the lead van turned off, he took a chance and followed it. He called Sparky. "Speed up and see if you can spot the other van. I think it's too far ahead but try anyway. If you can't find it, turn back, and wait for me at the Wible Road intersection." Sean took the turnoff and followed the van downhill. Sixteen minutes later, the slow-moving cargo van stopped. Sean pulled over but there was no movement from the van.

He wiped his forehead, gripped his pistol, and waited.

A few minutes later, a man he had never seen before got out, walked to the rear of the van, and opened the doors. Sean saw that the van was empty. He ignored the man and made a quick U-turn. He glanced in the rearview mirror after his turn and saw the man laughing. He gunned the SUV up the road, cursing all the way. He reached Skyline and saw Sparky parked as instructed. He motioned for him to get in his SUV. When the door closed he said, "This is bad, really bad." He shook his head. "The bastard has both of them."

The expression on Sparky's face was unlike any Sean had ever seen. His ever-present spark of life had disappeared. Sean called the Sheriff and explained what had happened. The authorities said they would look for the cargo van and they would also notify the Highway Patrol, but Sean knew there was little chance of spotting the van. They had no idea what direction the kidnapper might have taken. Moreover, they knew the kidnapper was shrewd enough to change vehicles again, which would drop the odds of catching him to near zero.

Sean grabbed a map of the greater bay area. "Okay, we're right here. I think we should drive down to Pescadero and start there. That's where the van turned off the day we followed him. Maybe he lives in town. If not, we can drive up the mountain."

"Punch it."

Sean pulled out and headed for the small town of Pescadero. While he drove, he tried to suppress horrifying images careening through his mind. It had taken him so much time and effort to get to where he was that any thoughts of losing Kelly and Cody were unimaginable. He tried to extinguish bad thoughts by concentrating on the road, but his efforts quickly failed.

Forty-two minutes later, they drove down the main street of Pescadero. The town was smaller than they expected, but it was a starting point. They passed a restaurant and went to the end of the street. Sean looked to his left and stopped. "There's a country store that also sells feed. Let's go in there."

Sparky nodded. "If anyone knows the populace around here, it'll be those folks."

Sean pulled into a parking space. "That's what I'm thinking." They went inside and walked up to the counter.

A middle-aged man, with a gray-streaked mustache and wearing an old beret, turned and asked, "What can I do for you?"

Sean said, "This is an emergency. My son has been kidnapped and we need your help."

The man's expression changed. "You're serious?"

Sparky said, "Very serious."

The man placed both hands flat on the counter. "How can I help?"

Sean said, "We recently followed a cargo van that turned onto Pescadero Creek Road from Highway 1. We continued south so we wouldn't be spotted. The driver might live here, or he could have gone up the mountain." He glanced outside. "Are there are a lot of vans around here."

"Not that many, really. This is more of an SUV and pickup community." He paused and then said, "What color was it?"

"White."

"Well, I know of two white cargo vans in town, but I can vouch for those folks. One is almost ninety and the other is my brother-in-law. There's no way it can be either of them."

Sean nodded. "Okay, another question. This guy had some kind of droppings on his shoes. I'm thinking chickens."

"There are hundreds of folks here, and in the mountains, who have chickens. It would be worse than finding the proverbial needle in a haystack."

Sean thought for a moment. "Thanks, anyway." He turned and started out.

The man said, "Hold on a minute."

They walked back to the counter.

"Chickens are skittish and too low to the ground to mess up the top of shoes much. But pigeons are another story."

Sparky said, "Pigeons?"

"Yep, they are generally on perches." The man rubbed his chin. "You know, I have one customer, an odd duck for sure, who regularly comes in here for pigeon feed. I order a special blend for him that comes in from Texas. Kind of expensive for feed. Well, one day my wife mentioned that his shoes had pigeon dung on them. I never paid no mind, but you know how women are. They pay attention to that sort of thing."

Sean and Sparky looked at each other, their minds working.

The man continued. "To tell you the truth, I don't trust this guy, and I make him pay cash."

Sean asked, "What makes you say that?"

"Spooky. The guy's real spooky."

Sean said, "Do you know where he lives?"

"No, but he doesn't live in Pescadero. I pretty much know everyone here." He nodded as he thought. "Up the mountain, but there are a ton of folks up there and a lot of them live off the road in the trees so you can't even see their houses."

"Have you ever delivered to him. Do you have an address?"

"Nope, we deliver some items locally but not up the mountain. It's pretty windy all the way up." The man tapped the counter. "One more thing. He usually calls to see if his order is ready to be picked up, and then he says he's on the way. It always takes him a good forty-five minutes to get here. That makes me think he lives quite a way up."

Sean considered the information and then asked, "Do you know if he drives a white cargo van?"

"Never seen him drive anything else."

Sean and Sparky said the exact same thing at the same time. "Let's go!"

They jumped in Sean's SUV and headed up Pescadero Creek Road.

Sean said, "Call the Sheriff's office and tell them what we've learned."

After a quick conversation, Sparky said, "They said they would look over the area, but they were pretty low key about it. I think that was because we didn't have anything specific to tell them. They also advised us to go home."

"Bullshit on that. He has Cody and Kelly. He can do whatever he wants whenever he feels like it. I'm not going to just sit around and wait."

"I'm with you, pardner."

They inspected all the visible houses as they drove, but most of the turnoffs were dirt roads that went through the trees with no structures in view.

Sean noticed that nearly half of the roads had gates and most of them were open. He turned to Sparky. "This guy's going to have a locked gate. Let's concentrate on those."

Sparky adjusted his seat pad and peered out the window. "Makes sense. Anybody in his line of work won't want folks nosing around."

Fifteen minutes later, they stopped at a locked gate. Sean got out and climbed over the gate. Sparky crawled between two boards. They eased into the woods to avoid the dirt road and pulled their guns. They walked about thirty yards and stopped at the edge of a clearing.

Sean looked at the vacant house, holstered his pistol, and said, "That's one a dilapidated piece of junk. Damn thing is falling apart."

"Well, we had to check." Sparky turned and started up the road. "Let's go."

They drove to where Pescadero Creek Road ended, and they turned onto Alpine Road. Sean became more pessimistic because the number of houses dwindled as they gained elevation. He saw a gated road and slowed.

Sparky yelled, "Stop! There's a goddamned bronze silhouette of a pigeon on that gate. I kid you not."

Sean pulled over and stopped several yards past the gate.

Sparky said, "This is the place. I can feel it in my bones."

"Every time I've heard you say that, you were right."

"I'm right this time too." Sparky looked back toward the gate. "Maybe we should call the sheriff."

"No phone signal. I already checked. We'd have to drive to Pescadero, and it would take them too long to get all the way up here. Anything could happen during that time." He paused in thought. "Remember, he doesn't need Cody anymore. The guy will just think he's in the way. If something happened to Cody, I would never forgive myself."

"You're right, but let's be awful damned careful. We have too much to lose if we screw it up." Sparky got out, opened the rear door, and pulled out his shotgun. He patted the barrel. "We may need an equalizer."

Sean climbed over the fence. "And we need some luck. Lots of it."

They moved off to the side and entered the trees on high alert. After a few yards, Sparky stopped. "Hold on; I've gotta piss."

"Damn, Sparky. I've never seen anyone drink as much water as you do."

He unzipped his fly. "We'll discuss that another time."

They continued in a stealth mode and moved through the trees and brush. They had attempted to move parallel to the road, but Sean had no idea how far they should go. He stopped and whispered, "Let's check the road so we don't pass the house." They turned and crept through the bushes until they found the road, which curved left, but there were no buildings visible.

Sean gave a hand signal and they moved back into the trees. After about twenty yards, they moved toward the road. They came to very thick brush and had to move branches aside with their arms. Sean came to a clearing and slowly stepped out from the brush.

Rick stood against a van with a shotgun leaning against the vehicle. The sound from the brush caused him to grab the gun and swing it up in a quick motion. He took a snapshot and the shotgun roared.

Sean felt pellets strike his leg as he opened fire with his pistol. Three shots rang out, and two of the bullets struck Rick in the midsection. The gunman dropped his shotgun and slumped to the ground.

Sparky said, "You got him, pardner."

Sean hobbled toward Rick, picked up the shotgun, and tossed it aside.

Sparky checked for other gunmen; then, he glanced at Sean's legs. "You're damn lucky. He shot so fast most of the pellets hit the ground." He took a closer look at Sean's left leg. "You okay?"

Sean rolled up the bottom of his pant leg and examined the wounds. "I'm good. Thank God he didn't use buckshot." When he saw that the bleeding was minor, he rolled down his pant leg. "Watch the house while I find out what this asshole knows." He grabbed Rick by the shirt and pulled him against the van in a sitting position. "You're gut shot, and you're not going to make it. It's time for you to do something right for a change. Where's my son?"

Rick looked at his abdomen. "Damn, I . . . I never should have hooked up with that crazy bastard."

Sean shook him. "Tell me where my son is, or I'll make your last few minutes hell on Earth."

Rick tried to speak, but a stream of blood flowing from the corner of his mouth made him cough.

Sean shook him again.

Rick's eyes blinked several times. "He said he would let the kid go but he . . . he's going to kill him. I don't want anything to do with killing a child. I've done some bad th . . . things but I ain't never hurt no kids."

Sean glanced toward the house. "Where is he?"

"There . . .there's a prepper cave back there that is sealed. He has both of them in there." Rick's eyes closed.

Sean shook him again. "What do you mean sealed?"

"It . . . it's sealed and there's a thick metal door. It's a goddamned fortress." The words came thick and slow.

"There's . . . ." He stopped and gasped for air. "There's a hidden vent above the main room but it . . . it's only six inches wide."

Rick's eyes closed, and he slumped to one side.

Sean said, "We have to find a way into that cave." He glanced at the van. "That door sounds pretty solid so we might need a little help. Maybe there's a crowbar in there." He opened the van door, looked around, and saw a toolbox against the wall. He opened the box but he didn't see anything they could use. He started to close the lid when he saw a flashlight. He grabbed it, turned it on, and flashed a beam against the sidewall. He pocketed the flashlight and climbed out the back of the van. "We might need some light if we somehow manage to get into the cave." He looked at a path leading into the trees. "The cave must be that way, but it's really dense in that direction."

"Yeah, and he probably heard the shots. Depends on how thick that wall over the entrance is. If he knows we're coming, it'll be a tricky setup."

Sean scanned the area. "I don't want anything to do with that path." He rubbed his left leg and said, "Let's circle around and find the cave." Guns ready, they moved on a parallel route with the trail.

After entering a stand of thick trees, Sparky stopped and pointed. "Down there. Two vans and a car. The vans don't have license plates, so I suspect they're stolen."

Sean glanced around and, then, continued through the trees. After about thirty yards, he held up his hand and stopped. He looked through some brush and said, "There it is." He shook his head. "This guy must be nuts. There's thick concrete all around the cave entrance, and that door looks like the ones on the back of Brinks trucks. I can see two cameras."

"We need to find a back door . . . if there is one."

"The guy mentioned a vent, but the opening is too small."

"We won't bother with that." Sean checked the open area and said, "Okay, let's go back in the trees and search. One problem is that a cave's interior can go in a few feet or hundreds of yards. Some caves have secondary, natural entrances but they're often small and hidden. Let's have a look." He turned and started up a tree-covered slope.

Sparky said, "Sounds like a long shot."

"I know, but that's all we've got."

They searched but found no other openings. They moved deeper into the trees and checked under thick brush. Sparky put down his shotgun and crawled through a thicket. A minute later he said, "I think this is one of those holes, but it won't do us any good. The guy's filled it with concrete. There's no way in."

They searched until they reached a fence that looked like the perimeter of the property. They went along the fence but found nothing. They headed back in a slightly different direction. After about fifteen yards, Sparky stopped and got down on his hands and knees next to two thick shrubs. He crawled inside the brush and said, "I've got something."

Sean heard rustling. "What is it?"

"There's a small hole in the rock under the brush. Very small but I can feel a slight flow of air from inside." He crawled back out and stood. "I think it's part the cave, but there's no way to know where it goes or if it's big enough to allow a person to maneuver down there. It's really small and narrow, and it could lead to a dead-end."

Sean said, "Time's running out."

"I know." Sparky looked back at the brush. He put down his shotgun and checked his pistol. "I'm smaller than you. I'm going down."

"You sure?"

"You said it best. The guy doesn't need Cody anymore. We've got to do something and fast." Sparky's emotions showed in his voice. "They're the closest thing to family I have."

"I know, and the clock is ticking." Sean looked back at the trees. "Okay, I'll go back and watch the entrance to make sure he doesn't leave for some reason." He handed Sparky the flashlight and picked up the shotgun. "Good luck and be careful."

Sparky gave a thumbs-up and disappeared under the brush.

———

Sean made his way back the way they had come. He had his pistol holstered, and he kept the shotgun ready. He came to a location where he had a good view of the cave's entrance. He settled down to watch when he heard movement from behind.

"Drop the shotgun. Now!"

Shit.

Sean did as he was instructed.

"Take your pistol out of the holster with your left hand and toss it to one side."

Sean knew he had no options so he obeyed.

Fagan moved to the side and looked at him. "I know you. You're the guy in the mountains. You must be the kid's father."

Sean said nothing as he searched for an angle.

Fagan looked in the direction of the road. "I thought I heard shots, but those walls are awful damn thick. I came out to see if it was the cops. I have a car in the back of my property, so I was all set to take off, but I waited to make sure. And along comes you all by your lonesome. How special is that?" He pointed toward the cave. "Move."

Sean said, "Is my boy okay?"

"Yeah, but not for long."

Sean's heart filled with anguish. He looked toward the cave and said, "Kelly?"

"Oh, she's fine. I have special plans for her."

Sean felt sick with grief. He had to do something, but the odds were too great. He could only wait and watch for an opening. He trudged down the slope and walked toward the cave's metal door.

Fagan told him to stand to one side while he unlocked the door, then he motioned for him to enter the cave. Sean stepped inside and saw that the cave split into two tunnels. There was a small, dark tunnel on his right but the larger tunnel, on the other side, had undergone construction and was sealed except for a closed door. He looked to his left, and saw Cody handcuffed to a metal bar. He ran to his son.

Fagan yelled, "Leave the kid alone and get down on your stomach."

Sean wanted to take a chance, but he knew if he made the slightest move, the devious bastard would shoot him. He had to wait and watch for an opportunity.

Fagan bound his arms with duct tape and then rolled him over. He checked to make sure Sean had no hidden weapons and then he handcuffed him to the bar.

Sean looked at Cody with concern etched across his face, then he looked at Fagan and said, "Where's Kelly?"

"She's locked in the main living area." He laughed. "You won't be seeing her again, but I will."

Sean cursed under his breath and scooted as close to Cody as possible.

CHAPTER 46

Sparky descended about twelve feet into the steep, narrow, craggy hole. When he reached the bottom, he looked up and hoped he could climb back out if he needed to. Due to the steep angle, going up would be far more difficult than going down. He knew that once he began to move through the cave, there was a chance that he might never see daylight again. It was a risk he willingly accepted.

He moved the flashlight from side to side and took his bearings. Though it was difficult to ascertain directions, he believed the tunnel went toward the cave's entrance. Even if he were correct, he had no idea how far he had to travel. He was able to walk upright for the first several feet, then he had to stoop. He continued until he came to a Y in the tunnel. The shaft on his left was much larger than the other side, so he went in that direction. After several yards, he came to a dead-end except for a small hole, less than a foot wide, at the bottom. He ran back the way he had come and took the other shaft. After only a few yards, he had to get down and crawl. As the seconds ticked off, he became increasingly concerned about what might be happening inside the cave's entrance. Was he running out of time? He forced bad thoughts from his mind and proceeded as quickly as he could.

The tunnel widened enough for him to stand, but the shaft began to angle down, and he had to move carefully to maintain balance. After a drop of what he believed to be several feet, the shaft expanded, and he came to a level area covered with water. He flashed the light from side to side, but there was no way to determine the water's depth. Having no choice, he inched into the cold water. After a few steps, he found himself knee deep. He flashed the light ahead to make sure the tunnel on the other side of the water was wide enough to enter. He crept forward. He took two steps and felt the hole deepen. He drew his gun and held it above the water line, which had now risen to his waist. With the flashlight in his left hand and the pistol in his right, he proceeded with extreme caution.

He was about seven feet from the opposite bank when he slipped and nearly fell. He steadied himself and started to take another step, but the bottom of the water channel was full of holes. He desperately wanted to move faster, but if he fell he might lose his flashlight or his gun. He took a series of small steps and inched forward.

He reached the bank and climbed onto a dry shelf. He looked back, shook his head; then, he moved into the small dark hole in front of him. He made good progress for the next few minutes; then, the tunnel narrowed significantly. He stooped and continued forward. Soon, he had to get down on his hands and knees. The rocky floor tore holes in his pants and scratched his knees, but he moved forward as fast as he could.

He had no idea how far he had traveled, and he wondered if he had gone too far. He began to worry that he might be in a separate tunnel that did not lead to the cave that had the metal door. He paused, but he knew he had no alternative but to forge ahead. He flashed the light forward and saw that the shaft narrowed again.

He lay on his stomach and inched along. After a few yards, he thought he felt an increasing airflow and he was able to stand. Encouraged, he started to continue but the flashlight flickered and went out. He tapped the flashlight but the light flickered and went out again. He checked the cap on the end of the flashlight and discovered it was loose. He took off the cap and reseated the batteries. When he attempted to screw the cap back on it slipped out of his hands. He tried to catch the cap and dropped the flashlight.

"Shit!"

He got down on his knees and moved his hands around. He found the flashlight and the batteries, but he could not find the cap. In total darkness, he moved his hands in a wider arc.

Nothing.

He began to move in a circle, searching with his hands as he went. He banged his head and felt blood running down his face. He was nearing panic when he discovered a groove at the bottom of the wall. He retrieved the plastic cap, which had bounced and fallen into the groove. He replaced the cap and turned on the flashlight.

He sighed; then, he crawled forward.

He had lost precious time and he was worried.

Several times, he scraped his knees and legs in the narrow, jagged tunnel He ignored the pain from the abrasions and continued as fast as he could. After several difficult yards, he looked ahead and saw that the shaft in front of him widened. He crawled forward, and he was soon able to get on his hands and knees. The tunnel grew wider, and he attempted to stand, but he scraped his knee on a craggy outcropping and bumped his head. He cussed under his breath, then he flashed the light down and saw blood streaming from his knee. He applied pressure to the wound while he considered his precarious situation.

After a moment, he moved ahead, and he was able to stand after a few more yards. Fearful that he was running out of time, he quickened his step. He stopped suddenly and tilted his head to one side. Had he heard voices? He crept forward with his flashlight pointed down. He saw a faint light and turned off his flashlight. He moved cautiously and saw an increasing glow in the distance. After a few steps, he put the flashlight down and tightened his grip on the pistol.

He heard voices.

He rounded a curve in the tunnel and crept forward. The light grew bright, and he knew he was only a few yards from the tunnel entrance. The shaft widened substantially, and he slowed at the sound of a man's voice. He moved to the edge of the tunnel, but he was careful to stay in the shadow. He looked into the open area. Anger surged when he saw Sean and Cody handcuffed to bars along the front wall. A gunman stood in front of Sean.

The man held a gun at his side and said, "I've got to hand it to you. I have no idea how you found this place, but it all ends now."

Sean rotated his body to shield Cody from the expected bullet.

Fagan aimed his pistol at Sean.

Sparky yelled, "Drop it, motherfucker!"

With incredible speed, Danny Fagan spun and fired four shots that would have formed a pattern around the heart of a man of normal height. At almost the same instant, Sparky fired three times. The first bullet hit Fagan in the upper chest; the second struck his neck and severed his spinal cord. The last bullet smashed into the concrete wall.

Sparky went to the fallen gunman to make sure he was incapacitated, then he searched Fagan's pockets. He pulled out a set of keys and unlocked the handcuffs securing Sean and Cody, then he removed the duct tape.

Sean jumped up. "Quick, Kelly's in the other room." He took the keys from Sparky and opened the door to the main living area of the prepper cave. He saw Kelly, wide-eyed, handcuffed to a bed. He ran to her and said, "Cody's safe. Everything is okay." He removed the cuffs and held her in an emotional embrace; then, he took her hand and led her to the other room.

She ran to Cody and threw her arms around him as tears streamed down her cheeks. After embracing each other, they turned and looked at Sparky. He stood, gun in hand, his blood-soaked pants in rags. He wiped blood from his face and said, "I need a drink of water."

Sean shook his head. "Well, of course you do. There's some in the main room. I'll get you a bottle."

Kelly wrapped her arms around Sparky. After a moment, he started to pull away, but she did not let go. She said nothing, but they knew the depth of her gratitude. Finally, she removed her arms and said, "Give our hero all the water he wants."

Sparky took a long drink of water and said, "I got a free haircut." He ran a hand through his hair. "I felt the force of one of those bullets as it zoomed over my head. Damned eerie feeling."

Kelly said, "If you had been taller, he would have killed you for sure."

Sean added, "The guy knew every square inch of this cave, so he knew right where you were. He shot so fast; I thought you didn't have a chance." Sean looked at Fagan's body. "But he didn't figure on your height."

Sparky said, "Being a little person has its advantages."

CHAPTER 47

It took four days for the authorities to complete their interviews. During that time, Kelly and Sean took extreme measures to support Cody. He was a resilient kid, but he had undergone significant levels of stress over the last few weeks. Sparky dropped by often with a ball and gloves. It was an obvious, and successful, way to speed their way to a normal routine.

On a hazy Monday morning, Cody heard the doorbell and opened the door.

Gordon Munson, Cody's Scout Master, greeted him with a broad smile and a handshake. "Hello, Cody."

"Hi, Mr. Munson."

"I need to talk to your mother, but, first, I want to say we are very proud of you."

"Thank you. I was glad I could help."

"You did more than help. You saved the day." Munson glanced around the room. "Is your mother home?"

"Sure, I'll get her."

Kelly came into the room and shook Munson's hand.

"Kelly, we've kept up on the news, and we were disturbed to learn the kidnapper used a Boy Scout disguise to seize Cody. The interesting thing is that I had submitted paperwork for an award before your ordeal. I just received the approval and I wanted to check with you for a good date for the ceremony." He looked at Cody. "We're very proud of your son."

Cody beamed.

She agreed on a date and marked it on the calendar.

A week later, Sean invited Sparky to the house. He shook Sparky's hand and said, "I wanted you to know Kelly and I are getting married." He smiled and continued, "I asked her at the beach where we had the sunrise breakfast."

"The perfect place. I'm extremely pleased for both of you. Congratulations."

"I want you to be my best man."

"It would be a great honor."

Sean picked up a large, flat, wrapped parcel. "I learned that Kelly is really interested in old, high-quality, black and white photographs, but she never had the money to pursue her interest except for a few small pictures she picked up over time." He placed the package on the table. "I bought this for a wedding present. It's an Ansel Adams."

Sparky's eyes widened. "Which one?"

"It's an original sixteen by twenty titled *Clearing Winter Storm*. It's a shot of the Yosemite Valley. An amazing picture."

"I know the one. She's going to love it."

Kelly walked into the room and tilted her head. "What am I going to love?"

Sean handed her the package.

She opened it and a thin film of moisture covered her eyes. "It's perfect. I'm speechless."

Sparky pounced. "I think he deserves a reward."

She winked at Sparky. "Don't worry. He'll be rewarded."

Forgiveness is the final form of love.

Reinhold Niebuhr

Made in the USA
San Bernardino, CA
20 April 2019